Praise for *In the Forest*

"[*In the Forest*,] with its economy of style, its lyrical moments and inexorable drift, achieves what no journalistic lamentation or public outcry could hope to do. It adds up to a memorial to innocence and beauty wantonly destroyed, whether the innocence of the murdered young woman and child, or that of the woodland itself, contaminated beyond recovery by the horrors it encompassed."
—Patricia Craig, *The Independent*

"*In the Forest* has all the ingredients of an ancient folktale . . . O'Brien allows herself an imaginative freedom which gives the story a new life, sharpening the sense of horror and the lost opportunity, while at no point allowing us to forget its truth."
—*The Economist*

"A rather extraordinary transformation of cold fact into lyric fiction."
—Melanie Rehak, *Vogue*

"O'Brien's work is deft, with subtle foreshadowing; an eerie, premonitory tone; edgy scenes; and taut narrative suspense . . . O'Brien is nimble and bold as she reaches into the belly of agony. Like her literary models/muses, James Joyce and William Faulkner, she is unblinking in the face of daily bigotries and cultural terrors. Her imposing novel laments the afflictions of an incestuous island colonized by Catholicism and the British empire, a place where national identity is authenticated by scars of suffering."
—Valerie Miner, *Chicago Tribune*

Mundo MacLeod

A NOTE ABOUT THE AUTHOR

EDNA O'BRIEN has written more than twenty works of fiction, most recently *Girl*. She is the recipient of numerous awards, including the Prix Femina, the PEN/Nabokov Award for Achievement in International Literature, the Irish PEN Lifetime Achievement Award, the National Arts Club Medal of Honor, and the Ulysses Medal. Born and raised in the west of Ireland, she has lived in London for many years.

In the Forest

EDNA O'BRIEN

PICADOR
FARRAR, STRAUS AND GIROUX
NEW YORK

Picador
120 Broadway, New York 10271

The author is grateful for permission to quote from *The Collected Poems of
W. B. Yeats, Vol. 1: The Poems, Revised*, edited by Richard J. Finneran
(New York: Scribner, 1997). Used with the permission of Scribner,
a division of Simon & Schuster, Inc.

The translation of Bryan Merriman's "Midnight Court" is by Frank O'Connor.

The Library of Congress has cataloged the Houghton Mifflin hardcover
edition as follows:
O'Brien, Edna.
    In the forest / Edna O'Brien.
        p. cm.
    ISBN 0-618-19730-3
    1. Serial murderers—Fiction. 2. Murder victims—Fiction. 3. Psychopaths—
Fiction. 4. Ireland Fiction. I. Title.

pr6065.b7 i5 2002
823'.914—dc21   2001051883

Picador Paperback ISBN: 978-0-374-53877-4

Designed by Melissa Lotfy

Our books may be purchased in bulk for promotional, educational, or business
use. Please contact your local bookseller or the Macmillan Corporate and
Premium Sales Department at 1-800-221-7945, extension 5442, or by e-mail at
MacmillanSpecialMarkets@macmillan.com.

Picador® is a U.S. registered trademark and is used by Macmillan Publishing
Group, LLC, under license from Pan Books Limited.

For book club information, please visit facebook.com/picadorbookclub or
e-mail marketing@picadorusa.com.

picadorusa.com • instagram.com/picador
twitter.com/picadorusa • facebook.com/picadorusa

1   3   5   7   9   10   8   6   4   2

For
Imelda Riney,
Liam Riney,
Father Joe Walshe

IN MEMORIAM

Turn back, turn back, thou Bonnie Bride,
Nor in this house of death abide.

—FOLK SONG

Cloosh Wood

WOODLAND STRADDLING two counties and
several townlands, a drowsy corpus of green, broken only
where the odd pine has struck up on its own, spindly,
freakish, the stray twigs on either side branched, cruci-
form-wise. In the interior the trapped wind gives off the
rustle of a distant sea and the tall slender trunks of the
spruces are so close together that the barks are a sable-
brown, the light becoming darker and darker into the
chamber of non-light. At the farthest entrance under the
sweep of a brooding mountain there is a wooden hut
choked with briars and brambles where a dead goat de-
composed and stank during those frantic, suspended, and
sorrowing days. It was then the wood lost its old name and
its old innocence in the hearts of the people.

Ellen, the widow woman, did not join in the search when
the men and women set out with their dogs and their
sticks, clinging to the last vestiges of hope. Yet she dreams
of it, dreams she is in Cloosh Wood, running back and
forth, calling, calling to those search parties whom she cannot reach, the tall trees no longer static but moving like giants, giants on their grotesque and shaggy roots, their
green needly paws reaching out to scratch her, engulf her,
and she wakens in a sweat, unable to scream the scream

that has been growing in her. Then she gets up and goes into her kitchen to boil milk. She looks at the sheen of dark beyond her picture window, the plants, geraniums and cacti, limp in their sleepiness, looks at her big new brass lock, bright as a casket, and then she comes fully awake, and as she tells it again and again, Eily, the dead woman with her long hair, walks towards her and says, "Why, why didn't you help me?" "The Kinderschreck," she answers back. "The Kinderschreck," and with her raised arm tries to blot out the woman's gaze, the light of the eyes a broken gold, like candles puttering out.

Kinderschreck

THE KINDERSCHRECK. That's what the German man called him when he stole the gun. Before that he was Michen, after a saint, and then Mich, his mother's pet, and then Boy, when he went to the place, and then Child, when Father Damien had him helping with the flowers and the cruets in the sacristy, and then K, short for O'Kane, when his hoodlum times began.

He had been a child of ten and eleven and twelve years, and then he was not a child, because he had learnt the cruel things that they taught him in the places named after the saints.

He was ten when he took the gun. He took it so as not to feel afraid. They put him away for it. It was his first feel of a gun, his first whiff of power. It felt heavy. When he stood it up, it was taller than himself. He did not know if he would have the guts to fire it. His hands shook when he loaded it, yet he loaded it out of a knowledge he did not know he had. Then he cuddled it to himself and gave it a name, he called it Rod. *I didn't mean to kill, only to frighten one man.* He wanted to say that, but he was not able to say it, because they were beating him and shouting at him and dragging him off. There was the guard, the sergeant, his father, and Joe Mangan, the bad man that threw the shovel at him and blamed him for cycling over his wet concrete and destroying it. It was not him that cycled over it, it was Joe Mangan's own son Paud, but they blamed him. No matter what was done wrong, they blamed him, and there was no one to stand up for him, because his mother was dead. They said she was dead, but she wasn't; they buried her alive, suffocated her. They brought him up flights of stone stairs and into a cold room to show her lying on a slab with no colour in her cheeks and no breath. It was snowing outside. It was the snow that made her white and made the world white. She was not dead. They only told him that so as to trick him, because he was her pet. They were jealous, they were. They put her in a coffin and buried her. He stole out at night and went and talked to her, and she talked back. He crept out through the window and ran across the fields to the grave at the edge of the lake. He was a cross-country runner and had won a medal for it. He scraped the earth back and made a hole where he could talk down to his mother and where she could hear. She promised to come back and save him when she was less tired. His plan was that he would run away until then, live in the forest and eat nuts and berries, and in the winter go from house to house to beg for food. He would give himself a secret name, Caoilte, the name of the forest.

The first time he spent nearly a night there he was dead scared and dead excited. There were spots before his eyes and shimmers, different colours. He got on his hands and knees and broke sticks, building a sentence around the totem words: "God hates me, Father hates me, I am hated." In the wood that night he saw things no one else saw, not Joe Mangan's sons, not anybody's sons, only him. He climbed into a tree and hid. A fox, a she fox, let out a sound that scared him. It was like a woman having her throat slit, only worse. The vixen was calling for her mate, her husband. She was in a bad way and so were the pheasants that were letting out cluck-cluck sounds to warn each other of the danger. He heard a badger barking and he ducked well into the branches because he knew a man that a badger bit and the man said it was worse than any dog bite. He swore then to live in the wood, to make a log cabin up in the trees, with a floor and chairs and a rope ladder leading up to it. He and his mother would live there, away from his father and everyone else. While he was thinking it, a princess floated by, flying. She was wearing a long white coat and had very long hair down to her ankles. She was carrying slippers. His mother was still in the house, his father attacking her with a poker. She shouted at him to run out, to run off to the woods, and she stayed behind to take the blows. He'd got one blow. There was blood at the side of his mouth that had run down from his ear, and he put a fob of a pine branch on it to stop it. The thing was to keep awake, no matter what. There were noises and there was silence. The louder the silence, the scarier the noise to come. A cock pheasant was warning all other pheasants of an imminent attack. He was waiting for his mother to come, but he was afraid she might be dead.

There was a full moon and it was walking across the sky, and in places the light spilt onto the ground, where there were no trees. That was called a glade. He knew that from school.

When his mother came he was fast asleep. Mich Mich Mich. He wouldn't let on he heard her and wouldn't let on when he came awake. She lifted him down and tweaked his nose and said, "Sleepyhead, sleepyhead." One of her front teeth was gone and she didn't look nearly as nice. He put his finger into the hole and felt the damp of the blood and tasted it and it was warm. His mother and he were not two people, only one.

"I saw a beautiful lady."

"Go on."

"She was on her way to her wedding."

"How do you know?"

"She had silver slippers."

His mother carried him back to Glebe House through the scrub, and the moon was a lamp to show the way. She said he was a brave boy to stay all alone in the forest and not scream like that silly vixen. She said he was a true son of the forest. Next day he wrote that in the front of his copy book at school: *I am a true son of the forest.* They jeered at him, called him a liar, a bluffer, said that he'd run scared from his own shadow, he that had to have his mammy walking him to school and waiting for him out in the cloakroom and sometimes having to sit in the back of the classroom because of him bawling. A mammy's boy, a patsy, a pandy, a sissy, and a ninny.

Soon after that, they had to leave Glebe House and went to live in a cottage far from the woods.

His father and the guard and the sergeant and his sister, Aileen, and Joe Mangan and Mrs. Joe Mangan are all in the court, and the judge is sitting at a big brown desk, higher up. The sergeant is telling the judge the terrible thing he'd done. The German man is on the other side, nodding about the terrible thing he'd done. His sister, Aileen, is beside him, holding his hand. His nose is streaming and his eyes, and he has no hanky. The sergeant is describing how he stole a bicycle from the doctor's shed, then rode it over the wet cement that Joe Mangan had just put down, and did it on purpose, and then rode and got the groceries for his sister and left them on the windowsill and ran off in search of an empty house where he could find a gun. The sergeant got very wound up when he came to the bit about breaking into the German man's house and finding the shotgun and the belt of cartridges and then painted the picture of him creeping back towards his own house, hiding in a ditch at the end of the garden and waiting for the opportunity to shoot. The sergeant told how he himself and the boy's father were behind that very door that had been shot at and were lucky to be still alive. There was more and more about his aggressive behaviour from a very young age, from the innocence of stealing apples to the non-innocence, the evil, the knowing evil of stealing a gun. He was listening to it all, but he was not allowed to speak. He had not cycled over wet cement, another boy did that, Joe Mangan's son Paud did that, but he got the blame and they called him dirty names at the time and told him what they would do to him. They would carry him off to the Shannon and drown him, and he'd never be found. He ran to his own house to tell his sister that, but she wouldn't let him in because she had a friend of hers there and she was ashamed of him. When he asked for a glass of orange, she poured it and put it out on the windowsill and told him to drink it there. That was when he ran away, because no one wanted him and no one believed him and he had no friend.

When the judge gave the sentence he didn't understand it. A detention centre. What did that mean? The judge's voice was very low, but his face was very red. The sergeant thanked the judge and they trooped out. His sister told him outside the court that he was going to be going away to St. Malachi's and it was lucky that there was a vacancy as it was a very nice place. He cried and screamed and ran down the street, but they caught him in a car park and lugged him back.

"If ever you try to escape, I'll hunt you down like a dog until I find you," Sergeant Wiley said to him, and there was hate in his eyes and in his spit.

His sister said that it was only for a little while and that it was a nice place and had a swimming pool, just like a holiday camp. He would be let home at Christmas and he could write letters, so he mustn't cry. *I didn't mean to kill, only to frighten one man.* She told him to shush it or they'd murder him for thinking such a thing, and anyhow, they had to hurry home to start washing and ironing and packing his things. She borrowed a suitcase from Mrs. Joe Mangan.

When they arrived there he wouldn't get out of the motorcar but clung to his granny's knee. She was the one nicest to him, along with his mother and his sister. The car drove past iron gates into a yard with big high walls. The sergeant sat in front and he in the back, refusing to get out, because the place was not a holiday camp but a big dark creepy castle. His granny kept telling him to be a good boy and do as the guard said and walk in there like a man. The sergeant lugged him out by the ear and led him past a whole lot of boys, boys his own age and boys younger and boys older, gawking and jeering. The sergeant passed him over to Brother Finbar, and Brother Finbar took him in and shut the door and bolted it. Brother Finbar had a long brown robe on him and a pair of rosary beads that swung in and out. They walked fast, with Brother Finbar telling him they would put manners into him. He was brought to a cloakroom to be fitted with clothes. He and Brother Finbar fought over his jumper, the one his mother had knit for him when she was sick in the hospital. It was purple and red, with navy cuffs and a multicoloured tassel at the end of a zip. It smelt of his mother, and when he wore it, he could feel her soft hands and her kiss. He would not part with it. He would not raise his arms to have it pulled off. Brother Finbar dragged and dragged, then found a loose thread in the waistband and started ripping it. He could see the colours breaking up, navy blue and purple and red; it was like his mother was being ripped up, and the threads were in wormy coils on the flagged floor. He was fitted with short pants, a jacket three times too big for him, and nailed boots. "You will wear our clothing whilst here," Brother Finbar kept shouting. Whilst here. Whilst here. Whilst here.

Out in the yard, boys cuffing and roughing each other. He stood apart with a group of boys studying him, making a ring around him. Where's he from? Ask him. Ask 'im. Down the country. Where's that? Where's down the country? Ha. Ha. Ha. A bogger. Has he got a cigarette? Hey, Rambo, got a fag? He doesn't smoke. Eejit. Bogger. Give him a hook. Test his mettle. Show your mettle, Bogger. Clinging to his mammy's knee. By the time the bell went, they had him down on the ground, kicking him, until a boy called Bertie pulled them off. The tea was in mugs and the thick slices of bread were streaked with lard. Brother Finbar stood at the head of the table as if he was an iron figure with iron rosary beads and an iron beard.

"Eat your tea, boy."

"I'm not hungry."

"The boot is on the other foot now . . . there's no guns here to scare people."

"I want to go home . . ."

"You'll go home when the boldness is gone out of you, however long that takes."

For two weeks he was assessed so as to be sent off to the other place. The Castle it was called, and it was run by the same order of Brothers and was miles from anywhere. The woman that assessed him sat him at a table and asked him questions, asked him if he had three wishes what they would be. He said he wanted to go home. Other boys told him he'd better get rid of the notion of going home. They said that once a person went to the Castle over yonder, they never got home. No use hoping. No use.

The Castle had the same big gates and the same rules and the same cabbagy smell. The boys were older, rougher. On the first evening he was late being brought over in the van and he had his tea alone with a young Brother. He couldn't swallow.

"I have stomach cramps," he told the young Brother.

"Drink a drop of hot tea, 'twill help you," the Brother said. He was a nice Brother and one side of his face was a raw red and he said that was called a strawberry face. He took different pieces of cutlery to draw a map of the country, and then he put the sugar bowl down to show where he came from, a scenic place with mountains and a famous lake. He missed it. He said he was very young when he joined the order, but they were a family of fourteen and with his face and everything there were no other chances for him.

"How long will I be here?"

"Years."

Brother Anthony ran off then, saying he had something for him. He thought it was a slice of cake, but it wasn't. It was a prayer that Brother Anthony had copied and that he read out to him: *"Jesus said to them, When you make the two one and when you make the inner as the outer and the outer as the inner, you shall enter the Kingdom."*

"A child and his mother are one."

"Ah, yes . . . but that's secular and I am talking of being with God."

"Will I not be going home for Christmas?"

"It's not for me to say. Who's at home?"

"My sister and my pet fox . . . I didn't get to say goodbye to it."

"No use crying over these things . . . these losses."

The rain was sliding down the window and plopping onto the flat roof.

He tried. He tried to keep awake so as not to wet the bed, but he always fell asleep and he always wet the bed, and he wakened with the smell of ugly wet and Brother Jude putting his hand in under the blanket and dragging him out by his mickey. You dirty thing, you dirty thing you. He brought him to a room that led off the dormitory. The strap was kept in a refrigerator there, to keep it cold and hard. It was a leather strap with studs down both sides of it. He was beaten on both cheeks of his bottom and on his legs and on his arms, but not his face. He was just punched on his face. When he got back to the dormitory, boys all came around his bed to know what happened, asking if Jude did any bit of fly-fishing or fiddled with his yoke. Lazlo led the interrogation. Lazlo was leader and they were all afraid of him because he was a schizophrenic. A schizophrenic meant that he heard voices and he could attack any boy if the voices told him to. Lazlo said that Jude was a wiggledy-wiggledy wanker. Lazlo trained boys to be tough. He took them into the lavatory and made cuts on their wrists with a flick knife so they'd get used to the pain. Lazlo said a boy had to teach himself one thing, to hate *them* with a worse hate than they had for him. The flick knife had a wooden handle with a picture of a Labrador on it.

In the morning he got another beating from the prefect on account of the plastic sheet being wet and smelly. That beating was with the back of a lavatory brush. At Christmas his granny would come for him and bring him home and he would tell her everything and he would never have to come back. In the letters to his granny he had to say that he was a good boy and learning his lessons and getting a star for his subjects. The Brothers made them say that, made all the boys say it. He would not tell her about the beatings when she came to fetch him in the car, he would tell her at night when she tucked him up in bed.

A psychiatrist saw him twice a week and asked him what he was afraid of. He said that he was afraid his grandmother would die, because he had dreamt it. He had dreamt that his mother would die and she did. He didn't say that he was afraid of Brother Jude or Lazlo because that would get him into a big mess. He was given the same three pretend wishes. He wished that his mother didn't die and that he could go home and that he would never use a gun again. Other times he wouldn't talk at all. Or he'd say funny things. He said, "Big fish eat little fish and little fish eat littler fish. Kangaroos have their own courts." Out in

the fields where he and other boys worked digging potatoes or pitting potatoes, he ate them raw to show how
tough he was.

One morning it was a priest that rang a bell for breakfast. Father Damien. Boys said that Jude had gone crackers,
had gone into the fields and stripped himself naked and run
off. His brown habit was found in the field and his beads
and his sandals.

Father Damien was home from Africa and had a tan
from all the sunshine. He was not cross over the wet bed
and called him Child—"What is it, Child, what is it,
Child?" Father Damien gave him a toffee. It was a white
toffee with ground nuts in it. Lazlo and the other boys
made fun of him. "Lick arse" they called him for playing
up to the priest.

Father Damien told him one day that he was a lucky
boy, he was going to be let help in the sacristy. He wouldn't
be an altar boy yet but he would train to be. He would fill
the glass cruets with wine and with water and get the vases
ready for the flowers. They were the first flowers he had
smelt in months. They were white with bits of yellow, the
colour of egg yolk, and they grew wild at home. At home
they were called bog lilies.

One evening after Benediction they were in the sacristy
and Father Damien was wearing a white garment, like a
gown, with big pockets in it. "Put your hand in my pocket,
child." There was a sweet in the pocket. Father Damien
told him to keep his hand there until he was told not to. He
felt the swellings, his own and the Father's, and his cheeks
got very red and he was hot and damp between his legs and
Father Damien clung to him until he was finished. Then he
said, "Good child, good child," and warned him not to tell.

. . .

Davey was his new friend. Davey was older, but not like Lazlo. Davey was fourteen, nearly fifteen. He ran the disco. They had discos one Saturday a month and Davey danced with the best-looking girls, "motts" he called them, and he steered them down to the back of the hall, where it was dark. The girls were delinquents like them, they came in a bus from a convent ten miles away and two nuns stood up on the platform next to the player so as to keep an eye on what went on. They couldn't see into the back of the hall where Davey and the big boys were lifting up girls' jumpers and blouses. He danced with the small girls. Boys danced with girls their own age. The girls knew the steps better than he did. The big girls were motts, and they had lipstick and fishnet stocking. Davey went in for the slow dancing and said he went through the girls like butter. "This is me new mott," he'd say of whatever girl he was dancing with. Once Davey had kissed a girl, it was on to the next, because the more girls a lad had, the greater his status. Status was a new word. Davey was his mentor. He said that. Davey said learning in class was only a small part of a man's education, fiddlesticks. The other thing Davey said was to drop a girl like a hot cake once she showed interest, got clingy. Hot cakes and hot crumpets were two different things, crumpet meant a girl's pussy.

The night of the Halloween dance he got his first drink, cider. A lot of the boys were dead drunk and gassing outside in the yard. Two boys broke into a factory not far from the school and siphoned cider from vats into lemonade bottles. It tasted of apples. Davey called him aside; he had a plan and it was thus: Davey said that every Saturday there were games in the grounds, hurley and football and handball, priests and Brothers and boys, all running in all directions, pandemonium. Davey said that young Mich would go into the chapel the next Saturday and open the back door that led out into a field and on down to the river. He wouldn't be playing hurley that particular day because he would have a nosebleed. Davey would pay a rough jackeen with a cigarette to give him a few punches and a humping nosebleed, dead easy. Davey said that they would probably find a boat or a canoe down by the river, and they would drift out for miles and miles until they came to the city. Then they could be stowaways on a ship or go into town, whichever. He seemed to favour the town on account of having mates there, criminally minded like himself. He said it was brilliant crashing a car, either doing it alone or with a crowd; it gave a great buzz. Best of all was doing it with girls in a car, because they lost their marbles on account of having such a big fright.

He left the games field with a handkerchief to his nose and went into the chapel and no one paid any attention to him. He unbolted the back door and then hid in the confessional box until Davey came.

Once out that door, they ran helter-skelter, down the fields to the river and along the river and over gates and fences and across fields, all the time hoping there'd be a boat moored at the next bend or the next, but there wasn't. He was proud of how fast he ran in the nailed boots. By the time it was dark they had come to an estate with a whole lot of houses and ponies in a paddock. There was a bonfire with kids around it. Davey said that they'd best chat up the kids. They were smoking and having a singsong. They were enjoying themselves, and then a boy said, "Jesus. Look." A car was coming into the field, the headlights full on. Someone had grassed. It was the white van from the Castle. The head Brother and two other Brothers and Lazlo and a boy jumped out. He ran to the river and jumped in, clothes and all, and he could feel the current pulling him along and he was happy because he was going to drown and he would never be going back to the Castle again. The boy that caught him was Lazlo, who got his own back on him for having dropped out of his gang and joined Davey's. Lazlo held him under the water until he nearly drowned, then brought him up and shook the water off him. Then he put him down again and held him, and he was smothering and his head and his brain were all water, and Lazlo wouldn't let him up until he nearly died. "Lick arse, lick arse."

He was put in solitary and had to write down how bad he was. He had to write it hundreds of times. Christmas would be soon, but he would not be going home. He didn't cry much anymore. And he could take the beatings. He stoppered the tears up, like putting a cork in a bottle. It got that it was just as bad between the beatings, waiting for the beatings. He never knew when they were coming for him. He was due a hundred lashes. He only cried when it came to Christmas, because he was not let home. Most of the boys were let home, even Lazlo. His sister sent him a card with silver salt on it and he licked it and it tasted gritty. She said the family hoped he was well and that they missed him. They had been told about his running away and his aggressive behaviour, and they were all praying that he would turn over a new leaf. She put kisses at the end. He cried at Midnight Mass because of the singing. A woman sang, but he couldn't see her because it was on tape. It was like hearing his mother singing in the kitchen, hearing her but not seeing her. Father Damien called him aside after Mass and asked him what he would like for Christmas. He said he would like a guitar. Father Damien gave him a teeny box of chocolates and a holy picture. He ate the chocolates on a garden seat and wondered if it would snow. The plants were all lying down, as if someone had beaten them and they had no strength to get up.

He was put working in the fields, after school, as a punishment. He and other boys were taking potatoes out of pits and putting them into sacks. Lazlo was in charge. When they'd finished they told him that they had some business with him, and they went to the opposite end of the field away from the school where there was an old plough with a car cushion on it. They knew what he'd done with Father Damien and they said they were going to cut it off. He screamed and held on to it and begged, and Lazlo said, "Okay okay, off with a caution." They put him facedown on the cushion and pulled his overalls off and they took turns.

He could hardly walk back because he was so sore. And he was bleeding.

He dreamt about running away because if he dreamt it, it would happen. Himself and another boy were sent to the top gate every other morning to collect the milk. One morning, the other boy was sick, so he went down alone. The routine was always the same: the driver got out the full crates, took the empty ones, and set off. When he was found out in the next big town, the driver said, "Holy heck." He told the driver that he'd been kept prisoner there, and his grandmother and himself made a pact that he would run away when the opportunity came up. The driver didn't believe him, but he knew the bastards they were, so he let him go.

He ran towards home, but he was not going home. Three nights on, soaked and scared, he was knocking on the door of Mr. Cleary, a man he knew. The man couldn't believe it, but he let him in and they dried him and gave him hot cocoa, and he slept in the room with two of their sons, who were afraid of him. He knew they were afraid, because when one went to the toilet the other went as well, so as not to be alone with him. The man had gone to the guards, because there was a warrant out for him to go back to the place he ran away from. He got a reprieve for seven days. Then he got sick and the doctor came, and he was going to be allowed fourteen days in all. He helped the man bring in the cows and do odd jobs in the fields.

One evening the man was milking the cows and he stood beside him in the cow house and told him the things that happened to him in the place and the man asked him several times if it was true. "God's honour," he said, and the man hugged him and stopped milking and the dribbles of milk went over the floor. The man said he would talk to his wife and that they would take it up with the authorities. He was in their house then, part of their family. They had their dinner in the evening and the woman ladled out meat and vegetables into soup plates. They had apple pie or jelly after. Then the man opened the door and made some sort of cluck sound, and his pet rabbits came out of their hutch and into the kitchen and ran around. The favourite, Dustin, climbed onto the man, onto his knee, and then up onto his shoulders, and nibbled at his ears. The others perched on the tiled kerb around the fire. Everyone laughed. He laughed, too. This was home, a dinner, apple cake, a calendar on the wall, and a record put on for the rabbits to waltz to. In bed, the sons would try to get him to talk, to tell what it was like in the Castle, but he wouldn't. He knew things that they didn't know. Then one night he boasted about getting a blade and slitting his wrist and being in the ambulance, hopping along the dark road to Casualty, and the twenty stitches he had. He told them how he bit the stitches and spat them out. He told them he was a head case and that Lazlo and the gang were scared to death of him. They knew he was sent away because of trying to shoot his father and the sergeant, everyone knew it. There was a hole in the panel of the door for everyone to see, for proof.

One day after planting cabbages the man sat him down on a wooden seat in the front garden to have a talk with him. He thought it was about going back, but it wasn't. The man asked him if he would like to be part of their family, one of them, a son. He said he didn't know.

"Would you like me to adopt you?" the man asked.

"I don't know."

"Legally adopt you."

"Can you?"

The man said it would take time, that he would have to go through all the correct channels, but he felt confident. His father had given the permission. His father didn't want him back and his sister was gone away. She was gone to live with her granny. He'd seen her on a bus; she'd waved to him from the bus window and he waved back, but the bus was moving. It was evening. The man asked him if he'd like a different name and he said he would, he would like to be called Caoilte, the name of the forest.

It was about a month later that it came over him. He began to hate the rabbits and the attention they got, the fussing over them, the cluck-cluck and oats put down on the kitchen floor for them, their supper. He hated other things too — the sons, pretending he was their brother when he wasn't. He knew the movement of the rabbits, the time of evening they came out and frisked around the fields and nibbled at grass, same time as when the crows cawed, and then the cluck cluck cluck and their trooping in to be petted. He went out to the field that bit earlier and took oats in a bit of cardboard and funnelled it out in little heaps. Several came across, but there was one in particular that he decided he would like to kill. A namby-pamby. A weakling. He struck the shovel down on the nape of its furry neck and it fell sideways like a glove. No one saw him. Next morning the dog brought the carcass and flung it on the step. No one said anything.

It was only after he killed the kittens that there was trouble. One of the sons saw him, was peeping from behind the hay shed, a peeping Tom. There were six kittens in all, cleaved together in their sleep, so it was easy; it was just like killing a mat except for the squeal that came out of them and the blood. The son ran into the house yelling and the mother came out and blessed herself and asked him why in the name of God he had done such a wicked thing. She stood above the kittens and asked him what harm had they ever done, what harm had they ever done to him. He said it wasn't him that did it, it was someone else, a boy that came on a motorbike and then scooted.

The father broke the news to him in the dining room. There was the father and him and a big jug of artificial flowers. The father held up papers, the documents about the adoption, and said it would have to wait. He would have to go back to the Castle for a while because his head was all scrambled up. He got on the floor and clung to the man's trousers, but the man said it was out of his hands now, it was in the hands of the state and the social workers and the people experienced in these matters.

They drove to another place, to where the local doctor had made arrangements for him to go. They'd made a special case of him. He was not going back to the Castle. A secretary took down the particulars and signed him in. The man told him to shake hands with her and say thank you, and he did.

"We've been trying to get him to eat for days, but he wouldn't . . . he's very weak," the man said.

"We can't have that," she said, and went off to see what she could raid from the kitchen.

When she was gone, a head doctor with a red puffy face came and looked at them, and the man handed him a sealed letter.

"Hang on, hang on . . . we might have a problem here," the doctor said, and went off to make a phone call. He came back and said they couldn't keep the boy, but that there was a place for young offenders about twenty miles away and he would be placed there.

"Can you make an exception?" the man asked him.

"I can't . . . he's under age . . . someone got their knickers in a twist." He kept saying that and a Latin phrase: *"inter alia, inter alia."*

"So what do we do?" the man's wife pleaded.

"St. Sebastian's . . . that's the place for young offenders, and it's not far. The only snag is, his father will have to meet you there to sign the admission forms."

"His father won't," the man said.

"I'll go and phone him and make sure that he does. He'll

be there to meet ye . . . I'll tell him exactly where it is." He went off to telephone his father and came back telling them to drive nice and slow but to keep their eyes out for a big white noticeboard that said St. Sebastian's, two miles this side of the town.

They drove, the man, his wife, and himself, without saying much, and when the town lights winked, the man started asking the way. One person said, "Straight on," and the next person said, "You've passed it." The man had to get out and make a phone call. The woman asked him was he cold and he said no. Then she asked was he sorry for the thing he'd done wrong and he said yes. Yes.

Two nurses saw him. One took his pulse and another put a stethoscope on his heart because he was shaking and twitching. Then one of them asked him why he had killed the kittens. He said, "I forget." The other asked him why he had run away from the Castle. He said he hated it. The nurse said hate was not a good emotion, especially in a growing boy.

His father had not arrived, so they sat in the outer hall and waited and waited, but he never came. Two more phone calls were made, and then a nurse and a doctor came out and had a piece of paper that was a dossier on him. The man and the woman stood with them, and he was standing nearby, next to a big green plant, and he could hear what they were saying. The doctor was telling the woman that it was not advisable to have him around other children.

"Why not . . . why not?" she kept asking. He held up the dossier again and showed it to the husband and the husband said "Jesus" and said he would rather not show it to his wife. The doctor insisted. He held up the piece of paper for the woman to see, and when she saw it, she screamed and said it out loud for everyone to hear: *This boy could kill.*

The man and his wife shook their heads at each other, and then the man came across to him and said that there was no room at the inn and that they would be taking him back to the Castle.

"Don't send me back, don't send me back." He got down on his knees and shouted it to strangers sitting in armchairs. It was visiting Sunday. A woman came forward with a biscuit and he refused it and shouted louder, louder, "Don't send me back there . . . I'll do away with myself."

He said it to himself when they drove through the night in the rain. He thought if he said it often enough his prayer would be answered, but it was not. They drove along dark country roads, where there were hardly any cars, and now and then came on a dead fox or a dead cat, outstretched, its fur and its guts strewn there, a pitifulness to it, as if there was something that cat or that fox badly needed to say.

Eily Ryan

I WOULD COME HERE for the mornings alone. Everything fresh, sparkling, the fields washed after rain, the whole world washed. Daisies and clover and blue borrage springing up, and the young cattle on the other side of the fence, frisking, kicking their hind legs and their tails, as if they have taken leave of their senses. The apple and crab-apple trees are coming into flower, apparitions of white, cloaked in green.

I went up the lane very early to give an eye to the ewes in Dessie's field, like I promised him I would. They are due to lamb. There was a fox padding over the far field, out for its breakfast, and I wondered what I would do if it attacked the ewes. First it drank out of the stream and then crossed over, lifting its leg every other minute, and came at a trot to where I was. Its pupils are vertical like a cat's. It's the nearest I have ever been to a fox. A big heavy ewe was cropping the grass, and it stole up to her like it was invisible. It was sniffing, sniffing, when our Smokey came and charged it and chased it back over the stream and up the opposite hill, the pair of them ferocious, a chestnut coat and a grey coat savaging one another, then the fox vanishing into a burrow and Smokey coming back frothing.

The nights can be long. My sister, Cassandra, says we won't stick it in the winter, Maddie and me. We'll have coughs and colds. We will stick it. We'll wear loads of jumpers and thick socks, and anyhow, we have the summer to acclimatise. I leave the door open for the clean, fresh smells to come in. The house has had no one in it for years, so it smells mouldy, a reek of lime and damp mortar. Apple Tree House it was named.

Up in Denny's pub they said that a cobbler lived here once and most likely I would come upon odd shoes. I did find a bracelet in an old coal scuttle where someone must have hidden it. It polished up nicely. And I have Maddie gabbling away nonstop. He says the daftest things. He says this house is "yucky" and that we should go back to the "apportments." That is his new big word. I say, "Wait until we have a bathroom and a tiled stove and a birdcage and a barbecue, just as in the garden of the 'apportment.'" People think I spoil him, carrying him everywhere, little hulk that he is, but the field to the road is a swamp. I bought a lorry-load of chips to make a path and just stood there and watched them being swallowed into the mud as fast as they rolled out. The driver kept telling me I should have put big stones, rocks, in there first — "Ah, don't let it get to you, missus."

Denny's pub is two miles away. He keeps a roaring fire no matter what the season. He did all the smithy work himself, the fire grate, the fire irons, and the ornamental eagles on his piers. He has two washbasins that are a feature for tourists. The pedestal of one is a lady's white porcelain legs moulded into black porcelain court shoes, and the other, in the gents, features a lady's plastered protruding buttocks. He escorted me in to have a look at both. I wonder what they make of me. Anyhow, they're all smiles. Once, he got a bit fresh and said that if I came at night I was to bring a change of underwear. Then to make amends he said he'd save me the sawn-off language some of them used.

The townland is named after goats, except that there are only a few around. There is a herd of cattle and a reigning red bull. In the evening they all come to the fence and bawl and bawl, and Maddie bawls back. He pretends to be thwacking them with his stick and shouts some important new word. He's the cop and they are the robbers. The "apportment" is a place we rented for two weeks before getting in here. More scenic than here, a lake, reeds, water birds, and cruisers that docked in the evening. Two city slickers invited Cassandra and me over for cocktails. The one with designs on her wore a ridiculous T-shirt, and mine took me on a tour of the inside, pointing to the amenities, the bunk beds, en suite, the cocktail cabinet, and the Scandinavian shower. He suggested that he and I motor over to Dromineer for a bite. Cassandra was miffed at being left outside and came in and said how naff that he served martinis from a plastic glass, then stormed off in her very high heels. She says it's the Mars in her.

Apple Tree House was waiting for me, or so Billy said. He had it on his books for nearly a year, but kept it for someone special, and that someone turned out to be me. He had to bring a slash hook to fight his way through the briars and the brambles across the field, the house itself and the chimneys smothered in ivy and different trees. He put a crowbar to the door and pushed it in, and as it heaved and creaked back, a startled bird flew out at us, a blackbird, a she. We'd scared it. It was then Billy said he would help me to find a loan, and he did. Cassandra always says that I was born with a silver spoon in my mouth.

The day we moved in, Billy helped us, brought things in his van, and Maddie and me drove on ahead in my little daffodil-coloured Beetle, hooting to let the world know. We had to park the car where the three grassy roads meet and walk across, lugging stuff. Billy brought an old sofa, pink velvet, with the nap worn down. I had cups and saucers and cutlery in a bucket. Maddie carried a lump of bog oak that Cassandra found for us. As we came around the house, there was our visitor, a dog on its haunches, a grey coat, the grey of steel wool, and the most pitiful expression in its eyes. It as good as spoke to us. Its coat had been burnt in places. It isn't a frisky dog, it's a thinking dog, and its hind leg is buckled so that it hops like a kangaroo. It took to us, jumped on us, yelped to make us welcome, and followed us up and down the lane while we got our bric-a-brac. Billy said it had been through fire, so we called it Smokey. It goes off nights and often isn't back until noon, but back it comes, because it wants to be here, guarding us.

We broke a bottle of red wine to launch our arrival. Billy only conked its neck and then strained it through a bit of muslin Brigit had left me to put over the milk. It's a little muslin cap with coloured beads dangling from the edges. Billy knew all the history of the house, told us how a shopkeeper in a market town owned it and thought he would retire here but found it too isolated, too run down. At times he believed that people had broken into it, on account of finding ashes in the grate and a mattress and an old torch. Billy made me promise that I would get a phone, said a woman alone would need it, shouted me down when I said an army of spirits protected me. He won. We sat outside on a broken wicker seat, Maddie hugging his new friend Smokey, us drinking, and the light of the sky changing colour, from one deep blue to another, like paint on a palette.

"Jaysus," Billy said when he spotted an old coal scuttle with jewellery in it. It was a silverish bracelet showing through the black dust, and he took it out and wiped it in the grass.

"Jaysus . . . it's the crock of gold," he said, spitting on it.

"Jaysus," Maddie said, and we laughed and laughed, and it was the beginning of everything, the buds on the trees, the birds scudding about in some sort of spring daftness, in the occasional gusts of wind, falling blossom, the very same as if someone had emptied confetti from a packet.

Twice I went indoors just to look at the letter again, to look at the words, to drink them in: *Thinking of you across two seas. Should one be upside down because of a beautiful crazy red-haired girlfriend. I guess yes. Your Sven.*

Homecoming

SERGEANT WILEY is fixing up his hedge to keep McCarthy's bloody bullocks out. It is a straggly hedge, hawthorn, privet, and different kinds of greenery tangled in together and sprouting with a will of their own. McCarthy's bloody cattle have made big holes in it and keep coming in, time and time again, and trampling on his wife's lawn and his wife's flower beds. With a slash hook he loops down the high branched bits, and with his hands knits them together and packs them into where the gaps are.

Coming across from the graveyard, he sees a youth in a bomber jacket carrying a rucksack, but he pays no attention, thinking him a hitchhiker on his way to the hostel. He has knelt to drive a peg into the ground when suddenly there is a face peering at him from the other side of the gap, the tongue forking in and out in obscene and apish mockery. The two faces are level, the one laughing, the other rigid with surprise, realising it is O'Kane, who should be in England, doing time for mugging an old lady.

"On maternity leave, are you?" O'Kane says, chuckling.

"Sure now, I retired from the force over eighteen months ago . . . I potter . . . I'm fixing my hedge because it's necessary to keep stock in or keep stock out."

"How far is the town?"

29

"You're looking across at it . . . you can see the smoke from the factory chimney."

"Didn't expect to see me, did you?"

"So you're home for a bit."

"For keeps. They were shit scared of me . . . my negativism. Define negativism," he asks, then answers in a gallop, "An act of striving against all attempts at contact, ergo, when a hand is offered I withdraw . . . Give me your hand."

The sergeant puts his hand through the gap, and the grasp is deadly, rage emanating and pulsing from it. Their faces are so close he can smell onions off O'Kane's breath, and him raving: *The inmate's behaviour is not likely to attract much publicity because of relatively minor offences, although it should be noted he is Irish. Reasons for refusing food, wants to die. Has no one to double up with. Sister, father, stepmother, staff all cunts. Fifteen minutes surveillance on wings C and D necessary. Shat in cell. Refused Mass visit. In padded cell for management purposes. Blood potassium fell. Laughs abnormally. Resents changing milieu.* Changing milieu . . . You're the bastard that had me put away . . . that started it all."

"It was for your own good. You were wild."

"Jail made me a man."

"I expect it did."

"And a monster. It's a mismatch between us now and it'll all end here," he says with a fiendish laugh, then vanishes sprite-like.

The sergeant, still kneeling on the ground, feels not the damp grass but the sweat pouring through his vest and the corkscrew vein on his temple throbbing.

"It'll all end here." He keeps repeating it as he gets up and goes into the house to phone the barracks, to warn them that the Kinderschreck is back to persecute them.

Druidess

DECLAN HAS COME to do the roof for Eily. Eager, rake thin, a cigarette at the side of his mouth, he is carrying something precious in a piece of cloth which he lays on the table with a certain ceremony. His sculptures. They are polished figures in black wood, embracing couples, a goddess with pendulous breasts, and a warring goddess holding a sceptre.

"Someone said you'd be interested . . . hope it's not cheeky. Bog oak . . . very ancient, over five thousand years old, petrified, I think they call it. It's how coal is made . . . What d'you think, missus?"

"They're lovely."

"Say hello to them. This is *Druid at Dawn*, this is *Morrigan the Bloodthirsty*, and that's *Diarmuid and Grainne*, lovers that died together."

"And who is this?" Eily asks, picking out a figure whose hands are folded chastely across her chest.

"Ah, now . . . she's my favourite . . . little Lena. She must be the loneliest child that ever lived. Came from a bog five thousand years old. You don't mind that I brought them to meet you."

"Not in the least. What's your name?"

"Declan . . . but I changed it to Shiva after I went to India," and he winks and fiddles with an assortment of silver earrings in his left ear.

"What was India like?"

"Most intense experience of my whole life . . . great soul . . . great dignity . . . and the dancers, Jesus, their whole personality dances."

"Well, we'll have to do a bit of dancing up on the roof, Declan."

"Jaysus, the roof, the roof. I'll tell you what, missus, miss, I went up there yesterday evening. I got the loan of a ladder, and I tell you, there are piles of slates missing. That's not the worst bit, it's the joists . . . they're like pulp, sawdust. You could puff them away in your hand."

"Oh no."

"It's an old house, you've got to remember that. Empty for years . . . rotting."

"I can't have a whole new roof, not this year anyhow."

"I'll tell you what we'll do. We'll patch it up, we'll put tarpaulin inside and we'll paint it with pitch and we'll get some new slates and tuck them in under the old slates, seal them with a bit of lead for the time being."

"Will that keep the rain out?"

"Well, there's always buckets, I'll bring a good supply of buckets. One question . . . what made you settle here?"

"Back to nature," she says with a hoot of laughter.

"Mystical . . . gorgeous." He grips her hand, apologises for the dirt, says it's on account of being a carpenter, a stonemason, a barman, a sculptor, and a small-time farmer.

"A barman!"

"I do weddings . . . me and my friend. We bring the barrels and we draw pints all night. I love weddings . . . I'm mad for them. Great craic, great singing . . . so if you're thinking of tying the knot, give us a shout."

"Have you a girlfriend, Declan?"

"Not exactly. There is a girl that kind of showed interest . . . Muriel."

As they are talking, Maddie comes whizzing in, puts down his big stick, and stands and stoops like an old farmer, one elbow on the table, looking at his visitor, sizing him up.

"So what do you do?" Declan says.

"I'm kept going . . . I make walls, I make lakes, I dig drains, I'm run off my feet," Maddie says, affecting a worn voice.

"That's terrible altogether," Declan says.

"But wait till I tell you . . . I met a man up at the ash tree and I'm after buying a tractor from him. I gave him ten pounds for it. I sat up on it and I drove it home."

"Go away."

"Yep. I have it up by the crossroads. D'you want to see it?"

"I'll see it in a minute . . . I'll have my tay first. Why don't you have a cup?"

"No time . . . I have to get my potatoes in . . . I'm always first with the spuds . . . June the twenty-ninth," and he goes out running, shouting, "Duncan, Duncan."

"Who's Duncan?" Declan asks.

"Someone he's made up . . . they have battles."

"Great little lad."

"He's dying to be five . . . that's his big agenda."

"What's your big agenda, missus?"

"To cut this bloody hair, to shave it all off. The plumbing here . . . well, it's primitive, a tap outside in the yard."

"That's kind of exotic, though . . ."

"When will you be able to start the roof, Declan?"

"It's like this . . . I'm freelance. I work for a fecker over in the mills and he's a right bastard, but the long evenings are coming in and I'll be home while it's bright and I'll be down here . . . Mr. Fixit. Do me a favour, don't cut that hair."

Dusk

DUSK, and the figure on the roadside barely visible. He is thumbing. What with the baby and being late, Moira Tuohey thinks not to stop, but suddenly O'Kane throws himself in front of the car and she has to pull on the brakes so as not to run him over. "God Almighty, I could have killed you," she says through the window. He is a young fellow in a bomber jacket with a rucksack, and he is holding an apple and an orange in either hand.

"Let me in," he says in a tough voice.

"I'm only going a mile down the road."

"'Twill do."

She feels nervous but realises she has no choice. She has to get out on account of it being a two-door car and the baby is strapped in the front seat. As he jumps in the back, she notices a wooden handle jutting from inside his jacket.

"I hope you're not going to hit me with that," she says.

"Hardly . . . a nice lady like you." Something about his speech along with his stare unnerves her. His speech is too slow, too clumsy, as if he has not spoken to anybody in a long time.

"I'm only going to the next town," she says, determined to be breezy, businesslike.

"Is that baby teething?" he says, and leans forward and tickles the baby under the chin.

"Don't wake him, he's only just gone off."

She notices how fidgety the passenger is, tapping on the back of the seat, looking out one window, then another, continuously wiping the mist off them and muttering to himself.

"What's worrying you?"

"The guards are after me," he says quite flatly.

"For what?"

"Robbery . . . I have to find somewhere to live. Do you have a sofa?"

"Oh, I don't live around here at all, I'm just back for a visit. Tell you what . . . there's a caravan site about two miles from here. It's supposed to be very nice, very clean."

"I'm a loner."

"What's your name?"

"O'Kane. Mich."

"Ah. My mother knew your mother," she says, determined now to get on friendly terms.

"Bastards. They said my mother was treated for depression . . . she was never depressed. She loved me. She knit me a jumper."

"You've been away?"

"I was in jail in England . . . They wire you . . . They put wires on you and then they prod you the way they prod cattle."

"That's terrible."

"That's why my fucking head is not good . . . they wanted my brain for experiments."

"Are you on your way home?"

"Pigs. It makes me mad the things they say around here about my mother."

"Don't mind them . . . they gossip. That's why I moved

. . . My husband and I, we have a little business farther west."

"Do you sell helmets?"

"No."

"Pity. A helmet is good cover for the face. I'm thinking of going to France for the summer . . . after I've done a few people."

Her driving is reckless because all she wants is to get to the town and stop outside the chemist and pretend she has to get medicines urgently for the child. She has already rehearsed exactly what she will say, rehearsed unstrapping the harness, and in her mind has lifted the child out and run to safety. She won't even put up a fight if he insists on taking the keys. It's an old car and Jason will understand when she describes the look in the man's eyes, the fidgeting, the crazy talk.

"I'll get out here, it's the cow walk," he says suddenly, and pounds her shoulder. The car comes to a screech and she places her hand across the child's chest to protect it. As he goes to get out, he drops the orange into the child's lap.

"No, you keep it yourself, you'll need it . . ."

"He'll need it . . . he's teething," he says.

As she stands to let him out he gives her an unbearable look of reproach. "You were afraid of me . . . that hurt me . . . I wanted so little . . . I asked so little."

"What's in the cow walk?" she says, as a kind of apology.

"The true answer," he says, and looks up into the rainy distance with something like longing.

As she drives away, he is standing under a cover of young trees, motionless, half hidden, as if he is planning something spiteful.

Stones

O'KANE SITS on a tree stump behind a high ornamental wall with crenellations along the top. Three men are filling potholes on a stretch of road at the outskirts of the town. His father is one of them. His father sweeps the dirt out of the hole with a yardstick, rooting and poking until every bit of dirt is nosed out, lifts it and scatters the debris into the kerb. Then he scoops the stone chips into the potholes, packs them down with a shovel while a second man sprays tar over them from a hose affixed to a tanker on the lorry. When his father has flattened the stones with the paddle of the shovel, patted them in, he adds a second heap, which in turn is tarred, and so on, in silent, sweating, unbroken tedium.

I'm nearer than he thinks . . . I'm within striking distance of him, O'Kane thinks as he watches through a chink in the wall, sees his father, the black sleeve, the braced arm, the thick hand holding the shovel, the face determined and gruff like it always was. The lorry trundles on as the next hole is filled and the next, and the patches of tar are like black flowers splashed on a blue road.

O'Kane decides to give his father a bit of a turn and lets out a hoot, half man, half donkey, his prison hoot, and his father looks around, sharp, baffled, and then runs his hand down his neck as if flies have landed on it. He's got fatter. The devil's work. The devil done that.

At lunchtime the lorry is driven onto a by-road and the three men go up the street to Nellie's Café for their grub. O'Kane leaps the wall and begins to take shovel loads of chips and throw them willy-nilly onto the road and onto passing cars, shouting, "Fucking provos . . . fucking provos."

Walking her dog, Mrs. Vaughan sees this and runs back into her house to hide. She draws her blind, drags a gas cylinder and puts it against the hall door, and goes upstairs to peer through a window, to wait for him to move on.

His task done, he decides to call on the parish priest. Going up the short drive towards the pink two-storey house with its green shutters he recalls things he had nicked there—altar wine, a nail scissors, money, and hair gel. He recalls His Holiness, like a big white owl in his fleece long johns, gagging for it.

"Oh, Enda . . . nice to see you," Father Malachi says in as level a voice as he can muster.

"Not Enda . . . "

"Of course. Michen. I heard you were home . . . Still on the road, day and night . . . always on the road. It will be time for you to settle down . . . nothing in those woods for anyone . . . there aren't even birds up there. I was talking to Cian Logan the other day, he's retiring, he's done his three-score and ten, and I said to him, '*Cian, tell me what was wonderful about being a forester,*' and I had to laugh at his reply: '*Damn all . . . midges eating you alive in the summer and rainwater drenching you in the winter every time you sawed off a branch.*'"

"You had me there," O'Kane says, standing by a low

bed with a red cover and a white linen antimacassar over the pillow.

"Yes, everyone thinks his or her own calling the most taxing," the priest says, pretending not to be unnerved.

"I want money."

"Now, why would I give you money?"

"Because I could have you disgraced . . . I could go to the bishops."

"It's you yourself that might be disgraced . . . Nevertheless, I will give you money if it means a hot meal or a decent pullover," the priest says, and looks towards the hall, reluctant to leave him alone in the kitchen and disguising his fears by muttering to himself, wondering where his overcoat could be.

"Shitting your pants?" O'Kane says with a grin.

"England has done you no good."

"Plenty of fist-fucking in the English lavs."

"No good whatsoever."

The priest returns, separating the new clean notes with his dampened thumb: "Today was my day for visiting the poor." He counts them studiously, then hands them over.

"Dirty money," O'Kane says, and pockets it.

"You should go on down home and make peace with your father."

"I'm not wanted there."

"Where are you wanted?"

"Nowhere," he says, and sits down at the end of the table as if he is about to be given food, staring out, his eyes like holes filled with vistas of nowhere. "I might go to the Low Countries . . . they have lots of woods there and caves," he says with a sudden spurt of excitement.

"Well, please God you'll find your niche," the priest

says, and holds the door open for him to go out, then lifts his hand in some baleful mimicry of a farewell blessing. He stands dismayed for a long while.

> A curse on the man who puts his trust in man,
> Who relies on things of the flesh,
> Whose heart turns from the Lord,
> He is like dry scrub in the wastelands:
> If good comes he has no eyes for it,
> He settles in the parched places of the wilderness,
> A salt land, uninhabited.

Father

ON FRIDAY, 15 April, at approximately four o'clock, I was working on the road down from the hotel. I was accompanied by Michael Burke. We saw a car, a fairly big family car, maroon-coloured, driving very fast. It was driven by my son. He was wearing dark glasses and had on a fisherman's hat. It swung around in a hand brake turn and backed up the same way as it had come. The driver did this a few times, and then he drew towards the digger where we were working at high speed and got through us. I am convinced that he was trying to drive through me and knock me down. I would have been thrown to the ground but for Michael Burke pulling me back towards the wall. He drove so close by me that a button came off my jacket. There is no doubt but that he was trying to get me. Two days later he drove the same car up and down the harbour front yelling, "Fucking provos, fucking provos." There was damage on the left rear wing of the car. Also, he was growing a moustache. The next time I saw him was when I was in my own car and stopped at the bottom of the hill outside the bank. While I was there, a silver-coloured car approached from the opposite direction. When he saw me, he picked up speed and tore off, shouting some "f" words through the window.

Aileen

THERE'S WORD going around that my brother is back from England, that he was spotted in the north drinking champagne, and then in Dundalk arguing in a car park, and then nearer home, thumbing a lift. He's beginning to be a bit of a legend, but I hope he isn't around, and if he is, I'm glad I've moved away from Cloosh and made my own life here. This world is not his world, and frankly I don't know what his world is and he doesn't know either, shuttled from one place to another down the years. No sooner would he be let out than he'd be caught again for some fresh crime, burglary or aggravated burglary, whatever that means. A wild young man. They couldn't tie him down, he'd escape through windows or police vans and one day he even ran away when he was out for a walk with a prison officer. He'd show up around home and ask to be hidden. It got so that even I was afraid of him, I that reared him. You could be talking to him and all of a sudden he'd be looking through you like you were glass and he was going to smash his way into you.

He walked in here one day and demanded a sandwich. I was changing my little boy's nappies, my little Ben, only a few months old, on a table. My brother jumping up and down wielding the bread knife, and I said to him, "Will you put that thing down, Mich, what kind of fooling are you up to?" He wanted a sandwich but wanted it there and then and I changing nappies and Mich yelling and roaring at me and saying, "Give it to me now," and I am saying, "Pipe down or people will hear," and I wrap up the child in a duvet and walk off towards the bedroom, and doesn't he follow me down with the knife aimed at me and says, "I'm going to cut your throat," and I say, "You're absolutely crazy, but I'll make the sandwich if you put the knife down," and he says, "I don't want your fecking food, it's poisoned, and I'm going to leave a permanent mark on your face, so's every time you look in the mirror you'll think of me," and I try fighting him, and he lunges the knife into my knee and blood starts gushing out. Next thing he produces a flick knife and digs it down into the duvet with Ben under it. The luck of God he didn't harm him. My leg is going from under me and I let on to him that I hear the landlady and that he better get out before he's sent back to one of them detention centres. I get him out the front door, and he starts kicking it and calling me every name under the sun. Then everything goes silent, even the child is stunned, and there's blood pumping out of my knee and I shout out the window, "Somebody come and help me." I shout it oodles of times, and the landlady calls up from below and I says to her, "Would you come up and help me, my brother is after throwing a fit and I'm bleeding." She comes up and she says we have to report it to the guards, and I say I don't want to, that I want to go to the doctor, and we leave Ben with a neighbour and we go out together. Up he hops from behind an oil tank with a hatchet, and I tell him to go away, that I'm only going to the doctor, and he says, "You're going to the pigs." That's what he called the guards. We try ignoring him, us going down the road and he on the opposite side with the hatchet, cursing us. He sees that I've gone into the doctor's and the woman with me and he scarpers. They bandage me up and then the woman insists that we have to go to the guards, and I say, "That's betrayal," and she says, "Betrayal or not, he assaulted you," and I say that they'll send him back to one of them places, and she says that if I don't she will, and we go out the lane and she heads towards home, and I go on up to the barracks and I report it. Because it's gone dark, I ask can they drive me back home because I'm afraid to walk, and they say there isn't a car available, and I walk up home lame and scared out of my wits. When I get in the house I call to the landlady and she comes up with a poker in her hand and says there's no sign of him and that he's probably gone to stab someone else. We're having a cup of tea when there's a knock on my door and it's him nice as pie asking would I have a drop of washing-up liquid, so I lift my knee to show him the big bandage and I say, "Look what you did," and he says he didn't mean to do it, it was them that told him to do it. I said who was them and he said the voices, the commands. That was the first I ever heard about them voices and I was puzzled, and I felt a bit sorry for him because he looked so lonely, a loner in life. I took his hand then and I said I did something awful, "I went to the pigs," and he got up then and went out.

I heard he was over in a caravan site by the lake for a few months, and next thing he stole a priest's clothes and a priest's collar and made his way to England. He wasn't long there before he struck again. There was a picture of him in the paper, with the priest's outfit, mugging an old woman at a bus stop. After that, the odd letter was from places with Her Majesty's name on the top of the stationery. That was the first time I heard mention of voices, voices telling him to be a desperado, to earn for himself the name and state of outlaw.

Froideur

THEY ARE in Otto's studio, a loft full of clutter, old floor lamps, picture frames, cane chairs waiting to be restrung, sofas to be upholstered, and a motorcycle from his tear-away days. A collection of china dolls on a high ledge look out at them with beady, unblinking, compassionless eyes, and from the rafters old pots and pans, ceramic jugs, and the pink baby chair with its abacus of beads from Otto's babyhood. Witnesses to his wayward and wandering life.

Otto is carpenter, stonemason, weaver, ladies' man, and bohemian all in one.

Each week Eily comes to paint with him, and over time she has heard fragments of his peripatetic life, born in a bunker in Berlin as the city was about to fall, an adoring mother who worked in a nightclub to rear him, weaned on whiskey, gaudy cellars, the bittersweet songs of love and disillusion, a world of women, bonbons, prostitutes, and, later on, actresses to whom he gave fans or shawls, waking up next to a ravaged face each morning, and always inside his head and in his urgent hands the powerful painting that was waiting to get painted. But he had deferred it and put it into life instead. Many a morning he has paced and with a childlike simplicity spoken to her of his torment, but on this morning he is in a sulk and has not yet saluted her.

"Say it."

"I do not wish my little woman to go away."

"It's only a few miles down the road."

"You shouldn't have left here. This is our valley . . . our Montmartre."

"I had to . . . my lease was up."

"Your house is not happy . . . it's gloomy."

"Don't say that. It's costing me all I have and haven't."

"For your whippersnapper . . . Master Sven . . . Prince Hamlet of the byways."

"The local people like him, they respect him, they call him the Scholar."

"You are a free soul."

"So is he."

"Not like you. You give off an aura . . . Even the dogs in the street know that."

"We'll still be friends, Otto, always."

"Always. What is always. Go . . . go to your shack with its no bath and no lavatory and no Otto to come across the fields to of an evening and smoke and have a drink and conjure Chagall's floating angels circling above our valley."

"I'm happy . . . don't you want me to be happy?"

"No, *nein, nyet.*"

"What can I do?"

"Let me paint you."

"Okay."

"Nude."

"Okay."

"A triptych — first nude, the young Eily, vibrant, hungry, her burning hair. Next, she is older . . . a little belly on her . . . mother of three in a chemise, and last a pilgrim woman going up a winding road."

"Why are you so against him?"

"Question . . . how come Otto has not been allowed to make love to the little Madonna?"

"Because it wasn't the right chemistry."

"I see. You will tell me next that you have discovered love. You will tell me there is no other love like it . . . never was, never will be . . . The stroke of his hand and you are electrified . . . you think a thought and he finishes it. You will tell me you have just discovered love and I will tell you you have just discovered disappointment. It is all illusion, fantasy, chimera."

"Why are you so against him?"

"Because he is young and nothing else matters in this crooked, lousy, beautiful world."

He kicked a few things out of the way and went down the ladder stairs and she followed, a bit crestfallen.

Parting

MADGE IS hanging out a double sheet, mustard-coloured. There is something amiss about her wave to Eily, something tentative, embarrassed. In that moment Eily thinks she should reverse up the lane, but then she thinks that would be hasty, unfriendly.

Madge and Eily have been friends since they met that warm day the previous spring when Eily had gone into the craft shop where Madge works, to see if she might display some of the postcard drawings she had done. They were all of nudes, and many were pregnant, with proud, voluptuous bellies.

"How about putting some clothes on them," Madge said, and they laughed, both knowing how the local people viewed them, their long skirts and their wellingtons, sloppy knitwear and ethnic jewellery. "Blow-ins" they were called, a name that had originated from the flotsam of wrecked vessels that had blown in from the sea. Blow-ins.

They went outside and sat on the window ledge watching the dilatory life of the street — a dog chewing a flat ball, young girls teetering in absurdly high platform shoes, walking up and down, expecting a group of boys to appear.

"I hate men," Madge said, but without conviction. She had separated from her third partner, had two kids, no money, lived in a leaky caravan, and had just set her cap on another heartthrob. They discovered that they both had a penchant for the Jesus types, men with long, straggly, unwashed hair, woodsmen appearing at dusk like shadow men. Madge had noticed her latest on the upper road delivering oil, and many a morning since was to be seen wandering up there, drooling.

"What hooked you?" Eily had asked.

"A silent bugger . . . I have this dappy notion that if they're silent they're deep. What about you? Are you solo?"

"I am now. I lived in England, worked in an arts centre, fell for someone, got pregnant . . . the old story. But I have a bonny boy."

"The old story," Madge said wistfully.

It transpired that they lived within a few miles of each other, Madge in her buckled caravan and Eily in a rented apartment surrounded by rolling hills and the landlord's thoroughbred horses.

When Madge visited for the first time, she marvelled at this harem, this Aladdin's cave: bright walls, Oriental rugs, shawls and throws flung around like props on a stage.

"I can see men enslaved here . . . Homer with the sirens," she had said, walking around, scrutinising the various treasures, little perfume bottles, tortoiseshell combs, donning a feather boa, and green with envy, as she put it.

In the month of the bluebells Madge asked if she could do a portrait of Eily and sat her on a kitchen chair in the middle of Allendara Wood. The bluebells everywhere, along the ground and between the rocks and up the tree trunks and even wreathed around the skulls of two dead horses that lay there perfectly preserved in a greenish mould. There was a harmony to it, the rich myriad life of the wood all about, the deft strokes of the brush along the canvas, little shadows that danced skew-wise across her face, under the brim of a lilac straw hat. It was Madge's hat and it was made of a silken straw. They jumped when a pack of lurchers ran through, chasing their leader, who had a hunk of raw dripping meat hanging from his mouth.

"You're to keep the hat," Madge said as they walked back in that filtered sunlight, stopping and starting, picking the odd flower, and concocting big dreams about buying land and selling it for a packet. That was the day they pledged to be always there for one another, but then Sven arrived and came between them somewhat. Farmers referred to him as the Scholar because he was so knowledgeable, knew so much about different types of land, diversified farming, lecturing them at length and sometimes a little boringly about environment, the pollution in their rivers and streams. The need for cosmic consciousness.

Madge had first sighted him in the hall dancing with an elderly woman, looking into her face and dancing the slow sedate steps that she knew, oblivious of the tempo around them. "I bet that boy loves his mum," Madge had said, and remarked on his arms that were a little too long for his body. It was Madge who spotted him and it was Madge who eventually threw them together. How inevitable it seemed once it happened, yet before that Eily had scarcely noticed him, had given him a lift the odd time, had once seen him in the landlord's grounds, the pair of them walking up and down the avenue debating heatedly. And then that spell, that flounder, an instant of capitulation and not a word uttered. It was his birthday, and while everybody was celebrating, Madge had sent them into the kitchen to make a pot of tea. Suddenly they were kissing and he was kicking closed a nearby door to avoid the inevitable guffaws from the other room. Accidentally they bumped into and overturned a heater, and as he told her afterwards in his confiding way, he left it overturned to prolong the sweetness of the moment.

Kilcash became their haunt, the oldest of all the woods, a timelessness in its rustle, in its vastness, in twig and leaf and bole, moss a thick bouclé of velvet on tree trunks, herds of wild goats fleeing at the first sight of an intruder. Their wood. Sven had fixed up a hammock inside a fort of trees and covered it with a canopy of green tarpaulin. Nearby was a well which he insisted was a magic well and where someone, other lovers perhaps, had left a little pewter egg cup for passersby to drink from. On their third or fourth visit she brought a holy medal and threw it into the well, and they wished, jointly wished, then watched the silver sparkle down there, the medal settling itself on a bed of fawn silt. . . .

"Hi, stranger," Madge said, fixing the last peg to the sheet with a snapping sound.

"I haven't been because I'm working on the place day and night."

"When is the housewarming?"

"Soon . . . I want to borrow that dream book from you. I had the oddest dream last night."

"What?"

"Monkeys. They were swinging inside my skull, frantic to get out."

"Sven borrowed it."

"Oh, he's back," Eily said, trying to sound casual.

"Yes, he got back last night. He called here . . . He

crashed out, but before you erupt, let me explain: he was tired, we talked, smoked a joint, I made a bit of supper and presto, it's midnight."

"I see," Eily said, but what she saw was a sheet hung up, water dripping from it in little piddles, a sheet she believed that they had slept on.

"Get a grip . . . you sulked when he left for Dublin, you sulk when he comes back. He's just a kid . . . he'll go off you."

"What makes you say that?"

"Well, his family think it's all wrong . . . an older woman, solo with a child. They have bigger things in mind for him."

"He told you that?"

"He trusts me, he confides in me, he runs to me, then you run to me . . . tea and sympathy . . . You're like children, the pair of you . . . Sometimes I wish I'd never flung you together."

Eily had been sitting sideways, half in and half out of the car, bantams, like little ballerinas pecking at the canvas of her shoe, when suddenly she swings her feet back in, trembling but adamant.

"Why are you doing this? Why are you so suspicious?"

"I love him, Madge."

"Oh Jesus. Love! All I meant was, don't be such a princess," and with that she reached in and tried to snatch the keys, and they bickered, Madge insisting, "I only want to be his friend. I want to do a painting of him, I don't want to make babies with him."

Eily reversed the car, startled some hens in the dust baths, and trampled over a new flower bed to get onto the rutted avenue, Madge hitting at the bonnet and pleading with her not to go: "I'm a blatherer . . . I know I'm a blatherer, but I love you."

The car shot away, Madge waving a teacloth and then shaking the garments on the line, imploring her to turn round.

When Eily saw Sven outside Jacko's Pub, sitting on the pavement, she almost melted. He seemed so young, so vulnerable, eating a choc ice, a punishing haircut, his tongue licking the drips of cream, beside him a bundle that held his few belongings.

She did not want to, yet she crossed towards him and handed him the tape that contained the storybook words they exchanged when they were alone.

"What's this?" he asked as he stood up. He had just read her eyes.

"I've decided that it's best you go home now . . . not in a month or two, as we said."

"I can't. I've told my parents . . . I've written to my professor . . . I've told them I'm staying on here."

"We always knew that you were going to go home . . . We knew it from that very first day in the Kilcash Wood, but we blocked it, because we're . . . simpletons."

He broke into his own tongue then, believing that the depth and truth of what he felt would be evident, and she, for her part, kept lolling her head idly as if she was about to yield to him. A little girl who was skipping stationed herself in front of him, wildly curious.

"Trying to find the right words," he said.

"For what?" the little girl asked, and he described seeing a beautiful princess on a dance floor, wearing a sailor suit, and then suddenly she was gone and he had to bribe one of the locals to drive him over fields and bogs, eventually arriving underneath her window and serenading her with bits of grass and loose pebbles.

"Don't, Sven," she said.

"Is it our age difference, then?"

"That . . . and . . . everything. There will always be people who will try to split us up."

"Let's go to a new place . . . let's drive farther and farther west until we find maybe an island with a few cows . . . me and my Gypsy girl."

"Your Gypsy girl's mind is made up," she said.

They are facing each other now, both shaking, each with a hand raised either to mediate or to remonstrate. The black hairs on his knuckles are like jet.

"This is some kind of false proudness," he says.

"It isn't . . . I've put down roots here and I've put them down alone," she says.

"To be honest, I don't know you now. I am looking at a woman I thought I knew . . . who has turned into a stranger."

"I don't trust you, Sven."

"I didn't fuck anybody in Dublin, if that's what you're thinking."

"You got back last evening."

"I hitched . . . it was raining. I walked the last bloody umpteen miles and I called to Madge . . . you're just jealous."

"Yes, just jealous."

"Explain to me, please, why you're making me go."

"I'll write it to you."

"So you really mean that you want me to pull out."

"Yes, I really mean that I want you to pull out."

"What do I do with all my feelings?" he asks boyishly.

"When we're sixty or seventy, we'll understand all about our feelings."

"I guess you're right . . . everybody moves on." He shrugged, then said, "Hey . . . let's make it bittersweet . . . let's kiss here on the street in front of all the busybodies," and his full lips, the wine red of loganberries, sought hers.

She did something other. She took off the chain and blue amulet that she was wearing and put it round his neck and tied it with infinite care.

"I'm in a rocket," he said, her hands so stealthy, so caressing.

"I'm gone," she whispered.

"Stay just one minute," but she was lifting the latch of the pub door, tall and tawny, disappearing with the abruptness of a sunset.

The Tavern

SHE SAT SILENTLY and drank slowly but deliberately. She thought, *I am seeing this place through different eyes.* She had been in Jacko's dozens of times, yet never before had taken it all in so acutely. She thought, *I've drunk with him here, I've danced with him here, I've flirted with him here, and now I am staring into the almost empty bar wondering why I sent him away.*

What she stared at were the high stools with their red plastic covers held down by regimented rows of brass studding, the one wall with a strip of embossed velveteen from Jacko's mother's time, the other walls white, the globes of light with segments of imitation fruits and a dented St. Anthony's box. Two men are farther over by the fire, arguing, grasping each other's coat collar, in an altercation. She knows them: Denny, a bachelor, small, with a grizzled goatee beard, and Huw, the swank, in a green corduroy jacket, with leather elbow patching.

"I'm not telling you and that's that," Denny says.

"All I'm asking is, have you a site to sell?"

"I wouldn't let you within miles of my place . . . with your women and your greyhounds."

"At least hear me out."

"I know what you want . . . you want to buy it cheap and then sell it off to another fecking foreigner."

"How many acres have you, a hundred, two hundred?" Huw says, baiting him now.

"More."

"Water frontage?"

"Water frontage, water view, water works . . . you're wasting your throttle, boy."

"I'll pay the asking price."

"I'm not selling . . . I told you last week and the week before and the week before that."

"What do you want with all that land and you an old bachelor?"

"How many illegitimate kids have you now . . . is it five or six? . . . the state paying for them . . . our poor little country bled from the likes of ye."

"You haven't done too badly with your water frontage."

"It was my father's before me."

"Look, half an acre is all I ask . . . I'm living with a Norse woman and she's mad to be by water. She misses the sea."

"Asleep on the job, are you?" Denny says, and winks to where Eily is sitting.

"And how is the princess?" Huw calls across to her. She had thought him attractive for a few minutes one night in another pub and she always regretted that she had let him see it, because he took sneering advantage of it.

"Fine, fine," she says distantly.

"Didn't poor Mrs. Burke go quick," Denny calls across to her in a friendly voice.

"And how are you, Denny?" she calls back.

"I'm getting old and foolish," he says, laughing.

"He's sitting on a fortune," Huw says, and suddenly Denny goes towards the door cursing, "Feck off, you and your foreign woman and them naked children, running wild."

"Oh . . . a major alcoholic," Huw shouts to him as he goes through the door.

Standing above Eily, he begins to read aloud what she has just written:

> Go up to the village and turn left at the village hall. Go on not too far and take the first left turning and you come to a little road that goes over a tract of bog, you pass a derelict house on the left and farther on down there's ponies, piebald ponies in a field, after that there's an old red caravan with a curtain in the window and you go on down until you come to a view of the lake way beneath you and you will come to a forked track where there is a rusted cattle feeder and you'll take the centre fork and see the house in among the trees. By the way, you'll have to walk the last bit of your journey.

He looked at her, looked to the copy book again, and whistled and said, "Jesus, you're a number-one Gypsy, plonking yourself like that in the middle of wilds. No one will go to a party down there."

"Look, Huw, cut it out," and she snatches the notebook back, and nettled by the rejection, he takes off his green scarf, dosses it with a spurious and condescending sarcasm, and says, "You're all candidates for Valium here."

She is unnerved when he has gone and orders another pint. Jacko says nothing. That is his way. He stands in the yellow artificial light, like a figure in a frieze, stands as he has done for years, drawing pints, never once remarking on his customers or entering into any conversation with them. The wall clock seems both loud and slurpish.

"It's not like you to have a third pint," he says, and she knows that that is his way of being friendly.

She thinks she will sit a while longer, then drive out to the lake road and Sven will be under a tree sheltering from the summer rain and she will stop and he will get in. At first he will be quite formal, talking with a kind of evangelism of some new theory of his, and in time taking her hand, holding it, and then they will park the car and go in their little lost road, the trees all in bud, catkins like feathered tapers, the blossom in mazed and snowy whiteness, thralling in the moonlight, bridal trees in the brief ravishment of springtime.

But he was not there and she wept at her rashness, her false pride, and her grandiloquent speech about being alone. Alone alone alone, the word galled her like the hungry cry of some cormorant, far out at sea.

Joy Ride

CISSY'S NEW CAR is outside her front door, a chocolate-coloured ornament, the sheer metal a mirror in which passersby can glance at themselves. Cissy doubles as sacristan and hackney driver, is run off her feet, and has gone in to grab a cup of coffee before taking a Frenchman to the airport. From the windscreen an ivory Virgin dangles down, a relic to protect her, and her rosary beads are in the glove box along with a bag of peppermints and a map.

O'Kane, sporting a new growth of moustache, jaunts down the towpath and stops to admire it, reaches in, and as he turns the key, the engine comes to life and he thrills to it. Within seconds he is tearing down the street and sees her in the rearview mirror, a grey-haired harridan, flapping like a turkey. Dogs and children scatter before him, and two older men on a street bench stand up and gape after him. He drives towards the next town, but bypasses it and goes on up towards the mountain, over the bumpy roads, where he can give her a good ride. Ursula he named her, after that cow in the jail. She is full of juice. She bounces and rocks and sways and swags as if there is no ground, as if he is flying it. Wild horses and wild ponies appear in speckled splashes, leaping and whirling into the air, the needle jigging, the engine racing, and a high that he hasn't had in over two years. Yelling with excitement he talks to himself, "Ride her cowboy . . . yonder yonder."

It is evening before he makes his way over the rim of the mountain and down a rough ravine to the edge of the wood that is his favourite, the wood where he hid as a kid, before the scumbags got him, and with a squealing and sprawling suddenness the car comes to a stop and he knows why it is that he has come there. He gets out.

"Welcome home, son . . . you did us proud . . . didn't let the bastards get to you." It is the wood talking to him, the trees thicker now, the trees where he hid and where his mother came and found him, the spot where he kept old cushions, the mass of cover dark even in daylight. He searches in his pocket for a rag, and finding none, he tears a strip from the tail of his shirt, unscrews the nozzle, and dunks the cloth in it, then lays it on the front seat, about to witness his first glorious spectacular. No sooner had he struck the match than the seat caught, as if it had been waiting for it, the flames breaking free and spreading, sheets of flame, flags of flame, orange, crimson, roaring and crackling. The tyres starting to burst, their bursts like priests farting, the windows beginning to crack, beads of glass falling onto the ground, flame flitting across his face and he sucking big scoops of air, flouting his importance, Davey and Lazlo and the other fuckers all cheering him on.

He decides to make a party of it, ask people up. He puts his arm out to catch a burning lady, an Ursula, a cunt. He's high, he's the devil's favourite son and they will never lock him up again or beat the shit out of him and into him. He's a man. He has grown to manhood in spite of the bastards and bastardesses. Better than eating, better than drinking, better than dope or screwing or anything. He hasn't screwed a woman yet. All he knows of women is from the juicy pictures in the magazines, passed from cell to cell, girls with their backs in suspender belts, one leg hoisted to show the pleat of their arses, or frontwise slung back over a table to show the pleat of their cunts, their throats waiting to be slit.

Soon he is smoochy and he wants to kiss a woman and get kissed. He debates about a name. He'll call her Veronica, no he won't, he'll call her Trish. He wants to hear a woman say, "I like your moustache." He feels her feeling the hard blunt hairs, up there in the dark, in the painted flame, and him feeling her back, up there on the edge of the empty forgotten woods.

When the fire had died down completely, he sat trying to figure out where he would go next.

Cissy's friends have foregathered to sympathise and to wait with her for the guard to come. They sit around the kitchen table lamenting that beautiful car that she had saved for, her chocolate ornament, her child, her joy.

"I even called it Cadbury," she says, and again she weeps, wondering aloud where it is and when it will be returned to her and in what state it will be.

"It'll be found . . . they always find them," one says.

"He's evil, I know he's evil," Agnes says, Agnes, whose mother asked her to pop in on her way home to see if Cissy was all right.

At the mention of that word they shudder.

"I'll tell you something I didn't even tell my own mother," Agnes says, and in a hushed voice describes how she and a group of girls were practising Camougie one evening in the sports field and O'Kane stood there watching them and his eyes met hers and the queer look from him sent shivers down her spine.

"Shivers," Oona said darkly, because they were all women and they knew what Agnes meant.

"Weren't you lucky you weren't in the car . . . or where would you be now, Cissy?"

"Tied up somewhere."

"Your throat cut . . ."

"I heard that he can make himself invisible . . . You can go up into your bedroom and find him there and not even know how he got in."

"Oh, Immaculate Heart of Mary."

"If the guards did their job we'd be safe and Cadbury would be outside the door."

"It's not the guards' fault . . . it's the government's . . . cuts cuts cuts everywhere."

"Tell you what," Oona says, "why don't we get down on our knees and pray . . . pray for two things, that Cadbury will be brought back safe and that Michen O'Kane will be sent back to one of them institutions."

Hoodlums

O'KANE IS ALONE in an empty chapel, white walls, the red flame of the lamp, a bare altar, by the holy-water font a poster of Jesus in white with a gold halo around him.

He had gone in hoping to find some Holy Mary on her knees, to get a bit of money. He hasn't eaten for two days, and his feet and his socks are soaking wet. Empty. Fucking empty. Nothing for it but to raid the box where the money for the candles is put. He finds a screwdriver round the back, in a shed where they kept tools and a lawn-mower, and begins to prise the metal mouth open, bit by bit, tongues of twisted brass curling out like an opened cunt. He keeps hacking at it until the hole is big enough to put his hand in. He rummages. The metal teeth snarl at him and he snarls back. Fucking nothing. Two coins, one of them foreign. He goes pitch and toss with them on the tiles of the floor when in walks a kid, a kid not unlike himself, younger and with rosy cheeks.

"Howdie, Gunner," the kid says.

"Who're you?"

"Not telling."

"Little gick . . . Got a fag?"

"They're all shit scared of you . . . They're locking their doors since you hit town."

"Why aren't you shit scared of me?"

"'Cause I'm a hobo like you . . . I can hot-wire a car . . . I haven't done holdups yet, but I'm planning. Did you know that Jesus is also called Emmanuel?"

"Who says?"

"It's written on the poster: *Dear Jesus alone in every tabernacle . . . poor Jesus.*"

"Could you get me chips or a bun?"

"I'm skint . . . but tell you what, there's a cure for hunger . . . the priest read it out on Sunday," and picking up a leaflet he hopscotches to the altar and reads in a manly voice:

> Elijah went into the wilderness, a day's journey and sitting under a fir bush wished he were dead. Lord, he said, I have had enough, I am no better than my ancestors, take my life. Then he lay down and went to sleep. But an angel touched him and said, "Get up and eat." He looked around and there at his head were scones baked on hot stones and a jar of water. He ate and drank and then lay down again. But the Angel of the Lord came back a second time and touched him and said, "Get up and eat or the journey will be too long for you." So he got up and ate and drank, and strengthened by that food, he walked for forty days and forty nights until he reached Horeb, the mountain of God.

"Would you come to the woods with me?" O'Kane asks.

"Which woods?"

"Any woods. We can track game and shoot and have barbecues . . . I'll get a guitar."

"Ah now . . . me mammy would die if I wasn't home for me tea," and at that he runs into the sacristy whistling, and out the door, then off under the yew trees, over a stile towards home.

O'Kane went out wet, sullen, and lonesome. He crossed fields and back yards shouting and kicking dogs that accosted him.

It was a shop called The Wren owned by the newcomers, the blow-ins. In the doorway there were sacks of potatoes and vegetables caked in thick brown muck. He stood outside and looked in at the plates of scones and small pots of jam and honey. There were women in there, talking and laughing, with their backs to him. One of them went behind the counter as soon as he came in and looked at him, suspicious. He was holding a single coin in his hand.

"How much is a scone?"

"Thirty pence," she said, then shook her head because he had only five. Her eyes were mean-looking and her hair was scraped back in a bun.

"Go on, Maggie . . . give him the scone," a second woman said, and rooted in her shoulder bag for the money. She was tall, hair all the way down her back, red hair, the ribs of it standing out, as if there was electricity in it, and when she turned, her eyes were gold spots, like the beam of his torch in the wood at night.

As he is given the bun he bows to her and blurts it out: "Elijah fasted for forty days and forty nights until he reached the mountain of God."

Maggie comes from behind the counter and holds the door open for him, then, pulling the bolt angrily, turns to Eily: "He's off his trolley . . . you shouldn't encourage freaks like that."

"Mother Margaret," Eily says, allowing a wisp of cigarette smoke to float in her direction.

Playtime

SHE WAS IN a cream, rackety little motorcar with a child in the back seat. O'Kane thought it was someone else's child that she was dropping off, because she looked too young to be a mother. Her hair was all hidden under a black beret and she was smoking and laughing. He tailed her in a stolen car, but kept a sensible distance.

She turned around a lot to talk to the child and on a bend nearly crashed into a haulage lorry. Suddenly she shot up a side road to where there was the new school. He put on his sunglasses and a knitted cap, and he followed on foot. The school was a huddle of single-storey wooden houses, some old and shook-looking, some very new. There were trees and flower beds and ornamental rocks. There was a sandpit with buckets and spades for the kids. In the windows there were paintings and mobiles: stars, dinosaurs, and fishes. He could hear singing.

Just by the vegetable garden a young fellow was emptying horse manure from a trailer and dumping it onto a pile.

"Howya," he said as he passed him.

"Shovelling shit," the fella said, and laughed.

He followed her to the very end building and then went around to the back to have a view through a side window. They were infants and they were all in little wooden armchairs around a table, as if they were grown-ups eating their breakfast. When she went in they jumped up and ran to her. The child she was carrying thumped her at being put down and then lay on the floor kicking.

From a cupboard she took out things that were not school things at all: mats and bits of coloured rope and sun umbrellas. Then she took off her shoes and started clowning, and they clowned with her. She walked a tightrope holding the umbrella, and when she fell they cheered and started clambering over her. Then they took turns walking the tightrope, and they fell.

Eamonn, the fellow shovelling shit, was standing beside him laughing as well. "It's a new kind of school . . . no curriculum, no beatings, no punishment."

"You want a hand shovelling that shit?" he asked, and picked up a spare shovel, and the two of them worked and whistled.

"Don't put the fork through it when you lift it . . . it stirs up the gas . . . gives out a rotten aul smell," Eamonn says.

"I'll split your skull," he says, aiming the shovel at him.

"Sorry sorry."

"Are you local?"

"I'm not . . . I work with a man that owns the equestrian centre . . . I muck out."

"Spend your life shovelling shit."

"Nearly. He's going to bring me to the horse show in Dublin in August . . . Jesus, don't put the fork through it . . . sorry sorry."

"What do they do with this shit?"

"It's great for rhubarb . . . they make a rhubarb bed."

A tall grey-haired woman came as they were talking, carrying a tiny mug of coffee. She was surprised to find that there were two workmen, but at once said she was

glad of the extra help, as many hands make light work. She
went on to praise the manure and the generosity of the man
who gave it to them for free. She said that it did wonders
for the rhubarb bed, the fruit trees, and the little birches
that were growing apace. She liked all trees, but the rowan
tree was her favourite, because of the bright red berries.
Suddenly she became very girlish and put a strand of hair
behind her ear and told them, "When I was a little girl in
the forest, my mother told me that the rowanberries were
poison, but they are not . . . they are bitter, but they are not
poison . . . You will get a wonderful dinner here with
rönnbärsgele, perhaps you have had it sometimes with
game or venison . . . no?"

"Game or venison," O'Kane said when she left, and they
sniggered and shared the mug of coffee. The rim of it was
white, with white dribbles leaking onto the earth brown
glaze. They had a few slugs each.

When he looked again the dazzling young woman was
wearing an apron over her jeans and carrying a skillet on
which there were little loaves of bread.

"Hi, Eamonn," she said as she passed them. The children followed in a drove, behind her, their faces painted
every colour and streaks of paint in their hair.

"They love you, missus," Eamonn says.

"They love anyone that lets them play and make bread."

She carried the tray of loaves to a clay oven that was
built on bricks and shaped like an igloo. She used a toasting
fork to open the slide door and a big blaze of fire leapt out
and lit her face, and it was all ruddy, as if she were blushing.

"What's her name?" O'Kane asked.

"Catherine, I think."

"You think."

"Maybe I'm mixing her up . . . bewitching, isn't she?"

"What the fuck would you know about bewitching."

Soon the smell of warm dough drifted across to them, and the children flopped around and the woman talked to them in a husky singing voice. She knew all their names.

It was a week before he followed her, and when he saw where she lived, he went wild. It was his house, his lair that summer before he went to England. He had slept upstairs in the attic room; he knew the foxes that came around there in the mornings, mothers and fathers and cubs, foxes that drank from the trough where he washed himself. He'd put the wind up the man that owned it. Left death threats. He loved sleeping there. Left an old mattress and things: an axe; souvenirs of his mother, her hairbrush and a pink bed jacket. His hidey-hole. The owner, a shopkeeper from Limerick, got afraid to come, complained to a neighbour about being burgled, his tinned foods eaten and his stock of paraffin oil used up. Now she was in it, her and the child. A sadness came over him, then rage, and he thought of hurling stones through the windows, but a voice said, "All you've got to do is make friends with her, son." It was a good voice and his heart leapt to it, and he felt something like hope, he felt he was coming home for her.

Watching

FROM THEN ON he watched her. He watched her eat her breakfast, watched her bathe, watched her bring out a mug of coffee to Declan Tierney, up on the roof, and whistle him down. She had a powerful whistle for a woman and a powerful laugh. She flirted. She carried furniture and bags of groceries, and she carried the child back and forth to the car, the two of them always gassing: "Hi ho, hi ho, it's off to work we go." In his daydream there was no child, there was only him and her.

He got to know her exact movements, the days when she taught in the school, the places she shopped in, the pubs she drank in, and the day she queued at the post office to get her child's allowance. He was about ten behind her in the queue, and the people on either side of him kept nudging one another and edging away from him.

"Hello, Michen . . . you're back," a bitch said.

"Piss off," he told her.

Eily turned and laughed, and then on her way out admired his jumper. It was a green jumper with berries on it that he'd stolen from a caravan. With his dole money he would buy her a present. When his turn came, a cow behind the counter told him he wasn't eligible for twenty-eight days, being as he was only recently returned.

"Eligible, what the fuck is eligible," he roared as he went out.

In a window across the street there were knitted things, shawls the colour of heather and belts with tassels on them. He went in, looked around, and picked up a flat grey stone with a sickle carved on it.

"Excuse me," a girl called out.

"Excuse me," he called back.

Later that evening he left the stone outside her door and hid in the field on the far side of the wall. The door was closed on account of it raining. He hid for hours and watched the turf smoke going up and breaking into shreds. There weren't many stars. There were clothes steeped in a big aluminium pot on the stove. The child was writing at the kitchen table. She sat next to him and from time to time went across and pounded the clothes with a wooden mallet and then took a drag out of a cigarette and inhaled it.

When she came out to hang the clothes, she was so close to him that he thought she would smell him the way he smelt her. She had a clean smell, like the smell of the clothes and the white flakes she had washed them in. He could have reached out and grabbed her, but he didn't. She had trained the tilly lamp towards the line, and the beams ran down one side of her face and neck and down the leg of the trousers that she wore. They were scarlet trousers, not the denim ones that she wore over in the school.

"Eily, where are you?" the kid called from the house. So she was not a Catherine, she was Eily, and he was within a few feet of her, imagining the scream she would let out if he sprung her.

Nothing was the same from then on. It was as if with some subtle, unspoken signal she had let him in.

The next night, she was standing up in the aluminium bath, blood running down her thighs, blood the bright red of fuchsia, blood like he had seen on his mother once and cried thinking she was going to die. It gushed. She poured the water from a jug, and the blood and the water got mixed in together and streamed down her legs, less ruddy, the rest of her body white as milk.

She went up to bed early that night, the child in her arms, already asleep. In his mind he went up the stairs behind them. He knew that stairs well, knew the missing step at the bottom and the steps that creaked. He knew the rafters where the thrushes nested in the spring. He saw a mother thrush sit there day after day and night after night, her eyes like glass beads. Once, when she went off to get food, he took the eggs and mashed them in his hands. The shells were a light blue.

In the mornings she washed outdoors in a big white bath, one that the Declan fellow carried across the field with three of his mates. It filled up with rainwater and sometimes the kid played with boats in it. The kid got on his nerves, the way she pandered to it, the way she kissed it for no reason, made chips for it and tumbled them in a wire basket like a lady in a chip shop. When they got into the bath together, she had a long brush to scrub her back and scrub the child's. She had a nailbrush with a frog handle. Before she washed the child's hair she undid the knots in it, picked them out one by one and then combed it and poured a jug of water on it, and Maddie rebelled when she poured on the shampoo and scrunched his eyes and kicked her.

One night she did something odd. She came back downstairs in the dark and lit a candle, then crossed to a wooden cupboard and turned the long, thin key and opened the flap doors. There was a golden figure inside, cross-legged. She sat in front of it, the same way as the figure sat, and began to pray. She folded her hands and bowed her head. She was praying for something very important, he could tell. It made him cry. When he cried he could not stop, it was like when he laughed he could not stop, except that it was crying and it went on and on. She was a sad woman that night, not laughing and not smoking a cigarette. She had a book that she read from, like a prayer book, and she kissed the page when she had finished.

He crossed the fields, climbed gates and walls, and then went along by the shore and past the empty summer houses to where his mother's grave was. He had not been to it for over a year, since he went to England, and he lay down on the mound crying and explaining. His mother heard him, but she did not talk back to him, probably on account of his having gone away and got put in jail for wrong things. Flowers and wreaths on a new grave caught his eye. He picked them all up in his arms and heaped them onto his mother's grave. He slept a bit. When he wakened it was light, and he decided to go back and visit the woman and bring some of the flowers and ask for a cup of tea and say he was lonely.

When he got there he ranted because she had gone out. He tore up the flowers, tore the petals, tore the stalks, and flung them everywhere. He knew where she kept the key under a flower pot, and let himself in. Even before he pushed it, he knew the creak of that door. Breakfast things were on the table. He ate cereal from a packet, held the packet above his mouth and funnelled it in. On the wall there was a calendar with a picture of a woman and a child, a golden child inside her chest. Underneath there was writing. He made out the odd word—ocean, deity, water, fire. The woman was all them things. Her folded tights were on a chair, and he picked them up and examined them and took them for company.

The following Sunday there was a session in the pub and she was there. Her hair was in small plaits, all over her head, like snakes tapping her. Surrounded by blokes. Blokes with earrings and leather jackets and guitars. She lapped it up. The blokes made much of themselves, getting out their instruments, setting them up, testing them, big pints placed down in front of them and in front of her, too. She was wearing the scarlet trousers that she had worn the night he saw her hanging the clothes. She had a matching jacket with some of the buttons open down the front. She had a necklace. A pouffe was set down for her to sit on. He stood outside the pub window, his eyes burning into her, burning into her smile and the open buttons and the necklace. She swayed in time with the music. The blokes reached over, whispering things to her. When she had drunk most of the pint, one of them picked up the bodhran and laid it into her lap. After a lot of coaxing she began to beat on the goatskin, bringing every dead hair, every fibre alive. She beat it like a mad woman, like an African woman that he had seen in a picture. He banged on the window, making the same sound, believing that she would look up and see him and bring him in and say, "This is my friend." He would bring her up to the woods, to his hideaway, and he would ride her there and she would ride him back, because she had already made eyes at him in the school and in the post office, had given him scones to eat, like Elijah got. He drew nearer and nearer, his nose puttied to the window, until a woman saw him and whispered to Gussie the owner.

"You bastard . . . you pup you, get out of here. Don't ever let me catch you here again." It was Gussie the cripple, with a beer mug in his hand and a posse of men behind him.

"Fuck you all," he said, and he turned, but he did not run. They were afraid of him. No one of them man enough to come out alone, but in a herd. He would have to act fast, because one of the earring bastards fancied her, his thigh smack up against hers for the session, his skin-tight leather thigh against her pleated, satiny folds.

Easter

IT IS a warm night, the sounds and the smells coming through the open door, the smell of grass, pigeons cooing in the trees and a donkey that has been moved to a nearby field whining to be let back home. Her friend Brigit's voice on the tape sounds so near, so intimate, as if she is there in the kitchen with them. On the table, the dozen eggs, the two needles, a big white bowl, and a whisk, all in preparation. Maddie is on her lap, and they lean in like schoolchildren to hear it.

More and more people here in Holland make an Easter branch. It is a custom that has been revived. First we empty the eggs, and then paint and varnish them and display them on a branch. It can be pussy willow or forsythia or any branch. To empty the egg I take a needle to the top and to the bottom, pierce a hole, and then place one of the holes to my lips. Then I blow with all my strength until the white and the yellow comes out completely through the bottom hole. It's nicer to keep the hole really small, but it makes blowing the eggs harder. Ever tried to blow a big balloon? This is the same. I use water paints, marker or glue glitter, cotton for hair and beards, and sometimes paper hats to make a funny impression. I looked up in my symbol book and found this:

"Eggs have been a symbol of spring since ancient times. Rabbits, too, are associated with the fertility of spring because of their ability to produce so many young. The lamb is an important Easter symbol. It represents Jesus and relates his death to that of the lamb sacrificed on the first Passover." Blow blow blow, dearest friends.

"Come on now, we've got to blow."

At first Maddie loved it, puffed his cheeks out and giggled at the splutter of the yucky egg coming out of the little hole and the puddle in the bottom of the white bowl. Yucky. Yucky. Yucky. He dipped his finger in the yucky and tasted it and ran into the yard to spit it out.

"I'm having a rest."

"I won't let you paint unless you blow."

"Eily can blow."

"Mr. Yucky can blow . . . he has lungs."

"Mr. Yucky's gone on strike . . . Mr. Yucky's on his bike . . ."

By the time he has come back, all the eggs are empty and she has got out the paint, the markers, the glitter, the cotton to decorate them with.

"Guess what. I think there's a robber out there."

"Really."

"I heard him . . . I chased him."

"How did you hear him?"

"I heard him running over sticks—the demon."

"Good thing I have you as a guard dog . . . Smokey is dozy."

"Is Sven coming?" he said overquickly.

"You are a nosey one . . . I don't know. Why?"

"I like Sven . . . me and him have good chats. But I like

Eily the most, then Cass, then Smokey, then Declan . . ."

"Then bed," she said, and had to chase him before she got hold of him.

The painted eggs hanging from the swaying branches are like jewels, red and yellow globes wreathed in glitter, and even as she steps across the kitchen floor, they begin to tinkle, their shells so light, so airy, as if they might shatter into smithereens.

Cassandra

I WAS MASTER of ceremonies for the Easter Egg Hunt on account of my years in puppeteering, knowing how to play a crowd, how to work them into a dither, terrify them and bring them back down.

Eily had bought the prizes in the pound shop—balloons, cheap little dolls, cars, and colouring books. When the guests arrived she had already set up a bowl of hard-boiled eggs and jam jars of water and paintbrushes. Every child was invited to decorate an egg. They did squiggles and dots, and we hawed on them to dry them fast. Eily went to hide them in the orchard, and when she hollered and they were let out, they charged like barbarians, roughing each other, everyone wanting to be first. Screams which meant an egg had been found, and another and another. Then a big lamentation from Maddie because he'd stood on his egg and broke it. He went in for one of his fits, turned blue in the gills, and had to be laid down on the grass for his mammy to stroke his tummy and tell him he was the best boy. Two other children couldn't find eggs at all, so two extra eggs had to be scrawled with a red marker and hid in a prominent place so that we could get on with the big attraction, the prize-giving. They formed a line outside the kitchen door, and each child in turn got a marzipan chicken, a chocolate egg, and a little prize. None were satisfied. Everyone coveted the top prize, which was a Transformer Robot and which Eily stupidly had put up on the mantelpiece. I knew it would lead to ructions. Me me me. Two boys tried to knock it over with a walking stick.

In the end the grown-ups had to have a secret ballot, and the prize went to a little chap with black curly hair who never spoke. It turned out he was a mute. Then they stuffed themselves with sweets and chocolate cake, then they fought, rival gangs, *Bang, bang, you're dead, I'm not dead,* up and down the wobbly stairs, into the garden, up in the trees, peeing on one another, one boy squirting the girls from his water pistol, and mothers walking around the garden, admiring it, out of politeness.

It was evening when we got ready to leave, the grown-ups drooping, the children more feisty than ever. Two daddies came to pick up their brood, and it was amazing the welcome they got. Kids descending on them, kids hugging them, kids jumping onto the running board of a vintage car that one of them drove. It was like the largest toy they'd ever seen, and the daddy basked in their admiration of it.

Eily didn't want the day to end. "Let's go to the pub," she said. Several of the ladies gave her that look, as if she was a dipso.

"We can't take children to the pub," I told her.

"Denny knows me . . . he knows Maddie. We're regulars . . . we go for a pint at six."

"They're tired, they'll moan."

"A girl's night out," she said with that soft pleading look in her eyes and the lashes fluttering a mile a minute and her saying, *Please please,* and me saying, *Another time.*

When I drove off, I could see her in my mirror waving goodbye, and in that wave I saw that she was facing isolation, and I thought, *Why did I ever let her bury herself in that strange old house with its haunted vibes?*

Blow, Lady, Blow ...

FROM BEHIND a tall iron gate, patched with sheets of aluminium and looped with wire of every description, Lalla, the little girl, is running as though she is shaped out of thin air, running between the snarling, yellow-eyed Alsatians, in and out between the several caravans and among the men who are engaged in their sullen tasks, welding and hammering and soldering, men renowned for their cussed manners and their fights outside pubs on Saturday nights. Lalla is wearing a tartan skirt and dainty turquoise slippers with fluffy pompoms. She runs, indifferent to the men who are cursing her for making the dogs so excited, runs for the sake of running, with the lightness of a bright streamer, and when Eily and Maddie arrive outside the gate, she calls out bossily, "You're late, you're late." The dogs converge on the gate and begin to leap up, their yellow eyes unblinking; they hurl themselves against the wire, drop back, and hurl again, barking with a fierce and lusty malevolence, and Lalla ordering one of the men to come and chain these savages up.

Inside the cramped and curtained space of the caravan, four mothers sit in a quiet inertia, smoking, staring at the television as brightly coloured balloons drift through the stale air with a randomness. Lalla's mother, Dell, cleans in the school where Eily teaches, and they have been invited to make it a special birthday party for Lalla, who is four.

A small table has been laid with mugs and an iced cake, and the room smells of cigarette smoke and a sickly sweet air spray.

"I saw you a long time ago," Lalla says, touching Eily's hair, the blue braid of her jacket, and then her hand.

"Where did you see me a long time ago?"

"In heaven."

"She's lying . . . she tells lies," her brother Shane says, and ignoring him, Lalla holds up her best present, a plastic wristwatch, the colour of raspberry cordial, and she licks it to show how much she loves it. Maddie is tugging Eily's hair at the other side, jealous, suspicious, and whinging to go home.

"We only just got here."

"Come," Lalla says, and takes Eily's hand and leads her to a smaller room crammed with bedding and boxes and two bunk beds where she and her gran sleep.

"Every morning we wake up at the same time and I say, 'Hello, Gran,' and she says, 'Hello, Lalla,' and it's always eight o'clock on my watch and it's eight o'clock at school and it's eight o'clock for the cows out in the fields."

"She can't count and she can't read," Shane says.

"I'll spit at you," Lalla says, and they have a spitting match, and her mother calls in that they are to behave themselves and remember they are not alone now, there are visitors.

"I like silver and gold and I like light blue," Lalla says, studying Eily's mouth now, in which there is one gold filling at the back.

"Where do you see silver?"

"Money."

"Where do you see gold?"

"Teeth."

"Where do you see light blue, Lalla?"

"In the sky. I like Mrs. Quilligan because she has no kids . . . she lets me play football."

"No, she doesn't," Shane says. "She's too scared to play football . . . she plays with Hilda," and from a cradle under the bed he takes out Hilda, a china creature in a pink fur attire from head to toe. Lalla snatches it from him.

"Watch this . . . she can smile . . . watch this . . . she can walk," and Hilda takes a few stalled steps and flops back onto the mat.

"Watch this . . . she's hungry," and as she presses on her, Hilda's mouth opens, her fawn tongue glides out, and with a little dropper Hilda is given some milk.

"Watch this . . . she needs to burp," and Hilda burps and Hilda says a croaky "Ta" and Hilda yawns, so Hilda has to be put down because Hilda needs lots of rest, and Hilda is put into her cradle and brought off to her dormitory. Lalla returns with pictures of her favourite toys and boasts of the many things they can do: play football, go to war, go to hospital, get married, have babies, and sometimes have twins.

"I gave her a scary spider book and she got goose pimples," Shane says.

"What's goose pimples?" she asks haughtily.

"Goose pimples are this," he says, and starts pinching her, and as she screams, "I hate you, I hate you," a startled mother comes in, dazed, wondering how she could have begot such unruly children. It is while they are fighting and their mother failing to keep them apart that Maddie comes in from the other room, holding something as if it is a trophy. In the one hand he has Hilda's fur outfit, which he has peeled off, and in the other the magic Bakelite box that enabled Hilda to walk and talk and eat and burp and yawn as she went to sleep. Lalla and Shane round on him, as he is the enemy now, the baddie that hacked Hilda.

"Let's chop his head off."

"Let's lock him up in the shed with the dogs."

"Let's put him down the well."

"Nah, let's fry him," and as they band together to pick him up, he retaliates with vicious thumps, and seeing that they will not be reconciled, Eily picks him up and apologises to the mother, who runs on ahead to get the dogs chained up once again, and all the while the balloons are drifting idly and harmlessly through the air.

"I want to go home, I want to go home," Maddie says, thumping her now, though in his temper he is still thumping them.

"We're going home."

"It wasn't a party."

"It wasn't a party because you mauled poor Hilda."

"Were you flabbergasted?"

"No. Annoyed."

"I'll never do it again . . . I swear."

Once outside the gate she looked around in dismay. Her car was gone. She found it farther up, driven off the road, hidden with overhanging branches, a fall of yellow pollen on the roof. It looked shaken to her. There was a note on the seat, and picking it up, she saw a mawkish scrawl on a torn bill from one of the shops. She read it twice: "Blow, lady, blow through the hole in your big fat duck egg."

"I've goose pimples," she said, and looked around, and Maddie rubbed her arms to do his magic, to rub the goose pimples away.

A Weapon

JEREMIAH KEOGH talks to his rifle, except that it is not there; O'Kane has just sped off with it in the night. He keeps going over its life, him and it together, and the day he bought it from the firearms dealer in Limerick forty-odd years ago, when he could scarcely afford it. A single-shot bolt action to it, and the dealer bringing him into the back room, where there was a sort of rifle range for beginners to practise. Giving him little tips on how to use it. He memorised the certificate number, in his head, the very same as a prayer, or a recitation, in case it should get lost. And now O'Kane has sped off with it in the night. His legs still hurt where O'Kane bound them with twine. He recalls dreaming of being in China or somewhere in the Far East, and having his hands and feet bound by men, pickaninnies with ponytails, and he wakened with the pain and found he was in his own room, and there was Michen O'Kane, the returned native with a mask over his face, his eyes wild, shouting, "Where's your fucking gun, where's your fucking gun," and him defying him and telling him what a pup he was to break into a house like that. Yes, he did defy him. He will tell that to his sister Geraldine when she starts to complain. When she sees the mud marks on the carpet and on the windowsill that she cleaned, she will ask how he gained entry and weren't windows supposed to be locked and why was he let get away with it, why was he let run off with a weapon to threaten others with.

He recalls the times with it, going out at dusk to shoot rabbits and hares, shooting weasels and stoats, and time and time again the magpies in the cornfield. One for sorrow, two for joy, three for a wedding, and four for a boy. Half his life stolen, with that rifle. He has only to show Geraldine the wardrobe with its front door smashed in for her to know the blackguarding that went on. He is lucky to be alive, his shins and his feet bound, and the hooligan with an axe, holding it above his head, swinging it, then smashing the lovely walnut panel of the wardrobe, and him saying, "You could at least have opened it, the key is in the door," and the vile language of the pup, every other word "feck," and the lunatic, flinty eyes in the knitted balaclava. Geraldine will say, "Go to the guards," and he'll say, "No," because if he goes to the guards O'Kane will be back to finish him off. Between two stools, the law and the outlaw, O'Kane's parting words, "You go to the guards and you're a dead man."

If he had a woman beside him now, she would bring in a basin of hot water to bathe his feet, but he has no woman, his Helena gone ten years, his rifle gone, too, and the ammunition, the live rounds of bullets, at least eighty, kept in the tin that used to have floor polish and that imparted to them such a clean, housewifely smell. O'Kane with enough ammunition to do his raids and his rounds and his housebreaking. He recalls the impudence of the pup as he lifted the weapon out of the wardrobe, wrapped in its bolster case, and said, "It's as old as yourself," then wiping the cobwebs off it and cocking it and sighting him and him trying to plead with the bugger, "I need that gun . . . it's my only protection. What else have I against marauders like you," and O'Kane digging him in the ribs like it was child's play. His torch taken, too, his blue torch that saw him home nights from the pub.

He has a good mind not to tell Geraldine at all, except for the fact that she will see the muddy footprints on the windowsill and on the fawn bit of carpet and see the ravaged wardrobe, the lovely walnut panel in bits, splinters on the floor and the top lintel hanging off where O'Kane found his money, his last little bit of security for a rainy day. "Where's your fucking money" and him saying, "I've no money . . . I'm a pauper . . . I've only a pension," and he'll tell Geraldine that, how he stood up to the bugger, and O'Kane repeating it and him saying, "I forget, I forget where I hide things," and then the bolt pulled back and the bullets put into the magazine, the chill of it, and O'Kane panting with excitement, the hunter in his blood coming out, and him pointing to the top of the wardrobe, to the money in a leather purse that Helena had made and thonged herself when she went to night school in the technical college and studied leatherwork as a hobby.

He can just see Geraldine, one hand in her apron pocket, wagging a finger, fuming, "Go to the guards," and him saying, "The guards are no friend of mine and never were," and not telling her, because it would scare her, of O'Kane's parting shot, "You go to the guards and you're a dead man." He can't tell that to the guards, can't tell it to Helena, can't tell it, has to keep it to himself, alone in his room, his faithful weapon gone.

Chase

IT IS DARK as the patrol car comes tearing down the lane and swings into Cooney's back yard, stones hopping off the kitchen window and Kim, their little terrier, yapping. They storm into the kitchen shouting abuse at Jim Cooney and his wife for harbouring a felon. Children who have been around the table back off and huddle on the stairs, nervous at the sight of two men in uniform.

"Bring him down," Corbett, the senior guard, says.

"The hell I will. You come in here like cowboys, scare the wits out of my kids . . ."

"We know he was here . . . we have proof."

"Look, Rambo . . . I'd agreed with Guard Tully that if O'Kane came in here again I'd feed him, talk to him, and Rita, my wife, would telephone the barracks and ye'd park the car up on the road and walk in the back door and I'd express surprise. Instead of that ye burst in . . ."

"So why didn't you telephone the barracks when he got here?"

"He stayed two minutes. . . . He wanted a sleeping bag that he left here before he went to England . . . and at this very moment he could be on the other side of that ditch resolving to kill me and my family for talking to scumbags like you."

"We have to bring him in," Corbett says.

"Ye took your time over it," Cooney says with a sneer.

"We had nothing on him until Cissy's car was found."

"A pile of ash . . . You won't get his dabs on it."

"Is he armed?"

"He says he has an axe and an iron bar."

"Where did he go?" Guard Corbett does not so much ask as fling the question from the doorway.

"Off."

"For feck's sake, cut out the fascism, Jim."

"Look, cut out your own fascism. He goes one direction, then he turns round and comes back the same way. There is no method . . . there's only chaos, madness."

"What's his mental state?" O'Herlihy asks.

"Hyper."

"So where might he be?"

"I'd try the Congo . . . he often calls to Minogue in a caravan up there."

"You hide him on us again and you're done," Corbett says, and goes out.

They are on the mountain road by the cow walk where Moira Tuohey had reported dropping him off. Desolate country. The odd light from a window only emphasising the long and tedious distances, neither dog nor man in sight. Sometimes they slow down to peer out at a bit of plastic or a torn coat on the wayside, both hoping and not hoping that they will find traces of him.

"I wonder what brought him back."

"To hurt the father . . . nothing more and nothing less."

As they veer off the road over a bed of rocks into a field, O'Herlihy whistles to give himself pluck. In the thick, sightless, mountain darkness the weak light from the caravan gives the appearance of a ship far out at sea, receding from them. Next to it is a second caravan, sunk into the ground, saplings forking out of the roof.

"Oh, state of the art," O'Herlihy says, then, "We'll park the car so that the headlights shine directly on the door."

They trip and stumble on stones and various bits of machinery, greeted by a growling dog and hens huddled under the adjoining caravan.

"Do we knock or do we call?"

"We shout."

Minogue opens the door of the caravan and extends his arms in mock crucifixion. He is in his shirtsleeves and wearing rubber waders up to his thighs.

"Have you seen O'Kane?"

"As a matter of fact I have."

"Bring him out."

"Come in yourselves and get him."

Then O'Kane appears. It is as if he didn't walk out of the back room but flew, abrupt and raving, holding something and shouting, "Get back or I'll blow your fucking heads away."

The light from inside the caravan gives a puny feeble glare so that it is impossible to say what he is holding, whether it is a gun, a hurley stick, or an iron bar.

"Put that weapon down," O'Herlihy says, edging forward in a youthful show of bravura.

"You young eejit, I'll put you in a bog hole," O'Kane says, leaping in a transport of joy and fury, wielding the thing with long, swinging thrusts.

"Come back . . . we're not going to die for that fucker," Corbett says, and the two of them take cover behind the car, watching as he races back and forth, the caravan bouncing, calling them cowards, assholes, threatening them and all those belonging to them. Then, as if he has wings, he floats from the caravan over barbed wire and into and beyond a copse of young evergreen trees. They move from where they have been crouching, vexed and confounded, listening for but not hearing the sound of his feet running through the dark. Corbett massages his stiff knee with a kind of weary fatalism. He is still going through the motions of following the fucker, of catching him, but he is not following. Instead, he yells at Minogue to come out and account for himself.

"You are harbouring a criminal, you pup."

"He called for a cup of tea . . . I was pouring it when you boys dropped by."

"We could arrest you, you know."

"You weren't fuck able to arrest him."

"There was a serious danger to Guard O'Herlihy and myself . . . his language, his movements, his stance were all threatening."

"That wasn't a gun, that was a broomstick," Minogue says, and he picks it up and rides it and starts crooning: "Gee up, old gal, for we've got to get home . . . to . . . night."

In the car they do everything to reassure each other.

"To have run after him would have been craziness."

"Oh, mad. The fight in him," O'Herlihy says.

"It looked like a gun, did it not?"

"You'd need to be a genius in that light to say it wasn't."

"We won't find him tonight . . . he's in some hole . . . but find him we will . . . the rat."

As they get back towards the town they are quiet, constrained. Outside the station they stand to stretch their legs. The same stars, a few dogs, the quenched string of fairy lights around the pub, not a sound and yet an unease. He could be anywhere, behind the stack of porter barrels, beyond the high wall of the youth hostel, up in the ash tree, anywhere and fucking nowhere.

"I feel kinda bad," O'Herlihy says.

Corbett does not answer. A sentence seems to grind repeatedly inside his head: *We let him go . . . we let the little fugitive go.*

A Letter

"QUEASY IN THE HEAD, queasy in the tum-tums, too much diddly-diddly-dee . . . queasy in the head, queasy in the tum-tums, too much diddly-diddly-dee."

Maddie goes around the kitchen, half singing it, then opens the door and shouts it out to the cows and the stocky red bull. Eily sits on the stairs drinking a mug of coffee, summoning the strength to go to the village. There will be a letter from Sven. She is sure of it. Her hair is all knotted from the reckless midnight swim and she has not the will to draw a comb through it. Snatches of the previous evening make her laugh, make her groan. The singing, the barbecue with Otto as head bottlewasher, and too much diddly-diddly-dee. Her head is splitting. She takes a scarf off the back of a chair and winds it around until she is slathered in it like a mummy.

"Eily's a mummy," she says wanly.

"Eily's a mummy," he says, and opens the door again to announce it to the herd, then slams it shut. He is jocular because there are no lessons. Every morning there is a lesson. He puts dots on a word in his colouring book and writes a name in English and in French. The French is on account of Elmer the elephant's being a French boy. Elmer is watching from the dresser, Elmer with his harlequin suit and his cloth eyes, who doesn't miss a trick, making sure that they don't go without him. Elmer is no fool. His droopy ears are all agog. He has a squeak box inside his belly. Eily loves bellies. Eily paints women with bellies. Bellies bellies bellies. He came out of Eily's belly and he was a giant.

Since she feels too queasy to carry him, he takes one of the big sticks from behind the door and they set out across the mud field, him jabbering nonstop. If only he would shut up. If only the birds would stop singing. If only a cold breeze would circulate through her head. Bits of the previous evening keep coming back, the excitement, the banter, the jokes the men made, the ice cold swim, the way it felt like getting born down there, then the warmth from the barbecue, their heated faces, a young boy singing a love song, keening it out to the lonely fields and the distant lilac mountain. Too much diddly-diddly-dee, like there was no tomorrow. Tommy, the soberest of the group, landing the van in a ditch and their having to walk to the house of the young accountant, and his coming out in his striped underpants and everyone getting the giggles. Much cajoling to get admitted, and then seven of them packed into a room, like children, unable to restrain themselves, still laughing, still intoxicated. The young accountant coming back every few minutes and threatening to turf them out on the road if they didn't stop their malarking. No tomorrow.

When she held the letter up, her eyes brimmed with emotion. She knew it would be there and it was. But for her own stubbornness he could be there himself, talking away, and they would be crossing the road to Ownies for toasties and coffee, Maddie plying Sven with pompous little questions about farming. It was a pale blue envelope with wavelets of paler blue, and it had a lot of stamps. She walked to the bench under the tree, saw how damp it was, but sat there anyhow.

"Can Elmer and me go for a walk?"

"Don't go far."

It was as if Sven were there talking to her, she could hear his voice, that soft bedtime voice reassuring her:

> So I am back in my old room in my parents' house in
> the eastern part of the country, close to the German
> border. From my window I have a view of a church
> steeple and a watercolour sky. It has been raining
> the whole week. Because I got to know you so much
> through our listening to music together, it is now
> very important to me. There was an old keyboard in
> the room here that I got tuned and I play on it, songs
> we played, if you remember. I am also getting on with
> my studies. I plan to be a bit more intensive in that
> part of my life, as it's a good way of forgetting. How
> is your place coming along? Does the roof still leak?
> Maybe not, maybe Declan came. My strongest mem-
> ory is our going out that night just to make certain
> no one had squatted in it and playing the car tape
> very loud and the music went off outside and down
> to the lake and we made us a dance in the dark under
> the stars: You can get it if you really want, you can
> get it if you really want, but you must try, try and try,
> try and try.
>
> I meet vibrant, red-haired, attractive, husky-
> voiced women every time I go down the street.
> Hahaha. That's not true. It's a shame people can't ex-
> press themselves better. Listen to the tapes, I guess.
> Of course I'm thinking about all things small and big.

She decides to write two letters, the safe and the unsafe, and would ponder over which one she should send:

> The other morning I went up the track to give an eye
> to the ewes in Dessie's field because they are about to

lamb. There was a fox coming across the opposite field, lifting its leg every other minute, and then it crossed a stream and I wondered if it saw me or if it would attack the ewes. Smokey, our stray dog, spotted it and chased it, the two of them flying like mad over the fields, barking, their coats a mirage of red and grey, rounding on each other, and then the fox disappearing into a hole and Smokey hurrying back, panting, waiting for his reward, the big, dozy, pregnant ewes oblivious of his valour . . .

She put it down and began her second letter:

Believe me, I did not want wedding bells. I hoped for something to happen between us that would be permanent, and maybe it has. Life is a roller coaster and we never know, do we?

A scream broke in on her thoughts and then the crunch of brakes and someone running and her turning to look. What she saw was a car veering onto the pavement to avoid an oncoming Jeep and Maddie thrown up into the air like a ball, then coming down again and dropping under the Jeep, then a deathly silence, and as she runs, the driver of the Jeep, a woman wearing a man's hat, has her head out the window perplexed. Fred from the garage comes running, shouting, "Don't move the car . . . don't move it . . . the fan is under there . . . it'll cut the hands off him," and as he grips the front wheels, he mimes to the woman that he is going to push them back slowly, slowly. Eily and those who have foregathered watch, aghast.

"Hello there . . . hello there," they hear Fred say as he stoops down.

"Is he alive . . . is he alive?" the women shout, and Eily drops to her knees, her hands reaching in to him.

As the Jeep is pushed back she sees Maddie like a trapped animal, curled up, his knees to his chest, his face a stark white, and then as he opens his eyes and blinks and reblinks, a wail of thanksgiving goes up: "It's a miracle . . . it's a miracle . . . he's alive."

As she reaches in, he begins to shake, his whole body convulsing. When she lifts him out he feels broken, like a vessel on the point of falling apart. The onlookers say that he must be left there, that she must not pick him up, that she could injure him even more.

"Leave me alone . . . leave me alone," she says, gathering him up in her arms, feeling his bones through his clothes, holding him tight, tighter, the onlookers urging her to bring him to the doctor and she refusing and just staring down at him, incredulous, her little mite, her parcel of infinity.

"It's all Elmer's fault . . . he ran out," Maddie says, basking in the sympathy all around him, and there in the middle of the road is Elmer, unscathed, strangely comic and plucky in his harlequin outfit.

A Will

IN THE OUTER OFFICE of the solicitor, Eily can hear him having an argument over the phone, saying intemperate things, then laughing at his own gall. His secretary, who is typing at the nearby desk, seems to ignore it, and a couple seated on a stool are so shy and so fearful they do not even look up, the young woman just staring down at the tattered magazines on the glass-top table.

Edward, the solicitor, comes out, laughing, rubbing his hands as if all the invective has cheered him up.

"I want you to act for Colm as well as me," the shy woman says, half standing.

"How the feck can I act for Colm if I'm defending you, Cora?"

"He says he won't do it again . . . he won't harm me."

"I want to hear it from his own lips," Edward says, turning to Colm, who is wringing the sleeve of his jacket, bashful, unable to speak.

"All right, then . . . whisper it . . . imagine you're in the confessional and making an act of perfect contrition . . . if that's not too hard for you to imagine . . . and you're saying, *'I will not go with that painted Dublin woman in her Mercedes again . . . I will not be her odd-job man . . . and I will not come home four nights a week dead drunk and I will not beat up Cora.'*"

"He means it . . . he bought me this ring," and she holds up a silver ring with lovers entwined. Edward glances at it, then at her, then shakes his head. "There's a stone seat under the bridge where the pair of you can sit and watch the ducks going quack quack quack and stop wasting my fucking time."

The first thing Eily notices is a vast unfinished jigsaw, occupying most of the table, his papers and documents on the floor.

"For the ulcer," he says ruefully.

"I'd like to make a will," she says, a little constrained.

"Are you single?"

"Sort of . . . I have a child. There is a daddy, but I'm by myself now."

"Fancy free," he says, and then less jocularly, "Are you worried about something?"

"I'm probably imagining things . . ."

"Well, whatever . . . you're doing the sensible thing. I'm always recommending it to people . . . the trouble I've had about wills . . . fisticuffs. You see that door there? Well, they broke it down one night . . . the sons or daughters of a certain farmer . . . I know it was them, but I could never prove it. They got the door down, ransacked the files . . . they didn't touch the kitty money . . . All they wanted was to get their hands on that document."

"I wonder what made her make a will . . . usually it's when people have the wind up," Edward says to Maeve, who is still typing.

"She left this," she says, holding up a diary with a cloth cover patterned with dainty rosebuds.

"Oh, we can't read her diary."

"I have," she says, and unprompted begins to read aloud:

> When they are all here, Declan and Cassandra and Ming and Otto and the others, and we are smoking and drinking and propounding our tinpot ideas, I am full of fun and even showing off a bit, and then after a few hours a shutter comes down inside me and I want them to be gone. I want my life back, my aloneness. It is the same when I fall in love. I fall in love and I become the creature that the man requires. I allow myself to be overruled, but already the love has cracks in it like cracks in a mirror. The hard experience of married life has made me afraid. Yet I tell myself that it will be different with Sven, free love, free thinkers, free everything.

Flinging it down, Maeve is suddenly petulant, as if something in it irks her — "These artists, these would-be artists . . . they're all haywire, full of complexes . . . If you ask me, they need to do a proper job and respectable work."

"A beautiful lady . . . but her feet are not on the ground," Edward says roguishly, mainly to himself.

Fiesta

IT WAS A PAGAN FEAST on the mountain, an old recitation, old lusts, debauchery and division between men and women amplified to the brazen beat of fiddle and pennywhistle.

Since noon they had been blaring, cordant and discordant. Calling the country people, saying, "Come, come and hear the old story, the hedge-master's recital of the Women of Munster upbraiding their pusillanimous menfolk." The barren field with its coarse grasses and weepy reeds had been transformed into a Mecca, the marquee like a pale temple set down there, torch flame, candle flame, and red-and-yellow fairy lights plump as tulips in the trees and along the hedges, revellers sloshing their drinks, a jig in their old bones at the novelty of it all.

They came to marvel at the audacity of the girls, the imperiousness of the Ruling Queen — Queen Eevul of the Grey Rock, draped with dead squirrels, leaves, and the accoutrements of the forest — and at the benighted husbands in their hobnailed boots, their hoary beards and torn waistcoats, side by side on a long stool, having to endure the taunts of these gaudy girls. There was Winnie in harlequin suit, Cindy in black corset and fishnet stockings, May in nun's habit, Agatha a dairy maid, Peg a scrubber with her battered bucket, and Eily the Princess poured into a lamé dress with a white fur stole, a silver handbag dangling from her wrist.

Harry, the master of ceremonies, told the audience how a poet who was also a hedge-schoolmaster fell asleep one day by the lake that was within spitting distance and had the most outlandish dream concerning the argument between the sexes.

O'Kane was there, too, at one with the dark, squatting outside, quiet as a cat, the marquee's canvas flap uplifted on this sight of her in a purple dress and purple gloves up to her elbows, tears streaming down her face, and that Harry spiv skimming them onto his finger as if they were pearls and asking the audience to behold "her tearful eyes red and hot, her passions burning as in a pot."

The fiddlers outdid one another accompanying her verse:

> Heartsick, bitter, dour and wan
> Unable to sleep for want of a man
> But how can I lie in a lukewarm bed
> With all the thoughts that come into my head.

The disgruntled husbands, loath to listen to these tirades, had to be held back from attacking her.

> There you have it. It has me melted
> And makes me feel that the world's demented
> A boy in the blush of his youthful vigour
> With a gracious flush and a passable figure
> Finds a fortune the best attraction
> And sires himself off on some bitter extraction
> Some fretful old maid with her heels in the dung
> Pious airs and venomous tongue.

Dissenting old maids hoisted on wires poked her with broomsticks, but she mocked them.

> *Couldn't some man love me as well*
> *Aren't I plump and sound as a bell*
> *Lips for kissing and teeth for smiling*
> *Blossomy skin and forehead shining*
> *Look at my waist. My legs are long*
> *Limber as willows and light and strong*
> *There's bottom and belly that claim attention*
> *And the best concealed that I needn't mention.*

Then one of the husbands rose, tottered, and staggered onto the rostrum to have his say. He decried the baseness of womankind, asked what were they but scratching posts outside public houses, tramps naked to the skies in empty bogs, turf cutters astride them. Pointing to the painted Jezebels, he said he could guess at the layers of dirt under their petticoats, singled out Winnie, his wife, with her brazen hips and her bullock's hide, who had tricked him into marriage and who had made him realise, on that very first night when he saw her stripped, that he was a father before he had even started.

The Queen poo-poohed his gripes, egged on the mutiny, as with shouts and hisses he was sent back to his stool to sulk.

The girls became more daring, did headstands and somersaults, flirted with the fiddlers, lampooned the husbands, and cheered at the secrets Eily admitted to.

> *Every night when I went to bed*
> *I'd a stocking of apples beneath my head;*
> *I fasted three canonical hours*

To try and come round the heavenly powers;
I washed my shift where the stream was deep
To hear a lover's voice in sleep;
Often I swept the woodstack bare,
Burned bits of my frock, my nails, my hair,
Up the chimney stuck the flail,
Slept with a spade without avail;
Hid my wool in the lime-kiln late
And my distaff behind the churchyard gate;
I had flax on the road to halt coach or carriage
And haycocks stuffed with heads of cabbage,
And night and day on the proper occasions
Invoked Old Nick and all his legions.

O'Kane on his belly, midges eating him, bats in eerie whirl, seemed to lose contact with the earth as the compere cross-examined her on her vices.

"Are you a witch, Eileen Ryan?"

"Maybe."

"Do you dabble in the black arts?"

"Maybe."

"Are you friends with Old Nick?"

She drew her stole down and Harry gasped in mock terror and marched her around for everyone to see and be horrified by the devil's hoofmarks on her breastbone, skewered in a vivid indigo colour. To the crowd it was all fun, make-believe, but to O'Kane it was real; she had stepped out of her own world into his, into his transmogrified dream of her, all-mothering, all-sinning, she-devil.

Then it was the duty of the Queen to give judgement as to which side was the most deserving, and she sided with the women, decreed that the mettlesome young Whelps of

Munster be brought into the chapel yard and tied with chains until they distinguished themselves in the bedchamber: "Mix and mash in nature's can, the tinker and the gentleman."

The crowd applauded, stood on chairs, whistled, clapped, finding in the beat of their hands a waiting wildness, their pagan impulses brought to life in this heady carnival.

By the Queen's divination, the hoary old husbands tore off their beards, flung down their waistcoats, and became mettlesome whelps, partnering the women in a violent instantaneous dance to avenge the slurs and insults that had been hurled. The nun came onstage, riding a donkey, whacking it with her rosary beads, and when it lifted its tail, misbehaved, and brayed, the crowd laughed until they cried, tears and laughter all one. Outside, O'Kane rolled around on the grass in a frenzy for it to end.

By the time the crowd spilt out, the moon had risen, and he stood, a raving shadow, to one side of the exit, knowing that she would come out, and she did, spivs congratulating her and jockeying to light her cigarette. She and they went on down to the lake, smoking and laughing, and he waited until people had scattered and the lights of the cars crawled along the road on the far side of the lake.

"Chase me, chase me," she taunted them, and suddenly she was running, running out of her clothes towards the water, the men chasing her and lifting her up, her half-naked body blanched under moonlight, a laughing queen being escorted on her litter.

"Isn't she plump and sound as a bell."

"There's bottom and belly that claim attention."

"And the best concealed that we needn't mention."

"Shame on her."

"Shame on you."

"She's a water baby."

"Let's throw her in." A shanty song started up as they swung her back and forth, and then O'Kane could hear the big splash of water and her scream, half terror, half delight, as she was thrown in, her voice gasping, "It's freezing, it's freezing, lads." The men were stripping and leaping in after her, snorting, currents of water being churned up. He ran with wild eyes and wild teeth, pulling his shirt off, ran to the water's edge and put his face down into it, peering to catch a sight of her, her white body, her trailing hair. They had stopped laughing and there was a silence down there. Six men and her. He couldn't swim, so he put his face to the water and drank it and spat it out, and the shoreline sucked the water too and burped it back and he called urgently, but none answered. All was quiet, their bodies gliding together down there, through the orgies of the deep.

In the Forest

O'KANE CANTERS across the several fields. O'Kane's reflection in the sheets of standing water, scummed with weed and dock seed. O'Kane's shadow, dark and furtive, scaling the lime-capped walls, in a jacket he has fecked from a shop. Flying it. The lull hour. Kids packed off to school, mammies and daddies gone their separate ways. Empty world except for her and the youngster and the smoke from her chimney. He knows the days she teaches and the days she doesn't. Fields and roads drying off after a night of rain. In a pool of brown rainwater he dunks his face and in another pool studies his smart new moustache. Suits him. Then he hears a car hoot and leaps jumping Jesus onto a gateway to catch a glimpse of her going off, except that it is not her, not her creamy jalopy. It is a sports car with a fall of rain on the canvas roof and a fucker skimming it off with a bit of a branch. Feck shit. An all-night visitor while he dossed in a hay shed because of the fucking rain. Clean-shaven, not the bearded bastard he'd seen her having a bit of a to do with in a pub. Her windowpane with a sheet pinned to it. Private. Keep out. Fuck shit. He is waving his arms in wild rotary fury.

"Top o' the morning to you." He is in the kitchen as Eily starts down the stairs half dressed, her top through her white slip busty.

When she realises that she has a visitor, she reaches back to the loft room, takes a sweater, and pulls it on over her head. Seeing the stranger, his movements manic, his eyes agog, she looks down, then looks back to think if they could escape through the skylight. Her hair is plaited and she is barefoot.

"Want to watch that last step . . . the bastard should have fixed it," he says, and dances across to confront her, wags his tongue because she doesn't remember him: "What's this? Don't tell me you don't remember me . . . we're old friends. Maybe it's the moustache . . . d'you like it? Goes with my mustard trim . . . So you forgot me, tough shit." The words come in a welter, as if his thinking is going too fast for him, pell-mell, bubbles of foam on his lip and his eyes rolling.

"Who are you?" she asks with as much composure as she can manage. She hears Maddie getting out of bed and coming to the top step of the landing to peer down.

"Put the kettle on . . . that's what a woman of the house does," he says, then turning to Maddie: "What's his name . . . Ben . . . Caimin?"

"No . . . his name is Matthew, but he's called Maddie."

"Maddie Baddie Daddie, and you're Eily."

"What's your name?"

"Never ask a man in my profession what's his name. As a special favour you can call me Iggy, short for Ignatius . . . you got the fireplace fixed, I see."

"So you've been here in the past."

"In the past!" He is walking here, there, everywhere, looking at things, his talk fast, furious; he picks a pair of stones from her collection in a basket and, rubbing them, chuckles at the sparks that fly out. The sparks are of his own imagining. While he is doing this, Maddie runs out and comes back with a handsaw, to attack him.

"We're not cutting wood now, darling . . . that's for later," she says, snatching the saw and putting it to one side.

Her visitor stands then in front of the wall calendar, which has a picture of a goddess, a flame infant a golden crocus inside her torso.

"That you?"

"Of course not."

"Read me what it says."

"Read it yourself."

"Haven't brought my bifocals."

He stands dreadfully close behind her as she reads: *"Thetis was one of fifty sisters and an ocean deity. Reluctant to marry a mortal Peleus, she changed her form to a wave, then a fish, then a burning flame. Chiron, a centaur, advised Peleus how to win her heart. She gave birth to Achilles and in attempting to avert his fate tempered his body with magical fire and water."*

"Won her heart," he says, and laughs a laugh that is bizarre.

"I'll make you a cup of coffee and then I'll drop you off in the town. We have an appointment there," she says.

Without once looking in his direction she can feel his eyes following her, his mad curious eyes watching as she reaches for a mug and a sugar bowl. Then he gives a little tug to her plait as she crosses.

"Now now now," she says chastisingly.

"I was fucked up and lonesome, and who walked in but long red hair."

"Look, there's a child here," she says.

"Okay . . . Okay . . . point taken. You won't see me losing the plot. Poor Jesus, poor fucker, he lost the plot. Number-one bloke. Him and me we did the odd gig. Like my trim?" and he brings his moustache close to her, then parts his lips to show his teeth, which are a fungused green.

"In case you think that's dirt . . . it's moss . . . not a rotten tooth in me head."

"He's a yucky," Maddie says, beside her now, pulling on her sleeve, asking to be lifted up, and as she lifts him, she goes to the open door calling Smokey, calling Declan, then goes outside to pull on socks and wellington boots.

Suddenly the visitor is hitting the table, pounding with his fists, no time for coffee, no time for a leak, time to go.

"We're ready, we're ready," she says as she grabs her shoulder bag and their coats.

"He's a robber," Maddie whispers, and she pinches him to be quiet.

Crossing the field O'Kane talked back to the birds, shouted at them to belt up. As they arrive at the grassy fork where her car is parked, he runs to where he has stashed his weapon and she sees the brown gauntleted handle of dark wood and the barrel covered in different-coloured plastic paper.

"I never let my child near guns," she says.

"Uncle Rodney . . . the boys in the north, the balaclava crowd want to recruit me . . . I'm a crack shot, but I'm no one's poodle . . . a loner . . . a lone cowboy, that's me."

"If that thing is loaded, I'd like you to unload it."

"Drama queen, are you . . . Get in the fucking car . . . we have business, missus."

Maddie begins to shout and kick, refusing to let the robber into the back seat.

"That's my seat . . . that's my seat . . . it's not his seat."

"Now now, darling . . . it's only a short journey."

"Darling," the stranger says, then grabs the long plait of her hair, runs it over his mouth, and nibbles it.

The car starts, stalls, backfires with loud swift bangs as they go off.

"You've got a small gun yourself in your exhaust," he says jokingly.

His arm is across the back of her seat, and he tweaks her hair from time to time.

"I wish you wouldn't do that," she says.

"Angry, are you . . . You should take a course in anger management . . . Noisy car you've got."

"Yes . . . they'll hear us coming."

"But they won't hear us going, baby. Baby. Into the sunset . . . had breakfast, have you?"

As they approach the town, he huddles down in the back seat and pulls his jacket over his head, and Maddie is howling, trying to undo the straps of his car seat, yelling to get out, because the robber has turned into a monster. She slows down outside the pub only to find it closed, the green blind drawn, nobody about except a woman in the distance going down the hill, walking her dog. Outside the post office Birdie's van is parked under the palm trees, and Birdie is in the passenger seat sorting a bundle of mail. With her whole being she wills the woman to look in her direction. Birdie does look and merely shakes her head to indicate that there are no letters for her.

"This is where we part company," she says, turning to him.

"Put your foot down . . . put your dainty foot down," he shouts from the shelter of his jacket, and she feels the cold graze of the gun slide down the side of her neck.

Once out of the village he begins to laugh, loud, gutsy peals of laughter, the laughter of somebody locked inside a barrel and frantic to be let out. They pass the town hall, the hurling field, the funeral parlour with a lit cross, ponies in a field, and clumps of yellow gorse just coming into bloom. A man at a gateway looks in her direction, then looks away as if he has not wanted to see her.

At the crossroads she swerves onto the tarred road towards the next big town, believing that their ordeal will end there. He is shouting at her to reverse, reverse, fucking bitch, fucking cunt. She reverses back to where there are two signs bearing the name of the wood—Cloosh Wood. One is high up and written in black on a white signpost, and the other is a fish-shaped oblong of oak with fancy lettering. At the first entrance to a dirt road there is a red-and-white barrier and he shouts at her to go on, go the fuck on. At the third entrance there is no barrier, and he leans forward and grasps the wheel, steering them towards a dirt road and a grid over which a carpet of young green branches has been laid.

"Where are we?" she asks.

"God's country," he says boastfully.

To one side is woodland, a sombre-green gloom stretching as far as the eye can see, the village, the showery apple orchards of home far behind them, an emptiness that is ghastly. She listens in vain for the thud of a hammer or the revving of a chain saw, but there is none, only him starting up a yodel as he runs around coiling and uncoiling an imaginary lasso.

"Wayyupwayyupwayyupwayyupwayyupwayyup," he keeps saying, and it takes her seconds to interpret it as "way up."

"That's how gamesmen lift the birds," he tells her, except that there are no birds, no birdsong, no evidence of life except a tub-shaped black barrel with POISON scrawled on its surface and a wooden toolshed, the very new wood syrup-coloured in the sunlight. Perhaps it meant that workmen came and went, and presently she expects to see a forester materialise out of that wilderness of green. On a nearby tree at the entrance to a shaded path is a round mirror with a rubber rim, his spyglass, and that along with the strewn branches over the grid tells her that he has planned this escapade. She jumps as a forked twig drops onto her jacket and he flicks it off.

"Is that kelly green?" he asks, fingering the collar.

"It's royal blue, actually," she says tersely.

"Okay Okay . . . wrong script . . . erase . . . erase . . . wipeout."

"People saw us, you know," she says, the calm of her voice in contrast with the pelting of her heart.

"There's no one out there for you . . . or me, sunshine," he says.

"I have friends . . . I do community work. I teach . . . They'll be on our trail," she says.

"Lonesome trail," he says. He is staring at her, his eyes both penetrating and dead-looking, like worn leather.

"Why don't we have a smoke," she says.

"Your shout," he says, and they sit on a log, their backs to the wood, facing a wasteland of tree stumps and ash-heaped earth. He watches her take the brown cigarette paper from its folder, make a trough, then flake some tobacco into it and roll it.

"Lick it . . . lick it," he says, and watches her moisten it, then tells her to light up.

"Top o' the world, ma," he says, grinning, then throwing off his jacket, and he leans back along a log, smoke wreathing across his young face and his mad chuckling eyes. He is not yet twenty, she reckons, his Adam's apple supple, like a yo-yo, his arm muscles thick and corded. The short hairs of his moustache, reddish brown in that light, have the bristle of a cornered hedgehog. Maddie has not said a word, his face buried in her lap, peering out at moments through the lattice of his outspread fingers.

"Ever see *White Heat*?" O'Kane asks.

"I don't think so."

"Top film . . . Cody's mother thought he was the little lamb of God."

"Every mother thinks that."

"Bollocks. Town bicycle, every mother."

"You'd want to watch your language," she says, and as she gets up and crosses to the car, he grabs hold of her ankle and squeezes it.

"Yonder," he says, pointing to the wood.

"I don't want to go in there . . . it's dark . . . it's dismal," she says, in a voice a little quiet, a little placatory.

"That's where you're going, goat girl . . . that's the deal."

He waits until they have crossed to the narrow entrance between a line of trees and then he follows, calling "So long" to the ash-heaped wasteland behind them.

How engulfing the darkness, how useless their tracks in the rust-brown carnage of old dead leaves. Pines and spruces close together, their tall solid trunks like an army going on and on, in unending sequence, furrows of muddy brown water and no birds and no sound other than that of a wind, unceasing, like the sound of a distant sea. But it is not sea, it is Cloosh Wood, and they are being marched through it. The ground is soggy underfoot, with here and there shelving rock sheathed in slippery moss. Not even an empty cigarette carton or a trodden plastic bottle, nothing: emptiness, him, them, insects like motes of dust suspended in the air, yet crawling onto her and onto Maddie, who is scratching and whimpering to go home. She is carrying him and hums to simulate some normality. She thinks before she turns, then asks, "What is this for?"

"They're after me."

"Who's after you?"

"Dublin gang . . . knackers."

"They'll find you here anyhow."

"No way . . . they're afraid of the banshees."

"Look, I'll drive you wherever you want . . . I'll drive you to the boat . . . I'll give you money."

"You've no money."

"I'm getting a loan from the bank on my house . . . we can go there and draw some."

"To the branch?" he says, puzzled, then a flying smile.

"To the branch," she says matter-of-factly.

"By the way, that's my house you're in . . . I dossed there . . . I left that bracelet in the coal bucket."

"You can have it back . . . you can have it all back . . . the house, the bracelet, the land, the lot."

"Trying to bamboozle me?"

"I'm not bamboozling you . . . this child is delicate . . . he has to have medicines every four hours . . . he suffers with palpitations. We were to drop you in the village, that was the deal."

"Your man stayed all night . . . under the sheets. Did you walk up his leg or down his leg . . . make any babies?"

"He is a friend . . . a platonic friend. He's helping me to sort the house out."

"Fucking prostitute."

Mick Rafferty is on the phone to his wife, in the shop where she does part-time work. He talks in a hushed, urgent voice and she talks back in the same way, not wanting to be heard.

"I think I saw the Kinderschreck."

"Oh Jesus, was he in our barn again?"

"No . . . in the back of a car . . . with the newcomer, the redhead . . . laughing like mad."

"Michael, are you sure?"

"I'm sixty per cent sure."

"Oh God, protect us."

"You're going to your mother's tonight . . . you and the children . . . you're to come now and pack the bags."

"And what about you?"

"I can tackle him . . . I have a gun . . . but if everyone is here yelling, I'm powerless."

"Why would he be laughing, Michael?"

"I don't know . . . maybe he was telling her a horror story."

"Maybe he was . . . maybe she'll fall for him . . . maybe she'll take him off our hands."

"I doubt it," he says, and slowly puts down the phone. He recalls the desperate look on the woman's face and the Kinderschreck laughing so bad that his back teeth were showing. He knows that laugh. He and his wife and children have heard it and trembled to it in the nights that the Kinderschreck slept in their hay shed and he had been too afraid to go out and order him off. The only traces of him in the morning being lavatory paper and empty biscuit packets.

They are standing arguing. O'Kane takes a round tin box from his pocket, a box that held floor polish once, and he rattles it jubilantly. Maddie listens with his eyes, with his ears, with all of him, as the lid is slowly turned. She jumps several paces back, staggers, and gasps at the sight of the cluster of bullets, brass-coated, their snouts close together. He picks up the rifle, takes out the magazine, puts the bullet in, closes it, then pushes the catch forward and holds it with his index finger, studying them.

"Please . . . please don't fire that gun . . . talk to me."

"Boom boom boom," he says, and as he pulls the trigger a sharp brittle clatter breaks the immense silence, the lead slug cutting through the treetops, the leaves swirling in its aftermath, and a burning smell.

"Imagine if you were a child hearing that," she says.

"Don't touch them . . . don't touch one of them, they're mine," he is yelling, bent over Maddie, who has crouched by the tray of bullets, studying them.

"Leave him alone . . . he doesn't know what they are . . . he's a child," she shouts.

"You will behave yourself whilst here," he says, and lifts Maddie by the collar of his jacket, and she stands between them, daring him to strike her, brave cowboy that he is.

He seems amused by her flaring up. "Relax, goat girl."

"Look . . . listen . . . put yourself in our shoes . . . our predicament."

"You know what your problem is?"

"What?"

"Your problem is, you don't trust."

"And what's your problem?"

"My fucking head isn't right . . . My heart is right, but they fucked my head up."

"All right, then . . . let's talk to your heart."

"Give us a snog."

"Don't be cheeky."

"We're not talking heart-to-heart, are we . . . we're talking shit . . . Are you wired?"

"Where are your family?"

"Family . . . that's funny. They killed my ma . . . the way they killed Cody's ma."

"There must be somebody."

"Only my granny and my sister."

"Where are they?"

"Loughrea."

"I know Loughrea. I have friends there . . . Why don't we go and we can call on your granny?"

"Too risky."

"What are you wanted for?"

"Larceny, robbery, possession of firearms . . . devil's work . . . Bastards want to put lead in me."

"But it's not fair to punish us . . . we're not your enemy . . . we don't want to put lead into you."

"You're the one," he says, and takes a folded brown envelope from his pocket and hands it to her. Her name is scrawled in pencil inside a crude drawing of a pumpkin. "Read it." She looks down at the daubed ruled page, the laboured childish handwriting she recognises as from the note that was left on her car seat outside the caravan site. She reads rapidly:

> I am asking you to go with me I know you might not understand what it means, but I would like if you say

yes please say yes do not show this letter to anybody or tell anybody because they would tease us don't tell anyone please understand if your answer is yes we will start now please say yes don't be embarrassed signed Michen.

"It's for you," he says as she hands it back.

"It's an old letter and it says Veronica, Dear Veronica."

"She fucking pulled back . . . she's for it . . . should've given her lead."

"I'm not Veronica . . . you know that."

Furious now he snatches the letter back and shouts, "Giveusthephone giveusthephone giveusthephone." He bellows his orders into it: "Reported on sick parade . . . metal in Vomitus. Released from medical centre. Reunited with family at front gates. Energy level terrific. Chlorophyll feed. C and D not necessary. Proceeding northwest as per coda. Over. Over." He is looking at them but not seeing them, arguing furiously with a host of voices, his answers clotted, indeterminate.

Mick Rafferty is bundling his wife and children into the car. Aoise, the youngest, is crying because the boogie man that slept in their hay shed is back. His father says that he is not in their hay shed now and never will be.

"Are you sure it was the Kinderschreck?" his wife, Tilly, asks.

"I'm seventy per cent sure."

"You were only sixty per cent sure an hour ago."

"I'm sure for definite."

"Maybe you should go to the guards."

"If I go to the guards it'll only bring him back on us . . . The guards are as afraid of him as you or me."

"You said he was laughing."

"The girl wasn't laughing. She looked scared . . . dead scared."

"Oh, God grant someone will tie him up soon."

They are walking again, Eily's face caked with mud and scratched because twice she has tripped and fallen. At moments her eyes seem to go blurry. Endless line of trees, tree trunks, thin branches jutting out like spikes. Maddie keeps slipping down onto her hip and gently she hauls him back, trying to fold him in sleep, because asleep he is not crying, not fretting, he is dreaming, dreaming of home maybe, of Elmer and his blackthorn stick for thwacking the cows. At moments the needles and branches appear to her to have gone inside her mind and inside her mouth. Tiny insects crawl in the corners of her eyes and nest under her clothes. The air is stifling. "Hold on . . . hold on tight," she whispers to Maddie each time he begins to slip. At moments she is weirdly calm, telling herself there is a particular place, a point they have to reach, for some bizarre reason, which will be the turning point, and they will be going back home. She even asks herself why it had to be, why her, some lesson to be learnt, some truth, some indelible truth. Other moments she begins to hallucinate, sees the apple blossom blowing through their garden, sees Declan and Cassandra and Sven, all waving to her, holding up a burned kettle. She remembers the harried drive along the road, the gorse coming into bloom, the postmistress in her van, the tall man at the gate ignoring her. As for the time, she has no idea. This is all time and no time. Her twenty-odd years condensed into this lunatic present. So it is the next step and the next and the next half step, and Maddie beginning to pee and taking him behind a tree, the steam, warm and sweet-smelling, his face stark white but his cheeks red as tomatoes.

"Mama." He has not called her by that name since he was tiny; it has come back to him in this extremity.

"I'm here . . . I'm here," she says, smoothing his sweating hair.

"Will Cass and Sven and Declan and everybody come?"

"Yes, they will."

"And tie the robber up?"

"They will," she says, holding him tight, tighter, willing him back into her, into safety. He looks so little, so helpless, with his dungarees down around his ankles, both knowing and not knowing what is going on.

"Up up up," she says, hoisting him over her shoulder. She thinks that if they can come through the darkness and out into a clearing that the worst will have transpired. Not yet thinking the unthinkable. She stops all of a sudden, falters, then her legs buckle, refusing to carry her any farther. Sunk to the ground and looking up at O'Kane, she pleads with him, "You wouldn't put your granny through this."

"I would if I had to . . . I nearly killed my granny. My voices were telling me, egging me on: 'Do her, do her.'"

"What voices?"

"Big tall man with horns . . . over in England after I got out of jail, I went to my cousin's . . . He wanted me to pick up a carving knife and cut my cousin Anthony up in bits . . . I went into the toilet to fool him . . . I counted . . . I counted to a hundred."

"Come on . . . that's what we'll do . . . we'll count to a hundred," she says, standing again. She starts counting, as if she is on a stage, then Maddie joins in, and so does he, a rousing trio, a choir of voices, ringing out in the emptiness of the vast, drowsing, unheeding, noonday wood. When they have reached several hundred they are panting and he stops and leans against a tree, a baleful look on his face. She knows she has broken through to him, to that human kernel in him and, as she believes, in all mankind. Even his eyes seem less threatening, bewilderment in them. He is trembling and she thinks that the fear which had run in her blood and run in her thinking runs in him too, and that it is a matter now of reaching to the child in him, the child cut off from the outraged youth.

"I was in the fear zone back there," he says, wiping the sweat from his face, from his palms, with a filthy handkerchief.

"We were all in the fear zone back there . . . but we're better now."

"I was seeing hazes. I was cracking up," he says, and looking up at the sky, laughs and says, "Doctor cunt rode his horse down the mountain in the snow, got a bag of messages and hung them on the side of the saddle . . . You don't believe me, do you?"

"I do believe you."

"He wanted attention. Do you want attention?"

"Sometimes."

"Near thing with my cousin Anthony . . ."

"You're fine now," she says gently.

"Send that kid tobogganing," he says, the toe of his boot squashing hers.

"There's nothing for him to toboggan on, and anyhow, he's exhausted."

He draws her towards him, an urgency in his voice: "We really didn't know, did we, how good it could be . . . them

times rolling around up here in the leaves and the muck . . .
knackered . . . stuffing the food into my mouth like a
mother . . . like a mother. I must admit I don't often fall in
love, but you got under my skin . . . animal magnetism."

"Tell you what . . . let's go back to the town and I'll buy
you a pint."

"What do you teach them kids in that school?"

"Games. Rhymes."

"Up came the blackbird and bit off her nose," he says.

"One two three four five, once I caught a fish alive. Six
seven eight nine ten, then I let it go again," Maddie pipes
up to surpass him.

"Bogger . . . behave yourself whilst here."

"Darling, tell him the poem you learnt . . . go on," she
says, coaxing Maddie, trying to mediate. Maddie mutters it
and she repeats it with a studied calm.

> *I went out to the hazel wood*
> *Because a fire was in my head,*
> *And cut and peeled a hazel wand*
> *And hooked a berry to a thread.*

"I'd like to learn that . . . The teacher learnt us a story
about a princess that pricked her finger on a spinning
wheel and was put away, and the prince had to come and
beat down the brambles to rescue her."

"We have that story . . . we'll loan it to you when we get
back."

"Who says we're going back?"

"I do, because I'm the boss . . . I'm the mother."

"Okay . . . free kick to you," and he goes into peals of
laughter, and Maddie stares at him, quite still, still and
white like a little snowman.

"That cow in your school is after me . . . said the name of the rowanberries in her lingo . . . ever tell you about my first kiss . . . she bought me a charm . . . raving slut . . . hope you're not going to ask me to dance."

"Not on this rough ground, nobody could dance here."

"That's one of the things I missed out on, dancing and scuba diving. You go through them jail gates and you're gutted. They drill a hole in you. Take your balls. I bullshitted them. Couldn't unmask me. Extremely attractive nurse on wing said I was malingering. My grimace was not the prodroma of genuine psychosis. They studied my laugh, my grimace. Jack Palance came by, stole it for *Shane* . . . never paid me a penny."

"Do you get help now that you're . . . free?"

"Help. Horseshit. I was misdiagnosed . . . I got my mind back second day after I was released."

"I worked with disabled children up in Dublin . . . Maybe I could advise you as to where . . ."

"Who the fuck is talking about disabled children. I'm a man. You wanna watch your language, lady, you could be prodomaed for that."

"I thought we were friends . . ."

"We are . . . I have a picture of you on my wall . . . next to a picture of my gun."

"What's all this fascination with guns?"

"You want to hear a secret?"

"Okay."

"In the street the men watch you . . . want you . . . your honey pot."

"I'm a mother first and foremost . . . my little boy is closer to me than anyone in the world. He was born premature . . . I was on a holiday with my sister, Cassandra, and the pains began and we thought it was indigestion . . . There we were walking along one of the canals in Amsterdam and I'm doubled over with pain and my sister starts waving a white handkerchief at the skipper of one of the ships and he stops and takes us in . . . my little boy came out in a big whoosh on the floor of a big ship, couldn't wait to come into the world, could you?" and she massages Maddie's scalp under the mop of damp sweating hair.

"I get very low and lonely . . . People leave out bread and milk for me the way they would for a dog."

"Where do you stay?"

"In the area . . . mostly up here . . . I hid here as a kid."

"What's your real name?"

"Mich . . . short for Michen."

"Michen, why don't we drive over to your granny, like we said."

"Boom boom boom," he says, pointing the rifle alternately at them, at the latticed leaves, telling some imaginary gang to keep out, verboten, piss off.

"You're all right . . . you're all right . . . they're just voices . . . they're just in your head."

"Fuck them . . . you and me will go and put that nanny goat out of her misery . . . break her hind leg. I'll let the kid pull the trigger . . ."

"You will not."

"It's along here," he says, pointing to a trail. "I have a pet fox as well . . . a dog fox, he has balls . . . he only comes out at dusk."

"You said we were going to Loughrea."

"This is on the way home."

"Home, Maddie . . . home on the range . . ." She is singing snatches of different songs, jumbling them together, knowing it is crazy singing meant only to get through the next minute and to the next, to keep O'Kane on the last rafter of sanity.

They come to a disused lime kiln and he stands and whistles. The goat has gone, only a twist of brown frayed rope evidence of its being there. In a slant of sunshine, a crop of tiny toadstools, their fawn mantles trembling like little globes, and a white flowering weed, a creamy lacework threading through the flaked and broken stone. Idiotically she breaks off a stem. It has a sweet sickly smell. She puts it in her pocket, as a keepsake.

He runs back and forth whistling for his pet fox, ogling it. Ruben . . . Ruben.

Back at home Birdie feels that bit uneasy, deciding she should jot down what she saw in case she is ever questioned.

> I am a postwoman by occupation and I live alone. I am responsible for delivering the post in a van owned by AN Post in an area which includes a radius of approximately one hundred miles. Much of it is very remote and includes a vast area of forest and mountain. I was sitting in the van which I had parked under the palm trees across the road from the post office when I saw a light-coloured car come round the corner. It could be called cream or beige but certainly not white. As it passed just beside me, I had full view of the interior of the car. The driver was Eileen Ryan and she did not look towards me. It seemed to me that she might be restrained from the side to prevent her looking in my direction. It reminded me of someone having a crick in her neck. I thought it strange

that she didn't pull over for her post, sometimes she would pull up when she met me and ask if I had post for her. The look on her face was one of anguish, of pain. Her hair seemed to be more tossed than usual. There was something on the front passenger seat, it would seem to be a child. There was a huge bulk in the rear seat. This bulk was a greeny canvas colour. This bulk did not show its face.

Her car slowed and swerved to my side of the road after passing me and then raced up and seemed to move faster. When the car swerved, the person in the rear seat was visible to me. I realised it was Michen O'Kane, him they call the Kinderschreck. He had a tight haircut and a new moustache. I know him since his mother died. From a week after her death until a short time before his father remarried the whole family including his father, himself, and his sister came to my house five days a week for an evening meal. I am not related to the family. As a devout Christian it is my duty to look after someone in need. When he got into trouble at first and was later released from some reformatory, I heard he was hungry and living rough. I used to leave milk and biscuits on a gate pier. After a few weeks I heard that he was caught again for something and was put away again.

As time went on, I had no contact much with him, and for the first time in two years saw him last Easter Tuesday. I was going to deliver post when he appeared from behind a tree at Derrygoolin Bridge and waved me down. He told me he was starving and hadn't eaten for two days. I felt pity for him. He said he had a few bob in his pocket and asked if I would get him food. I said I would pay for it myself. He said he would hide there and meet me on my return. I bought biscuits, sweets, buns, and oranges. He had asked for these items of food, as he had no knife to cut bread or make a sandwich with. He said not to tell anybody that I'd seen him and said, "I know I can trust you . . . you were good to me as a child." Most likely he thumbed a lift from the woman, who may be moving away, as people are always coming and going in this neighbourhood nowadays, not like the old times, the decent times.

He is lying on his belly, the gun cradled to his chest, pressing his nose into the earth, shreds of clay at the end of his nostrils, his eyes black-looking as he stares into the distance.

"Let's go to Loughrea," she says for the umpteenth time, her voice weak and hoarse.

"Can we?" he says, excited, like someone just coming awake.

"We must. This little boy is dropping and he's hungry."

"Hungry," and he looks at Maddie as if he had been oblivious of him all along. From his pocket he pulls out a few loose biscuits. They are chocolate-coated, with a white putty filling. They taste stale and musty, but they eat them out of duty.

"I took rat poison once . . . I bit my stitches . . . reason for refusing food, wants to die . . . denied martyr status . . . fuck them. Not wired, are you?"

"No . . . I'm not wired . . . It's just that it's all been a bit of a shock for Maddie."

"He and me get on fine . . . I'm okay with him . . . I'm cool," he says, scruffing Maddie's hair.

"As I told you, he has to take medicine every four hours . . . and we haven't got it with us."

"He'll have it."

"You wouldn't hurt a child," she says.

"Only an animal would hurt a child," he says, and seeing there is feeling in him, way inside him, she weakens, and suddenly she is crying, her head on her lap, tears streaming into her hair, onto her clothes, saying "Sorry sorry" and Maddie patting her in dismay. She had not shown her weakness before, not since morning, since the drive, passing the ponies, the post, the man at the gate, taking the main road, and him telling her she was a fuck bitch and a messer and having to reverse. She had trembled, but she had not cried, staring out at the wasteland of tree stumps and charred branches with the realisation that something drastic had commenced.

"They're at me again," he says, and he plugs both ears with his fingers and runs around the trees, hitting them and yelling at his assailants.

"I can't hear anything," she says, going up to him.

"He's whispering . . . so as no one can hear."

"Whispering what?"

"He's not pleased with me."

"How do you know?"

"He smiles when he's pleased, but he's not smiling now . . . He's fuming . . . he says we can't turn back."

"Tell him that we will give him a reward, a big reward."

"Ssh," he says, and shuts his eyes to listen.

She kneels and prays, not the known prayers, an interceding to God, each silent word plucked, eked, from the pit of her being, and then he turns, shakes his head, and picks up the gun: "If it was up to me, I would turn back."

"Who is it up to?"

"My master."

"I beg you . . . I am at your mercy and I am begging

you," she says, as if she is still praying, but he hustles her on.

They are moving again, crawling through a tunnel, dark within dark, scrambling on their knees, her breathing jerky, Maddie's face burning and the rest of him quivering.

"He hasn't a pet fox," he whispers to her.

"No, but don't let on."

"Redhead," O'Kane calls as he emerges, and she knows by the suggestiveness in his voice that he wants her alone.

She takes Maddie across to where there is a trough of muddy water, with bits of broken stick, and picking them up, she says, "Look, you can play boats."

"They're not boats."

"Just pretend . . . just be a champ for a little while more."

"I want to go home."

"I know. When we go home I'll make you a big pan of chips."

"I don't want chips," he says querulously, vexed with her because she is leaving him alone. "I don't love you . . . I don't love you anymore."

Crossing back, she sees O'Kane haul something cumbersome from a grove of young saplings, drag it, then prop it up for her to see. It is a glass casket with the figure of the Virgin Mary, such as she has seen on roadside shrines.

"That's Our Lady," he says.

"I know."

"Have you been devoted to Our Lady?"

"When I was young at school."

"Top woman. Never known to fail. She baked me a fruitcake at Christmas."

"So you're devoted to her."

"Oh, she's the business," and he runs his hand over the

folds of her plastered body and then throws her aside. "Fuck you, Our Lady."

Next he takes out a bunch of withered lilies and scatters them on the ground, then a crumpled green dress, a scarf, an umbrella, a large white comb, and a cassette with a tangled tape spilling out of it. He unfolds the dress and holds it up in front of her, the creased sleeves dangling down, as he watches for her approval.

"You like it."

"It's very nice."

"When it comes to fashion I know my stuff . . . Put it on."

"I won't put it on now . . . I'll do it later."

"You're getting married in it."

"Ah no," she says, overgently.

"Let your hair down," he says, and hurriedly she starts to unplait it, to keep his hands off her.

"To your bum," he says, and runs the comb through it, breaking the teeth in his frenziedness.

"Am I fat—am I ugly?" he asks.

"No . . . you're not."

"Running around your kitchen naked . . . There's man eating maggots in that swamp near there . . . gagging for women . . . Monaghan fella told me . . . nasty customer . . . schizo . . . high risk . . . high high risk . . . So how do you feel about the future?"

"Hopeful," she says. When she sees him take out the wedding ring, she almost screams. It is thin, with a brassy lustre, and she makes a fist as he tries to put it on.

"I have a ring from the father of my child . . . I can't have two rings . . . that's bigamy. Keep it for your own . . . sweetheart."

"Sweetheart shit. Why do I go to this trouble . . . haul this stuff up . . . this gear . . . flowers . . . music . . . beef or salmon, madam . . . you know what I'm saying?"

"Yes."

"Then say yes."

"Look, I'm not who you think I am . . . you're confused . . . you're confusing me, with others . . . your mind is in a ferment."

"Are you on my wavelength, are you on my ECG?"

"Not completely."

"I'm talking to you, goat girl."

"I know, I know."

"Tell me what that means, yes or no?"

"I can't," she says, and thinking it might pacify him, she takes the bit of flowering weed from her pocket and offers it to him.

"Cunt . . . you don't give a shit about me . . . didn't even come to my birthday. Go. Just go."

She picks her steps nervously but unerringly to where Maddie is, lifts his hands out of the muddy water, and takes him in her arms. She starts to run. The ground feels light, like it is on springs, and her head terrifically calm as she begins to recall different landmarks: the tunnel, the toadstools, an old sock, the churned-up roots of the fallen tree and the long, steep path that led from the entrance.

He has almost caught up with them. He calls furiously, like some demented general egged on by the heat of battle. It could be heard for miles, it must be heard for miles.

She turns, then Maddie turns. "He's going to shoot Eily," Maddie says.

"I won't let him and I won't let him shoot you . . . I know what to do . . . You just hide here and I'll be back in a minute, minutes." She tucks him down, covering his head in a camouflage of pine needles, kisses him, says, "Not a peep . . . not a peep."

A quiet has come over O'Kane when she goes back, a deathly quiet that seems like deliberation but is not, his jacket on the ground, the rifle on top of it, his sleeves rolled up, the eyes a molten black, absorbing her.

Motionless, barely breathing, she knows she has come to the rim of horror, but still, still trying to reach the inner crater of his mind, she says, "Spare me . . . spare me and I will make it up to you." But he is not hearing, the grand plan had commenced long before, the grand plan evidenced in the round bit of mirror hanging from the tree, the strewn branches over the grid, she the instrument of something outside herself, iconic, picked from a thousand faces for wanton ritual.

"What are you going to do with me?" she says.

"Everything."

"God is watching you," she says, in a flat, hushed tone.

He pushes her forward towards a raised mound under a horseshoe of pine trees, their branches a young green, softly swaying as if they are saying something to each other. To one side there is a shovel and a furrow newly dug, an inevitability to it all. Her blood freezes, because there is only there and only then, the taller spruces slanting against the slope, the stagnant air itself waiting to scream.

"Will you leave the child outside the shop?" Each word said slowly, overcalmly, with quiet, grinding emphasis. He appears to be heeding it.

In that suspended second, her thinking races ahead, and looking through the trees, she says, "I hear someone coming." As he turns to look, she steps on the gun, bounces on it, as on a trampoline, her strength prodigal, her determination supreme. He lunges, appalled that she should have tricked him, and now the ultimate flood of rage that has been waiting is loosed from the wrenched and bloodied sockets of his fucked life as he tears at her clothing in an ecstasy of hate, as though tearing limb from limb all womankind.

When he flings her down she feels the harmlessness of damp earth, his craziness shutting out all of life, all of light, a tiny pearl button of her blouse skivving off, his mouth, his mucus over her, still begging him, her words being swallowed: "Promisemeyouwillleavethechildoutsidethe shoppromisemeyouwillleavethechildoutsidetheshop promisemeyouwillleavethechildoutsidetheshop."

All earth, all air, all forest is filled with Maddie's cries calling her, running, kneeling by her, child and warrior in one, throwing fists of clay at her attacker, clay that falls in splotched medallions; a warring triptych, flailing and furious, her yoked body, Maddie clinging to her, their desperate cries as one, going up to the trees and down to the wisps of dew that have outlived the morning, rising and expiring, dying and perpetuated in that catacomb of green, up there at the edge of the world, on the point of sacrifice.

Wild Ponies

PRE-DAWN, the grey woozy world, a horn of a moon going back in, and rain dripping off the branches.

O'Kane wakens in the back of the car, pulls the blanket down, and sits up crumpled: he looks around, feels for the rifle, and listens; then he gets out.

His piss against the green lichen of the tree rises in a prolonged and steaming arc, and he breathes deep and slow into the neutral greyness, allowing not even a chink of a thought, saying, Time to move on.

The car bounces over the narrow slash of tarred road, swaying on the bends, uphill and downhill, past the odd bungalow, a gateway, a red letter box, a caravan, cows. Another mile or so and he is on the dirt road, and after that on a mountain pass, lurching and bouncing among the ruts. No guards, no lorries, no scumbags, bandit country. He is in his element, whistling, cheering, as if he has won a race, a tremendous high, his energy gathered and transferred into the driving, the last drive in that rackety little yoke, soon to pass into another county, a deserted outback, the end of the little yoke, its last hooray in a whoosh of flame. He is untouchable.

When he has to slow down he thinks, Fuck shit and reaches for the rifle. Crazed ponies everywhere, bucking and leaping, and he thinks of finishing them off, pictures their heaped bodies all over the road, then thinks the fucking car will be stuck and the scumbags able to trace it. They are Shortie's ponies, brown and fawn and grey and spotted, bouncing in the air, butting the car in ones and in pairs, neighing, wild-eyed. He thinks, nothing for it but to drive them off the road, and he ploughs through them with a hectic speed, and they scatter towards the mountain. He stops the car on the broken bridge near where Shortie lives. His van is gone. The yard a scrap heap of junk and Shortie's jaunting cars for gigs in the summer, hens, and two foals at the front door leaving their cards and swishing their chestnut tails.

From the booth he takes some clothes and the yanked-off number plate, smells the clothes, flings them in the back seat, and then stands on the rickety bridge of iron and cement blocks and looks down at the water, which is the colour of porter and frothy like porter too. He is about to pitch the plate in when a whelp comes up behind him and grabs the calf of his leg through his trousers. He roars. It is the dog from her place, looking at him with a wolf's venom, one brown eye and one blue, not growling, not barking, just staring at him.

"You devil," he says, and strikes it on the snout with the metal plate, but it crawls away, yelping, and each time he tries to catch it, it slips from his grasp as if it is covered in oil or car grease. Then he tries another tactic, which is to coax it, to bring it closer. From his pocket he takes a few biscuit crumbs, holds them in his paw, calling, "Smokey Smokey." It doesn't come. It is on its belly now, crouching, the lips lifted over the blackish teeth. He kicks it, and it takes the kicking, and when he has kicked it unconscious, he jumps the bridge, slides down the slope, and hurls the number plate into the river. He watches it go, bobbing between the stones, in and out of the froth, swept in the current, turning a corner where there are willows, when the fecking dog reappears and jumps in and goes on downriver along with it.

Back in the car he is huffed and he is hungry.

To Fiona, the young assistant, he looked crazed, spinning into the shop, his arms flying it and laughing at nothing. She had come in early to unpack stuff and shouts, "We're not open, we're not open." There was muck on his boots, pine needles in his thick crop of brownish curly hair, and one sleeve of his anorak rolled up, like he had just been in a fight. A maniac.

"We're not open."

"You're open now, pussy," he says, racing around helping himself to cartons of cigarettes, biscuits, cream cakes, toilet rolls, and she keeps staring at the gap in the shelves and imagining how Mrs. Morrissey will fume and scold her when she finds that they have been robbed. As he stood by the chilled drinks cabinet he jerked his head for her to come over.

"Fanta," he said, and when she hesitated he shouted, "Santa Fanta, you stupid cunt."

She hauled out as many bottles and cartons as she could hold and slung them into a wire basket for him. Lifting a big haunch of ham in its muslin cap, he plumped it onto the slicer and chuckled as she almost cut herself from nerves slicing it. He lifted off the slices as fast as they came and gobbled them down.

"What's your name, pudding face?"

"Fiona," she said. It was the first sound of her voice

since he had come in, and it was squawky, like a chicken's.

"Open the till, Fiona."

"There's nothing in it," she said, and drew out the steel drawer with steel clips empty of notes and the several cavities empty.

"You're not getting my drift, Fiona."

"I've nothing for you," she said shrilly.

"You've plenty for me . . . Open your purse, cunt." As she tumbled the contents of her handbag onto the counter, a tiny blue medal rolled onto the floor and ridiculously she shouted, "Don't take that . . . it's for a novena."

His right hand slid along her throat, that and a splutter of obscenities into her ear, yet she did not move and she did not scream but began to feel her legs go, under her long tweed skirt.

She was unable to tell Mrs. Morrissey the exact time the lunatic left, as by then she had blacked out, and they found her slumped on the tiles just underneath the open till.

He drove out of that county and into the next. Stone walls instead of woods and trees, no cover. He drove for hours and passed through bogland, in teeming rain, and while it was still lashing, he drove across roadside streams and much later on into a field, empty of everything except emptiness. A rotting wooden grid led to another field and another, and he was sitting inside the car, waiting for the fucking rain to let up.

It was a slow, sulky burn, the flames wouldn't suck, wouldn't hiss, wouldn't boil. They kept stopping and starting in the drizzle. He had to douse it again and again. The wadding didn't want to burn, there was spite in it. The high was not so high now and he was freezing cold.

He sat by the ugly black burnt-out shell of the car say-ing her name as if she might answer to it. When he tried to leave he was stopped. Fog walked into the field and all around the field, and he was trapped in it. He tried going through a gap, but it was foggy in the next field too, and then the voice came: "Cover your tracks, son, cover your tracks, son." He was a big tall man in a hard hat and he was leering: "Cover your tracks, son."

He ran to gather her clothes, which he had flung up into trees and into ditches, and he brought them back to the embers and made another fire and crouched there and watched them burn. They smelt of chicken feathers being burnt. He'd covered his tracks, son.

Vigil

CASSANDRA IS in Eily's kitchen pacing, the front door open, the better to call out when they get back. There is something about the kitchen that is not right. A kettle has been left on the gas ring, a new kettle at that, and there is an aftersmell of burned rubber. Then there are Eily's purse, the medicine that Maddie has to take every four hours, and Elmer propped on the dresser, all evidence of their leaving in a hurry. In a corner his purple Rolls-Royce, his "Vintage," as he calls it and a stack of wooden bricks. She thinks that maybe Eily has had to bring him to the doctor and considers going out to ring the surgery, but stops herself.

To be in Eily's kitchen without Eily is quite unsettling. She misses the laughs, the smokes, the bit of bickering. In the basket are the several stones that Eily collected on her journeys, stones sometimes chosen in the vertigo of love. She picks one up—round, squat, grey, inscrutable, its stony life locked within it, so that it tells nothing of its former whereabouts. She is jittery, stroppy at moments, and in the tiny mirror her eyes are stricken, as if someone had tried to scratch them. Then she jumps with relief at the sound of their arriving by the side of the house. It is Smokey, black and slimy, as if he'd been dipped in a barrel of oil, letting out short weird whelps.

"Smokey . . . Smokey, where were ye?" she says, and listens for the footsteps coming across the fields, the pair of them humming and chatting, and rehearses her own scolding voice saying, "You stood me up yesterday, you bloody stood me up." Eily and herself had arranged to meet in the town that morning, to go to an auction room and buy a few pieces of furniture.

During those next hours while she waits, she invents reasons for Eily's absence, says how wilful she is, often taking off on the spur of the moment, maybe gone to the city, or maybe gone to meet Sven, who might be reinstated. She climbs the stairs to see if Eily's Turkish travel bag is in its usual place under the bed and flinches at the sight of it. She telephones three friends, finds only Hildegard at home, and voicing her anxiety she feels ridiculous. She has to listen to a homily on Eily being a free spirit, a changeling, probably at that moment walking along some riverbank with Maddie and a new admirer paying her court.

She cannot stay indoors a moment longer. Hours have gone by, smoking, scouring the kettle, making cups of tea, some mindless cleaning of this and that. At the fork where the grassy paths join, she notices a man's glove, thick and black, like a boxing glove, a menacing purposeful feel to it, as if a fist were bunched inside. She draws back, too fearful to touch it or pick it up.

It is getting dusk, big sulky clouds threatening to rain and the newborn lambs in Dessie's field bleating. It feels like a maternity ward, mothers bleating too, running around after their idiotic young, who can barely stand on their buckled newborn legs.

"Shut up, shut up," she shouts, but it is to Eily she is really shouting. She remembers when they were young and how they used to play hide and seek in an old fort, and Eily was always the one to find the most covert place.

"I can't play this game for a second longer . . . Come back, come back from wherever it is you have absconded to," and saying it she puts her palms up in a gesture of prayer, and as the clouds break and she feels the first big spatters, she believes they are in answer to those wretched hours, her mind askew, imagining the worst.

In a tender reversal now of her spleen and impatience, she thinks how grateful she will be to see them, how deep that river runs with Eily and herself.

When they had not returned by morning Cassandra drove to the barracks, only to find that it was shut. She had to turn an iron handle and speak into a machine, then communicate her desperation to a faceless guard six or seven miles away. He is dismissive, reminding her that a grown lady, ergo her sister, has probably gone off for the long weekend and who wouldn't, what with the gorgeous weather that was forecast. She formed a picture of this young man, callow, restless, and irritable because of not being out in that promised gorgeous weather.

"She's missing," she says emphatically.

"A missing person is not a missing person until seven days have elapsed."

"She's very responsible . . . she would not disappear without letting me, her sister, know."

"Oh yeah . . . I stopped her for speeding a few times . . . Arty, isn't she?"

"What's wrong with arty?"

"Next thing you'll be asking me to give her Housewife of the Year award."

"Oh please . . . please this is serious," she says, trying to reach him now, trying to smother her anger, and suddenly and pitifully she is kneeling on the gravel, her mouth to the face of the machine, begging him to at least drive out and go with her to Eily's cottage to see if there is anything suspicious there.

"I don't have a patrol car . . . and I can't leave the station. You see, we're short-staffed on account of the bank holiday."

"What do I do?"

"Go out searching if you want," he says, and then the connection is cut off and the machine has that terrible deadness of machinery. From behind the barracks she can hear a lawnmower start up and knows that a guard or a sergeant must be there so she calls out, her voice shrill and warbling above the solid whirr of the blade in its near and less near precision, someone beyond that fence who hears her cry but is ignoring it. She climbs onto the fence and sees him in his shirtsleeves, impassive as a plank, and when he turns he shows no recognition, his eyes empty of seeing as he stoops and empties a scuttleload of young grass, the lime green specked with bits of chopped daisies.

That night a strange thing happens. Cassandra lay waiting for sleep, knowing that she would not sleep, her mind in splinters thinking of the machine she spoke into and of the guard who met her in another station who also seemed indifferent to her plight. She is thinking of the moment when she will have to break it to her distraught mother and father, picturing their faces, their disbelief, their shock.

When she hears footsteps in the garden she's not surprised; it is as if she has been waiting for this nameless person to come and take her, too. Naked, she pulls the quilt up to her chin, with only her eyes listening, hearing the knocking on the door that is quite timid. The caller has not struck the knocker, merely tapped tentatively on the wooden panel. She waits for a voice, a command.

She is in the kitchen now, the light from the hall shedding only a faint beam, so that to the person outside, the kitchen is a sphere of dark. The telephone is over by the fireplace, the green light of the answer machine like a little bead. She believes that she will be shot as she crosses to it. The knocking grows more persistent, but is still gentle, as if the person on the other side is pleading with her to have trust in it. She kneels by the side of the door and in a strangled voice asks, "Who is it?"

"Can you open the door?"

"Who is it?"

"Declan."

"Declan who?"

"I'm a friend of Eily's . . . I was doing the roof for her . . . you met me." As she opens the door she sees a young man, his gaunt face terrified and a cigarette about to drop off from the corner of his lips. "We think that the Kinderschreck might have taken them."

"The who?"

"A local . . . a wild man . . . He's only out of jail a few weeks. Since he got back home, he's created mayhem, stole cars, beat up a pensioner . . . took a gun . . ."

"Why do you think he would have taken Eily and Maddie?"

"If I tell you, will you promise that you won't say it was me? A man saw them around noon last Friday . . . the day they went missing . . . his wife let it out in the shop. The man is demented ever since, he's too afraid to go to the guards in case the Kinderschreck came back to kill them."

"Who is the man that saw them?"

"His name is Rafferty . . . They live a mile outside the village . . . on the right-hand side . . . a lovely flower garden."

"And he saw Eily driving with this wild man?"

"Don't say I told you."

"Why not? Why not, Declan . . . we must all band together."

"It's my mother . . . I'm out all day working and she's afraid he will come and take revenge. You see, he's sworn to paint the town red . . ."

She feels cold, forewarned, knowing that the suspendedness of the last three days is a mere prelude to something terrible. She knows. Yet she still thinks of them as alive; Eily's spirit would have spoken to her, sent her a sign of some sort, some premonition as she lay in the coiled darkness anticipating footsteps on the gravel under her window.

"We'll have to get the guards to track down this wild man," she says.

"We'll have to storm heaven and earth," he says sheepishly.

He did not leave, he vanished, like a fish darting down into the depths of a river, and she stood and watched the sky, a tapestry of stars, and she could hear seagulls crying, the lonely, icy, almost human shrieks of seagulls who had come sixty or seventy miles in from the sea. And why.

They stand as one in Mrs. Rafferty's cement path, appealing to her in her doorway — Cassandra, Delia, Hildegard, and Kim. It is evening, as they have had to wait until Delia finished teaching school, Delia round and strong and complacent, a link between the local people and the outsiders. The garden is a shower of colour, tiny blue flowers faint as drizzle, big white daisies, and devil's pokers a flame red, with red-bonneted gnomes in the flower beds, like bucolic guardians. The pebbledash of the house a mosaic of ornamental shells and wedges of deep blue glass holding lakelets of blue light. Mrs. Rafferty is vague, uncomprehending, her eyes averted, insisting that she does not know a thing, cannot understand why they have come. All of a sudden she seems animated, says by far the best places for their enquiries are shops, post offices, bars, and restaurants. She even recalls the name Celine, the proprietor of a new international bar who would be familiar with the comings and goings of travelling folk.

"Eily Ryan is not a traveller . . . she moved here," Kim says.

"Is that so?" Mrs. Rafferty says vaguely.

"Your husband saw someone in her car," Cassandra says.

"I'm not my husband."

"I'm her sister . . . I'm desperate . . . my mother and father are desperate . . . put yourself in our position . . . help us."

"I can't," Mrs. Rafferty says, retreating backwards into the house and almost colliding with her husband, who has obviously been listening. He salutes them with a stricken look, as if their arrival bespeaks doom for him. He speaks rapidly, as if in a witness box giving a prepared statement: "I saw her drive past here at approximately twelve noon last Friday. There was a man in the back aged about twenty with dark brown hair and he had on a green jacket," and pointing to the wellingtons Hildegard is wearing, he deems them the same green as the man's jacket, an army green, yes, army green.

"Can you name him?" Delia asks, sympathetic.

"No . . . all I can tell ye is the registration of the car . . . it's the same as my pickup truck. TZY."

"Was it O'Kane?" Cassandra asks.

"I couldn't answer that."

"But you know him, Mick," Delia says.

"Many people know him . . . you know him yourself, he's a pest."

"I taught him for a short while," she says. She has taught Mick's children also, and somehow she feels that he is better disposed towards her.

"I've told you all I know," he says, and puts his hand out to shake hers in conciliation.

"It was my idea to come to you," she says, her big brown saucer eyes gazing into his, begging him.

"Unease quickly spreads," he says in a droning voice, like a man talking in his sleep.

"Which direction did the car go, Mick?" she asks.

"Maybe Portumna . . . or maybe up there," pointing to the swath of evergreens.

They drove to the forest then, a place of unyielding solitude, vast, quiet, and they got out of the car and stared into a hinterland of green, trees stacked close together, the trapped wind like the sob of a sea, stared at it and then at the charred tree stumps on the other side, and throwing up her hands Cassandra asks, "Where do we begin . . . where do we begin to search?"

"We begin by getting the goodwill of the guards . . . the

local people, the foresters, people who know these woods, know them backwards," Delia says.

They stood in silence, reluctant to leave, each thinking it some kind of dishonour to go.

As they drive back down the road, they see Mrs. Rafferty away from her own gate with a cardboard box over her head. She gestures for them to slow down and in a galloping voice says, "My husband is sixty per cent sure it was the man you named."

"Sixty per cent," Delia says.

"That's how he worded it to me . . . it's on his conscience," she says, her sloe eyes darting in every direction.

"Will he go to the guards?"

"I'm trying to get him to go, but he's afraid . . . we're all in fear of our lives," she says, and from deep inside her comes a strange racking cough, like a death rattle.

Kim debates aloud to herself whether she should or should not tell them something that only she knows.

"For God's sake, Kim."

"A year ago last September I was off down near Eily's place, picking blackberries, and O'Kane came on me in that sneaky way of his and he made me go across to the house . . . He said it was his headquarters and that it would be up for sale soon, but if anyone else bid for it he would shoot them."

"There we have it," Hildegard says, and blesses herself.

"Can we speak to you in confidence?" Delia says to the tall guard on the other side of the counter.

He knows that they have come concerning the missing people, and he is already resistant.

"Go ahead," he says, but he makes no attempt to bring

them into the back room marked PRIVATE. That he is impatient is evidenced by his clicking the barrel of a biro, rearranging sheets of paper while pretending to listen.

"We want a search in Cloosh Wood," Cassandra says.

"Cloosh Wood . . . you're talking of over a thousand acres. It takes forty minutes alone to drive there and drive back . . . We've only four officers in our entire unit."

"It's got to be done," she says.

"Why there?"

"It's O'Kane's area," Kim says.

"O'Kane fever . . . why has everyone got that scoundrel on the brain? We're not treating this case as an abduction . . . They are simply a mother and a son who have taken off somewhere."

"He was seen in her car last Friday," Delia says very quietly.

"That doesn't mean anything . . . he's always thumbing lifts."

"But he's dangerous."

"He only does Mickey Mouse crimes."

"Burning Cissy Slattery's car isn't a Mickey Mouse crime . . . Kicking a pensioner unconscious isn't a Mickey Mouse crime."

"Who saw him in her car, some visionary?" he asks testily.

"No, a farmer outside the village . . . Mick Rafferty . . . but he's being cautious about it . . . His wife broke it to us."

"Well, that might be a link," he says, pausing, reaching now for a pad to jot down the farmer's name and address and cursing locals twice O'Kane's size for giving him bed and breakfast instead of turning him in.

"Would he be armed?" Kim asks.

"Not a firearm . . . maybe an axe or a knife."

"If he has her, what might he do to her?"

"Not that much. He's a loner, he'd use her to get him from A to B and then he'd vanish . . . Women are not his thing," he says, a little abashed at the necessity to broach such a thing.

"That's not true," Kim says abruptly.

"Why so?"

"I was in a caravan site two years back and he spent some time there . . . We used to all sit outside at a picnic table in the summer evenings, and one evening he said a thing I would rather not have heard."

"About women?"

"About women and what he would like to do to them," she says, and lowers her head with shame.

"Would you come out with us and talk to this Rafferty man . . . it's serious," Delia says.

"I'll go out later on . . . I'll have to refer to someone higher up to get the okay, and then I'll go out and take a statement from him."

"That's my sister," Cassandra says, holding up a photograph of Eily, thinking it will melt him, enlist him, those huge trusting eyes, the face pale and moulded under the brim of a straw hat.

"Good-looking woman," he says.

"We'd like it in the local newspaper."

"You'll pay dear for that unless you have an in with an editor or a subeditor."

"What about television?"

"She'd have to be missing for at least a week for that crowd to cotton on."

"Guard Tighe," Delia says, putting her hands flat on the

counter, her ample body softly feminine, her pleading eyes staring directly into his, not letting him slip from her, "you see, Eily moved into a house that O'Kane thought was his."

"His lair," he says soberly.

"His fox's lair," she counters.

"And finds Mrs. Fox at home."

"And Baby Fox," Delia says, her voice tapering out.

His voice ceased, but his thinking quickened and his thin, sallow face was a map of tiny creases.

Suspicion

AT FIRST GLANCE, Aileen could tell there was something wrong with him; she sensed it the minute he came in, soaking wet, his hair plastered down, his eyes caved in and black as soot. It was back and forth, back and forth, from the kitchen window to the side window, from the back door to the hall door, on edge, listening for the slightest sound, kicking the cupboards open in case there was someone inside them. He wanted clean underpants and wanted them fast. They sparred over that. She said he was not in an English hotel now, meaning an English jail, and that his granny was not a laundry girl.

"Where is my granny . . . This is her house, not yours."

"I come every Tuesday to give her a hand."

"Where is she?"

"She's down the fields dosing a sick calf . . . A woman of her age doing things men should be doing. Where have you been?"

"In the woods."

"What were you doing in the woods?"

"You'd love to know, wouldn't you?"

"I can see you're in one of your hate moods."

"Hand me the fecking underpants," he shouts as she roots in a clothes basket and hauls out different garments, socks, pillow slips, rags. He takes off his jeans and wrings the wet out of them onto the floor, jumping at the sound of a passing car and rushing into the back hall shouting at her to lock the fecking doors and keep the pigs out. When he draws the striped underpants on over his dirty white ones, she asks him if he is stone mad and tries to pull them, saying that if anything happened to him, like he had an accident, people would think he was kinky. He laughed at that and drew them up above his waist, and for a split second she saw the prankster of his youth in him. When she lifted his anorak to dry it before the fire, she nearly dropped it on account of its being so heavy.

"Jesus, how can you carry it . . . it's a ton weight," she said, and he grabbed it from her and told her to leave his stuff alone, to mind her own fucking business. "What in the name of God is at you?"

"They're coming, they're coming for me . . . they're taking me away."

"There's no one coming for you . . . there's no one out there . . . it's only rain dropping out of a gutter."

He made her open the door and go out and walk around to the gable to see if someone was lurking. It was then she noticed it propped against a pipe, bagged up with different colours of plastic and tied with different twines. She stood looking at it and called to him, "What is this yoke?"

"A fishing rod."

"A fishing rod . . . you're not a fisherman."

"It's the season . . . the mayfly. French and German and Dutch people in the hotel, they'll pay me to be a gilly."

"It's not a fishing rod," she said, studying it.

"It's a curtain rail."

"What in feck's name would you want with a curtain rail and you sleeping rough in the woods."

"I got a nice place . . . I'm doing it up . . . me and some-one."

"I hope she'll straighten you out. Father rang here and said you nearly ran him over on the road, him and three others . . . you tore past them in a car. Still whipping cars are you? One of these days you'll be in trouble again."

"Never . . . I'm a big player now."

She pleaded with him not to bring it in the house be-cause she well knew what it was. He laid it on the table with a braggishness and untied the knots slowly, unwrap-ping it more slowly still, as if it was Christmas and he was opening a toy. His eyes lit, watching her watching it. She screamed when she saw the grey muzzle of a gun. Once he had unwrapped it completely, he put his hand on the trig-ger and held it, playful, tantalising, and for that intermin-able minute she stood watching, not daring to speak, merely looking at it, waiting for it to go off. When he was satisfied that he had frightened her, he let go of the trigger and unbreached it, and it lay there like a broken ornament, the brownish wood handle with writing on it, stained in black, a silvery pin and the metal barrel like the eye of a tel-escope taking in her and the contents of the kitchen.

"Gather it up and get it out of here," she said.

"You want me caught, don't you?"

"I don't want you caught, but I want you to talk to me . . . I want you to tell me if you're getting yourself deeper into something you won't be able to get out of."

"I'll never do time again . . . me or Uncle Rodney," he said, and bent his cheek to it and caressed it, and she knew then there was something very wrong, very weird about that.

"Why didn't you bring this girl along?"

"She sleeps all day."

"Oh, a Sleeping Beauty."

"A Sleeping Beauty," he said to the mirror, and asked it if it thought he was good-looking or if he was too fat.

Hearing her grandmother and the dog, she told him for feck's sake to get that thing out of sight, to cover it up. The moment his grandmother arrived in the kitchen she ran to hug him, asked why he hadn't been sooner, why hadn't Aileen given him his tea, and why a new moustache and a little fledgling beard. She kept looking at him, regretting that he looked older, and please God wasn't he out of trouble now and starting a whole new life.

"They fucked my head up bad in England," he said.

"Don't use bad language, son."

"But not my heart," he said, letting her touch the outline of his moustache.

"Your soft heart," his granny said, and recounted that day in the morgue when his poor mother died and it was snowing outside and him sliding down the banister and out into the grounds to bring back a snowball to run over his mother's face, to give her the kiss of life.

"The kiss of life!" Aileen said, watching him watching the doors and the windows.

As a car swung into the yard he shouted at them to lock the door.

"It's only Tom . . . it's only cousin Tom . . . he's coming to fetch a lawnmower," his granny told him, and ordered him to sit down.

"What's that thing outside the door with plastic over it?" Tom asks as he comes into the kitchen and sees O'Kane with a mug of tea and apple pie placed before him.

"It's a long gun," Aileen says tartly.

"A long gun!" his granny exclaims.

"I wouldn't use it to hurt anyone . . . never."

"Well, you'd better get it out of here . . . I passed a patrol car a couple of miles up," Tom says.

"Where were they going?"

"Looking for you, perhaps," Tom answers, and opens and closes the oven door to show his disquiet, then goes to the dresser and takes the news cutting out of a tureen and places it on the table.

"Nice work," he says, holding up the picture of O'Kane attacking an old lady that was caught on video.

"A poor woman . . . the same age as myself," his granny says, tears in her eyes.

"I didn't do it . . . I was framed . . ."

"You've no business coming here," Tom tells him.

"I came to see my granny."

"I'm glad you did, love. We went through a very hard period. You gave us a fright when you stabbed your sister that time, scared us all, and you're always running away."

"Will I be able to stay until it gets very dark?"

"I don't know . . . things are different since you went to England."

"No one wrote to me . . . not even you."

"I didn't know what to say to you, son . . . I realise now I should have written."

"I'll be gone before daylight." He looks at his grand-mother, tenderly, the look that promises to do no wrong, and she looks back torn, then reaches into a drawer and takes out money and puts it in his pocket.

"I burnt a car up in a wood a while back."

"Whose car?" Aileen asks.

"An old banger . . . the gears weren't working . . . there was a hole in the exhaust."

"Come outside," Tom says, taking the heavy jacket from the back of the chair.

He is in the back of Tom's car, the gun on the floor with a sack over it, Tom speeding and the radio on full blast.

"What's that gun for, anyhow?"

"Shooting rabbits."

"How did you come by it?"

"I bought it off a man called Gleeson . . . I paid twenty quid for it."

"You mean you stole it."

"Is this a setup . . . are you driving me to the barracks?"

"Christ Almighty . . . I'm giving you a lift to the roundabout."

"Stop the car. I'm going to do a legger."

"You're welcome to do a legger," and as Tom slows, the music is stopped abruptly for a news flash. They hear how a woman and a child have gone missing in a district ten miles away. The announcer gives the woman's name, her height, her age, her occupation, and the type of car she was last seen driving, along with the age and colouring of the child.

"That's a sacred bond, a mother and a child," O'Kane says.

"What would you know about a sacred bond," Tom says, and keeps the engine running as he thrusts him out of the car, cursing him for the trouble he brings on them.

O'Kane walks, concealing the gun, jumping as cars whizz by, uncertain as to whether or not he will risk the town, the tall man's voice back, saying, "Sort this out . . . sort this out . . . Son." When he sees the streetlights, he stops and thinks. He remembers a chip shop and the priest's house where he mowed grass.

The priest's house is at the approach to the town, with a short avenue leading up to it. The lights are out and the car is not there. He thinks of breaking through the back window, but then decides it might get messy, so he goes behind a low wall to wait. He kneels there, the rain driving into him, a rush of rain down out of the trees, clean rain, washing him out, and he lifts his face and his body to it, allows it to soak into him and through him, making of him an innocent son.

It was a different priest, young, dark-haired, wearing a gold watch and a natty suede jacket.

"Will you help me?" he asked.

"Who are you?" the priest asked, a bit tetchy.

"I knew Father Hayes . . . I did jobs here . . . I mowed the grass."

"Father Hayes passed on. What can I do for you?"

"There's someone in a bad way in a wood . . . you have to take me there."

"How do you mean a bad way?"

"He fell and broke his neck . . ."

"But why come to me and especially at this hour of night?"

"You're a priest . . . God's brother."

"But I don't even know you."

"If we don't go, it will be a black night."

"What do you mean by that?"

"He needs the last rites."

"Well, if it's that bad . . . then I expect we have to go," the priest said, and opened the door cautiously to let him in.

Father John

I AM WRITING this in an empty house while the young man sleeps beside me. Beyond the shutterless window a lonely quiet and the vast wood, the scene of some awful secret that he won't tell me. At one point he threatened to kill me. I don't believe he will. To ask him why he wants to kill me is quite useless, might as well ask him why his eyes are a dark colour or mine are grey. However, he claims to like me, to have got to like me after our little contretemps because I did not show fear. I feel sure that he has broken out of an asylum and is being searched for, in some county or another.

He looks so young sleeping there on the floor, with the cake crumbs at the side of his lips. It was a sponge cake that Baba Melody gave me when I was leaving her house earlier tonight. A sponge cake and eleven duck eggs. He was waiting for me in the rain when I drove over the grid into my gateway. I could scarcely believe it. He said he was home from England and that there was someone in trouble over in his own area and needed the last rites. Driving along he said, "It was all to do with the devil's work," and suddenly he ordered me to turn the car around. At first I thought he was joking, then he lifted the muzzle of the gun out from under his anorak, and I don't know which gave me the worst fright, it or his disjointed talk or the so-called jokes he made. Passing the grounds of a hotel with its tall cedars, he threw the duck eggs out of the window and laughed boisterously. He asked if the sponge cake was a gift from a lady friend. I said I don't have a lady friend, I'm a priest who has taken the vows of chastity. He mocked that and said we were all the same under our habits. Then he asked who won the match and I said there was no match, that it was a weekday and not a Sunday. He said he'd lost a few days, scrunched up in a hole somewhere, and that one morning he wakened and there was a young foal licking his face. He said he needed to be in a forest, they were the only safe places.

The first forest we tried had a locked barrier and he said they'd regret that, the keeper would regret that, and he would be back to get him. He was talking, talking, talking. The odd thing is, I discovered later on I had a connection with him through his sister. I had baptised her child, his nephew, and he appeared in one of the photographs in a clean suit, holding the child. He asked me did I consider him good-looking. I said very. He said he'd been in a lot of jails since then and picked up a lot of hooliganism. Kept telling me to speed up.

When we came to the track that led into Cloosh Wood he got very agitated and asked if I would help him. He made me promise to help him no matter how terrible the shock. I gave him my word. We walked, or fairer to say, we stumbled, through a very dark, very soggy wood, treacherous underfoot and seemingly endless. Then he ran to one side and came back with a torch which I presumed he had hidden there. The light from it was sputtery and soon expired. All of a sudden I felt myself go stone cold. I cannot say what it was, because he would not let me any closer. I just had the sensation that I was approaching a scene of calamity, and instinctively I began to say some prayers for whoever might be lying there in that loneliest of spots. He went berserk, said that I wanted to frame him like all the other f*****s. I somehow managed to calm him, and we found our way through the undergrowth and through the dark into this empty house where he claims to have lived as a child. He said it was the happiest time of his life because it bordered on the woods. I believe that he brought me to give the last rites to someone and then changed his mind. He kept saying, "I'm an animal . . . I'm an animal." The moment I proposed hearing his confession, he went ballistic, told me to mind my own effing business, said I was part of a ring out to get him. I reminded him of the secrecy of the confessional and said I would not break his trust to anyone. He said then that he had misled me. The person that was in danger was in another wood altogether, held captive by a gang. I felt that he was lying. I told him that the best thing we should do was sit down and talk things over until daylight. I said everything was worse at night, fears were worse and suspicions were worse. I asked him was he hungry and he said yes he was starving. I sent him out to the car for the remainder of the sponge cake, and he was eating it as he came in. It was unnatural the way he pawed at the cake, and as he ate it he was also sucking it, as if it were both food and drink.

We sat on the planked floor and I tried to get him stable, telling him news of the parish, children about to make their first Holy Communions, a hurling match I had been to on Sunday, and a holiday I will be taking in the autumn to the Holy Land. All of a sudden he picked up his gun and put it to his head, and I jumped and grabbed at it to wrest it from him. We fought like soldiers all around the room, him asking me to shoot him, begging me. He said he deserved to die and that he would be better off out of this world. I asked him what he meant by such a remark and unfortunately inflamed his temper again. He grabbed the rifle, cocked the hammer as an expert might, and with his hand on the trigger pointed it at me and said, "Happy Christmas . . . this one is for you, Santa." The crackle of it and the speed of the lead going through the panel of the door, then the tiny hole all happened in an instant. How quickly life can be taken and how thoughtlessly. I asked why such an outburst. He said I had it coming to me, that I was caught up in bad work, associated with the devil, especially some she-devil, and that I was about to baptise the devil's children. I pointed out to him that if that had been so, I could have killed him in that vulnerable moment when he asked me to. He thought about that and seemed satisfied, but nevertheless he took out a box of bullets and reloaded the gun before my eyes. I hid my fear as I thought it would have made him more threatening.

He apologised for choosing me, kept saying there was no one for him, then repeated the names of Christian Brothers and prison officers that were supposed to have been brutal to him. He asked me if we could go to his mother's grave in the morning, because he wanted to speak to her and to pray, he wanted to unburden everything. Before nodding off to sleep he thanked me and said I was brave when he fired that lead. I don't believe he will kill me, that is why I have stayed. I believe that at the deepest level he needs a friend and that I will become that friend. He did say that a dog would have a better life than him. My whole priesthood, I now believe, was intended for this, for this dark night of the soul, watching over a young boy whose soul is in torment.

Shadows

THEY JUMP at their shadows' shadows and the thicker shadows of the headstones that seem to collide into one another in the enveloping dusk. It has begun to rain again and the lake has the turbulence of a sea, rough waves pounding in and out, the old bent thorn trees creaking, letting out little squeals like the squeals of field mice.

They are all women, all edgy, tired, footsore; their mistrust has deepened since they commenced their search that morning, scouring vacant houses, caravans, outhouses, horse boxes, unused lime kilns, and inlets all along the lakeshore where small boats bobbed and sidled in their beds of reed.

They had come to his mother's grave, some approving, some not; they encircled it, as though believing there lingered evidence of O'Kane's having recently been, expecting from the tall tombstone and the damp mound of earth something to float upwards, a whispered message from the other world, a deliverance. At the same time they are in fear that he might be behind one of those headstones about to take a shot at them. Gladys, whose brother is a guard, says how he told her that once a person has shot or maimed, it is quite simple to do it again.

"Who's talking of shooting or maiming. No one," Lorna says, nettled on account of her being a third cousin of O'Kane's, on his father's side.

"Let's ask his poor dear mother," Martha says, and kneels and gestures that they kneel with her.

"Ask her why she reared him so rotten," Nancy says.

"Ssh."

They are about to start the rosary when Ming suddenly stands up, looks out at the water, and in a shrill hysterical voice says, "Why are we here in a graveyard. It is so negative."

"It is essential," Lorna snaps.

"You are all crazy women . . . you are all judgemental women," Ming says then, and they are disbelieving, hearing accusations from her who had always been so polite, so reserved, so courteous that if she called at their houses she would not step over the threshold, ever.

"Coming here was stupid," she says defiantly.

"How can you say that. Some of us gave up our work . . . We've left our children with others to mind," Nancy says, nettled.

"You are all doing it for obligation . . . for reputation . . . you are hypocrites . . . you you you," she says, her face chalk white, her wet black hair streaming, like some tragedian in a play.

"What is it, Ming?" Martha says, offering her a hand.

"She is not anywhere here near water . . . I am one hundred per cent sure of it."

"You're just het up . . . you're just a little bit overwrought."

"She's a foreigner . . . they don't feel like we do . . . they've no hearts, they've no religion, they come to our beautiful little country to rip us off," Lorna says.

"Don't, Lorna . . . don't . . . there's enough anxiety hanging over us."

"You all walk so fast," says Ming. "You know the countryside . . . I don't know the countryside. I was left alone in a wet field facing to the north. I asked you to wait, one of you said yes but disappeared . . . I was frightened . . . scared."

"We don't know north from south. We are not compasses, we are human beings," comes Lorna's retort.

"Eily is putting us through this," Ming says.

"You are angry with her . . . you, the one who knew her, her friend, her confidante!" Gladys says.

"I didn't know her . . . no one knew her. She had secrets that she never talked of."

"Such as?"

"I can't say . . . please excuse me . . . my mind is working crazy at this time," and she bows contritely to each one.

"So are our minds working crazy, but we cope," Martha says a little wearily.

"You stayed with Eily, didn't you?" Nancy asks.

"Yes, that was last year. There were strange noises in my back garden and I couldn't sleep . . . probably foxes. I mentioned it to Eily, and the next day I found a letter on my doormat inviting me to stay in her flat, near here, overlooking the lake. She was very kind . . . she made me very welcome . . . But then one evening a young man came, a young man with short blond hair, and she tried not to introduce me . . . She didn't want me to know that he was her boyfriend, just as she didn't want him to know that she was a mother . . . she was very secretive."

"So . . . maybe you agree with the guards. Maybe they have a point when they say she's just off on a dirty weekend."

"That is not what I meant at all. She was a secretive person, but she is not a harlot."

Ming is wishing now that her jangled nerves had not betrayed her. She feels that she must say something to redeem Eily's name, and almost pompously she says, "She had a strong spiritual side . . . there was a sacred book she used to read before she went to sleep."

"Huh, with a boyfriend in tow."

"Excuse me, but you have no truth," Ming says to Lorna.

"What do you mean?"

"She was on a quest."

"What kind of quest?"

"Goodness . . . spirituality."

"She liked a good time."

"That is how you see it . . . but in the Buddhist teaching, the blank scrolls contain the true meaning."

"You're nuts."

"She's nuts."

Suddenly they are all shouting, rounding on her, each racked by her own fear, imagining their own children spirited out of their beds and buried in some bog hole. At the sight of a figure beyond the lych-gate they jump and listen to the scrape of metal over the grazed stone step.

"It's him. It's O'Kane," Lorna says.

"Keep together," Martha says, gathering them into a huddle.

"Let's call out," Nancy says, and they stand in a huddle as the figure comes slowly towards them, his hat slouched over his face, magnifying their terrors, halting by the gravestones, until Lorna twigs that it is her husband, Milo, and shouts, "What are you doing here?"

"I'm hungry . . . the kids are hungry . . . there's no dinner on the table."

"Giving us the fright of our lives," she says.

"Anyhow yer search is called off."

"Are they found?"

"No, but her car is . . . burnt out twenty-five miles away in a field."

"But that shouldn't stop us searching here . . . in this area."

"The guards say they have a lead anyhow, and that vital evidence can be interfered with because of footprints and so forth . . . So the search is off."

"Who ordered it off?"

"It was on the local radio, although I met a young guard in the town and he didn't know about it . . . He said the dragnet was in place."

"Who knows what . . . who is in charge?"

"All is unclear."

"All is a fuckup," Milo says, and they troop out after him with a sense of failure and frustration, not even realising that they have left Ming behind on the grave.

She did not follow. She was afraid of them, afraid of their girth, their hardness, the way they all seemed to swoop down on her. She wanted to cry, because she was crying in her mind, but something told her that she must not cry. "If I shed tears, tragedy will happen," she said aloud to the grave and the moaning trees. If she withheld her tears, Eily would be safe.

Looking up, she saw human faces between the tombstones, joking faces that were laughing, and she knew that at that moment she too was going mad. She stood up, looked out at the dark water that was a Prussian blue, and kept telling herself that she must not cry, because if she shed tears, tragedy would happen; kept repeating it, staring out at the iron blue of the water.

Searching

ANOTHER GROUP of women set out very early the next morning, the mist a cottony white, a presence, so that walking through it was like breaching net. They were heading towards Cloosh Wood.

In there, whispering, moving quietly, cautiously, sometimes having to crawl under a shelving of fallen and leaning boughs, in fear of every stir, dreading what might be behind the next tree trunk and the next, a little breathless, the air sultry, silent, and as a game bird rises, the speckled feathers in a frantic unnerved flight give them the jitters. Afraid, and yet driven by a kind of blind intuition, certain that their determination will lead them to mother and son, proud of having eluded the guards and the other local volunteers.

They have fanned out, promising each other to call every so often in solidarity. Immense solitude, the trees like pillars, solemn and solid, trees which seemed to have been planted by no man; trenches of brown water scummed with hordes of insects, a suffocating place.

Suddenly Josephine is heard to shout, "Girls . . . girls, come quick." They run through the undergrowth and see her pointing to something on the ground with her umbrella. It is a child's shoe, pink canvas and caked with mud, its lace missing. The sight of it chills them. They form a circle around it, clasped now, and it speaks to them of a child recently there, losing its shoe and not being allowed to stop to put it back on. It speaks of haste and captivity and even violence. They search now in the scrub, they kneel and delve their hands into years and years of packed damp pine needles, they reach into the lower branches of the trees and shake them, hoping to find a second shoe, a cardigan, a coat, any clue indicating that they might have passed that way.

It is Anya who calls first. She says, "Maddie," then she says, "Eily." Her voice is subdued, nervous, expecting almost to be chastised, and then gaining courage she shouts the names boldly, the others follow, and the drowsing wood is wakened from its inertia with the repetition of the two names, Eily and Maddie, hope and fear alternating in those who are chanting them. "Where are you, where are you?" Their shouts carry from tree to tree, from furrow to furrow, up and beyond, and their echoes come back to them in a wan, despairing mimicry.

They decide to bring the shoe back to the barracks, carrying it on the umbrella as if carrying a trophy, and they arrive in the town and make their way slowly and a little triumphantly towards the barracks.

Dread, hysteria, and mounting speculation. The shoe rests on the sergeant's desk, absurdly small and muddy, and does not constitute a clue of any kind because he has established that it is a shoe for a child of six or seven and moreover the missing child wore blue wellingtons.

The woman's belongings, the few bits of jewellery, garments, and undergarments are in a cardboard box on the floor, and tucked far inside his desk is her diary, which he has read and which at times induced in him a moral repugnance because of certain confidings, hinging on men and desire.

"She played with fire," he says to himself, looking down at the garments and out at the crowd around the gate, craning, inquisitive, and soon to start haranguing because enough was not being done to find the missing people. They stand out there, some of them in their Sunday best, as if they are waiting for a miracle. He recalls once being on a holiday in Italy with his wife and how by chance they had formed part of a crowd that waited in a church for the solidified blood of a saint to start flowing again. It happened once a year in the month of August. He remembers the dark nave of the church and coming upon a huge painting of the Virgin and Child, so lifelike that the Virgin's blue cloak seemed to stir from her breath; flowers in vases, fresh roses and withered roses not thrown out, all kept in preparation for the miracle of the flowing blood of a Madonna. His wife, Sally, with the help of the dictionary, had gleaned this from the expectant crowd, and so they waited too, and at dusk as candles were lit, all eyes were fixed on that cube of blood, solid sealing wax in an oblong glass case. Then the air went cold, a shiver ran through the atmosphere, and people started to tremble and break free from behind a tasselled rope, pressing forward to weep and gnash at the impending revelation.

He did not hear the footsteps, simply saw his wife standing above him in a dither.

"There's a priest gone missing now."

"Where?"

"Over in Eyre Court . . . a young priest . . . Father John Fitzgerald."

"Who told you this?"

"He didn't show up for Mass . . . he was supposed to rehearse the little children soon to take their Holy Communion, and when he didn't show up his housekeeper went across and got very suspicious because the eleven duck eggs and a sponge cake she'd given him weren't in his fridge . . . So she alerted the parish priest and he called in the guards."

"Who told you this?"

"A young guard from there come over to liaise with the guards here."

"I should have been briefed first."

"There's something else."

"What?"

"The rumour is that Father John knew Eily Ryan . . . that they were lovers . . . he was seen going into an empty house in Tipperary with a red-haired woman . . . that they had planned their disappearance . . . and maybe now they're in Berlin or Paris or Amsterdam," and as she is saying it, he sees the excitement mounting in her, that strange, giddy, prurient, unwifely grin, and tells her to go out and bring in that skittish guard, bring him in to account for himself.

He opened the drawer again and took out the diary, innocent seeming with its flowered paper cover, in contrast with the warblings within. He resolved that in due course he would burn it. He felt he would be doing the right thing by burning it. Woman's filth, Eve, taken from the rib of Adam, to wreak unchastity upon the world.

An auction room has been converted into an incident room in which the search parties could foregather. They have come with sticks and food and water and dogs, the dogs mostly setters, yelping and whining to be let loose, to be let into the woods. To one side of the room a little classroom has been set up, crayons and copy books and boxes of puzzles, as Vanessa, a student, has been appointed to mind the little children while their mothers join in the search. All around, the wardrobes, sofas, mirrors, hall stands, and ornaments add to the surreal feeling as people mill about, impatient to get moving. They are annoyed with the guards, yet Bobby, the American woman, is the only one to vent her fury. She has been the bane of the sergeant's life since she first set foot in the county. First it was to complain of the pollution from the factory, then it was an objection to a new streetlight as not being in keeping with the quaint mode of the others, and now it is why he hadn't got his act together sooner. She stands close to him, wagging her index finger to smite him.

"We're getting our act together . . . well over a hundred guards are being recruited . . . army, infantry, helicopter backup, house-to-house enquiry, underwater unit, sniffer dogs . . . What more do you want?"

"Three and a half days since Eily went missing . . . twenty-four hours since you learnt that O'Kane was seen at close range in the back of her car . . ."

"I have heard she looked very relaxed when she was seen with him in her car."

"Bullshit . . . she was scared to death, but she was simply not a priority for you."

"We treat every case with the same degree of importance."

"But you did nothing."

"Look, we have no evidence of any abduction . . . none . . ."

"So where do you think she is . . . by a hotel pool? And where do you think he is?"

"Bobby . . . I run this show, not you."

"One of your officers told her sister that next thing we would be asking to name her Housewife of the Year."

"That does not reflect gardai policy."

"Only when the priest went missing did you sit up . . ."

"As I said on the local radio, and I will say it again, any case that involves boundaries makes things more complicated . . . gardai in one station or another having to liaise with their colleagues."

"So where is O'Kane?" she asks.

"There are two or three woods that he frequents . . . he's in one of them."

"Get him," she says with a vengeance.

He turns away from her and defers to Joseph, one of the foresters, who has his back to the crowd and is bent over a series of maps, marking out particularly dense areas with a red pen.

"Why did you call off our search yesterday?" Vera asks him, a little nervous and a little piqued.

"Because you were all going criss-cross up there . . . it was useless, you were getting nowhere . . . no organisation, no strategy . . . Today we have a strategy, and Joseph is best suited to mastermind it. He knows those woods, he planted those trees, he patrols there," and turning to Joseph, he asks him to brief them.

Joseph is a little shy and coughs a few times and begins: "What we do is this . . . we form lines about one foot apart . . . ten to a line. Now the person in front of his or her line takes the lead and goes into the forest and after about fifty yards shouts ALL CLEAR . . . The second person picks that up and follows and repeats the coda, and so on to the third and fourth and fifth . . ."

"Might she have jewellery on?" someone asks.

"That's a good point," the sergeant says, and asks those who knew her to recall things they'd seen her wear. Vera remembers a leather thong with a wooden pendant, and Madge starts to speak but, succumbing to emotion, keeps saying, "I'm a blatherer . . . I know I'm a blatherer . . . but I am her friend."

"Are we talking a doomsday scenario here?" Declan, a little drunk, asks as he staggers to where maps of the forestries are spread out on a desk.

"No . . . bad as he is, O'Kane would not kill," a young guard says, and turns for confirmation to the sergeant, who is already counting and herding them into groups of ten. At that moment a stranger rushes into the room in a thrall of excitement, waving a sheet of paper and carrying a rowan branch as if it is a wand. He is tall and sallow, with a long white robe under his raincoat and his hair tied in a ponytail.

"She is there," he says, pointing to a star on a drawing which he has made, a perfect depiction of a country area with green colouring for the forest, brown for the humped bridges, and an outline of an empty house with creeper hanging from the eaves.

"Where is there?" Vera calls out.

"I am not familiar with the place-names . . . I've never been to these parts . . . I was guided here."

"It's been in every paper . . . a woman and a child and a priest are missing . . . it's on every radio station," he is told.

"I don't listen to radios . . . I listen to my dreams . . . I meditated and the answer came to me."

"What answer?"

"A woman in a swath of woodland who is prevented from screaming."

"Who are you?" the sergeant asks, irritated by his arrogance, his sandals, his John the Baptist robe.

"I am a link in the chain . . . a bond of connection between the missing woman and yourselves," he says, unruffled, and goes out with the same smiling rapture as when he came in, propelled by some inner calling.

Donnagh

IT'S LIKE we are looking for a wolfman who leaves his traces and then vanishes. The question now is will we ever catch him. Has he powers beyond the natural, that is what is being said. The truth is, we're all feeding on our fears, men and women both, retreating into blindness like into a dark cave. When Liam Purcell and myself came on an empty cigarette carton and banana skins on the cow walk, our antennae were out.

We stopped first at Glebe House, which has not been occupied for years. There was a good newish caravan cushion on the floor. It was brown corduroy with leather buttons. Liam said it was not there two days ago when he looked in that window. He has cattle up that way and fodders them morning and night, so he notices anything unusual. On the side of the track into the wood there was a lady's black sweater, and I picked it up with a stick and put it in the back of the car to bring to the guards. Then two hundred feet into the forest we came on the remains of a lunch—an empty biscuit packet and a tin that had sardines. I also picked them up for evidence. Farther on I found a blue torch with a red battery submerged in a pool of water. When I switched it on, the light was weak. Nearby was a fertiliser bag. Things.

My wife, her friend Josie, and myself visited our cousin

Mary Kate down at the shore, as she feels in real danger there because Eily Ryan lived in that very same apartment for a short while. The whole conversation hinged on the disappearance of Eily and her child and a priest and the possible connection with O'Kane.

"I wonder will he come for me," Mary Kate said. She kept looking towards the window.

"Don't say that . . . in God's name don't say that," my wife said.

"I know he will," Mary Kate said, and went up the stairs for the umpteenth time to look to see if her child was safe.

We sat there smoking, drinking cup after cup of coffee, turning on the wireless at news times, expecting some bulletin. At one point I just sensed that O'Kane was nearby. I don't know how or why I felt it, but I just knew. I opened the window in her living room and heard movement to the right and told them to shush.

"Is he there?" Mary Kate asked.

"There's someone there," I said and I called out and we switched on the outside light and we went out with sticks, the four of us shouting, but he had disappeared. We stayed an hour longer to give Mary Kate courage, but finally we had to leave because of work in the morning.

When we passed Tuohey's milk parlour, their security light was on and I said I found that odd, as it was worked by sensor and no vehicle had passed up or down the road while we were in Mary Kate's.

"That's not normal," I said.

"Nothing is normal now," my wife said, and Josie and she huddled together in the back, screaming, as if they were going to be shot.

At Houlihan's pier we saw a blue flame, about twenty

feet high off the ground, and I thought at first it was a lifebuoy on fire, and I wanted to swing to the right and investigate, but the women wouldn't let me, they said, "Drive on, drive on." They kept insisting then that it was a crowd of drunks who had lit a fire on the harbour and that it would be awful to call the guards at that hour of night.

Deep down we believe he has been sent by God, as punishment upon us.

Houlihan's Pier

"CRIPES . . . a dancing girl," Frank says as he slows down the car to look.

"A mermaid," Paddy says as they stare at the ball of lit blue that seems to be above the water, skimming it.

"It's a gas explosion on that houseboat . . . We better call the fire brigade," Frank says, a little less skittishly.

"I'm one of the fire brigade," Paddy says, and splutters. They are both half drunk and they are enthralled by it. It is well after midnight, and each had promised the other that they would leave the pub after the next drink, and on and on it went, Frank's uncle looking at his watch and begging them to bring him home to his bed.

"We better get out and investigate."

"We had not . . . we better be going back to Lawler's Pub and ring the brigade . . . The funny thing is, it wasn't there five minutes ago when we were driving down . . ."

"That's the thing with fire . . . it's a phenomenon," Paddy says, his tongue tripping on the big word.

On their way back to the village they come on Charlie, who is carrying a pregnant sheep into his yard, and they shout out to him about a boat being on fire and how they're going up to Lawler's to ring.

"Ring from here . . . it's faster," he calls back.

While they are waiting for the fire brigade to arrive, the

three men decide to go back, and getting there, walking in a closed knot, trampling their lit-up shadows, they find a car halfway in over the pier, as if someone has tried to push it but failed. They are drawn to it, closer and closer, like men seeing fire for the first time, the lick of the flames dancing across their faces, their hands blackened by going too close to it, and already they guess the worst.

"It's O'Kane's style," Paddy says, and as they gape at it, the sharp and brittle crack of a gunshot is heard and a bullet lands somewhere in the ornamental bushes around the ruin of an old house.

"He's around . . ."

"Let's get the hell out of here."

They waited in Charlie's house until the guards came, and when they returned the fire had almost ceased; the car a black shell with nothing to show of itself, no windows, no seats, no number plates, just a cavity in which rosary beads dangled inside from a charred dashboard.

The fire engine arrived soon after, but without its siren on, and the firemen jumped out, still half asleep but fully togged, ready to do their gallant work and a little crestfallen at finding they had come as the last puttery flames were ebbing, dying out. They walked around it saying the same commiserating things, and the fire engine itself, its silent bells, its roped ladder, and its coils of hosing looked like a big toy, faintly ridiculous in that scene of catastrophe.

One of the guards found a registration branded into the glass of the rear window, and they took turns to peer at it with a torch, then with the naked eye, to read the letters and the numbers, with collars of soot around them. With infinitesimal care he removed the soot with some sticky tape, and the other men watched in a strained, admiring raptness. They deliberated, then each man called out the lettering and the numbering as he believed it to be and their guesses matched.

Charlie's house was suddenly like a canteen. Neighbours had gathered because of hearing the cars and the fire engine, and Charlie's wife, her hair loose and flying as if she belonged in some ancient drama, kept plying them with warm scones, repeating the miracle that had happened while the men were gone, that a sick sheep that they were sure was going to die had given birth to twins. She marvelled that it was twins and that the sheep, poor creature, had had a dropped womb and wasn't it a good omen. It was only when the guard came back in from the hallway where he had been ringing the station that she seemed to take in the gravity of what was really happening.

"It's the priest's car," the guard said.

"Father John's car . . . Father John's car." The evocation of his name sent shivers through them, and one who knew him spoke of his kindness, his down-to-earthness, the way he mixed with the people and played hurley like any ordinary bloke. She was pressed for more information and all she could think to say was that he had a good dress sense and wore a beautiful gold watch.

"It doesn't look good," Charlie said.

"We've dragged our feet too long over them missing people," the men said, eager now to go on a reckless search in the dead of night.

Around the cold jetty in the sad dawn, twenty or so people converged to see it, and what they saw was a crinkled plastic sheet covering a shell of a car like a shroud. They knew it was the priest's car, just as they knew of the rosary beads that had not burned up and the shot that had been fired a few feet away after midnight. With a terrible constraint they kept looking towards the lake, believing that Father John was down there among the ghosts of others who had drowned, fishermen caught in a squall, drunk youths coming home from a disco, and Fidelma, who had left her husband after the first night of marriage. No one said so, but each felt he was down there, and standing in the cold, they looked up at the first sight of the helicopter, rackety, invasive, a big threatening bird, bringing unease to fields and meadows, to lanes with gorse bushes all in bloom, to that soft-seeming haze of the biding mountains.

Capture

"THE FOX IS INVISIBLE." He keeps shouting it from the depths of a ditch where he has hidden all night, shouting it and emptying the rainwater out of his boots.

The heat is on. They are searching boats, harbour front, fields and sheds, shitting themselves because they can't find him. He has seen his picture in the newspaper next to the woman, like they are a bridal couple. She has both her eyes, gazing. There is a picture of the fecking dog with the number plate in its mouth. A picture of the priest, a lock of hair down over his forehead, holding a hurley stick.

In that ditch before the dawn, he has his first fill of the chopper coming in to get him. He can feel their desperation in the way they tear over the fields, zoom up and down, in and out, skimming the treetops, trying to sniff him.

"You could get me, but you're afraid of me . . . scumbags," he shouts up to the helicopter as it whisks off over to the lake and the island where the butcher grazes his cattle. He gets out of his hole and walks across to a gateway, leans on it, waiting for someone to pass. A creamery lorry drives by, and the driver gapes at him with fear and semi-recognition and drives on. He leaves an old bucket upside down in a field, another trick to confound them.

"The fox is flying it," he says to the bushes, to the hawthorn, and across to the house that he has already targeted.

He is merely waiting for the man or the woman to come out, to walk up the road, to open a gate and let the cows make their own way on down to the milking parlour. He has watched them do it each morning, either one of them going up to open the gate and the other going down to the milking parlour to get the machines ready, and Kitty, the daughter, asleep. She is a redhead too, but not golden like the woman, raw, foxy. He bursts out laughing at the thought of her scream.

At the sound of something breaking Kitty sits up startled and thinks, *Jesus, the dishes, I didn't stack them right in the press, my mother will eat me.* Her younger sister, Deirdre, and her grandmother in the far wing of the house, and her parents gone milking, same as always, then not the same.

The bedroom door is kicked in and she screams, she screams at a face masked with black nylon tights, telling her to get up fast. Behind the gauze of the nylon she recognises O'Kane, his eyes like coals, spittle along his lips, and every other word fuck, fuck. To save her grandmother a heart attack she gets out of bed and says pluckily, "There's nothing for you in this house, O'Kane."

There are splinters of glass all over the kitchen floor where he has broken a panel, and she has to pick her steps to get the car keys that he has asked for out of the drawer.

"Take them," she says, and flings them across a worktop.

"You're coming too, Ginger," he says.

"I've an exam today . . . it's a very important day for me," she says, that little bit less insolent.

"It'll happen without you."

"At least let me get some clothes on," she says, pulling the lapels of her pyjamas across her front.

"Get the fuck out the door and stop messing."

He sits beside her, the gun across his sprawled legs, and a couple of minutes beyond the gateway she sees her own mother seeing her and flinging her hands up, aghast. He has already mapped a route in his mind.

"Go left.

"Go right.

"Go along the pier.

"Go up to the ash tree.

"Go to Dick's Cross."

"You think my mother didn't know you . . . you think that mask disguises you . . . well, it doesn't," she tells him.

"You're a fecking useless driver . . ."

"You were only a class ahead of me at school . . . such a shy little lad . . . you wouldn't come in the playground . . . waiting for your mother . . . and look at you now . . . having the country at gunpoint."

"Stop the fecking car," he orders her, and as he gets out, she thinks she will have a few seconds to bolt, but he has already anticipated that, and levelling the muzzle on her forehead he backs out, opens the back door, and lobs the gun above her head as he settles into the back seat and pulls the tights off. He allows the legs to dangle on his shoulder and gives them a little mocking toss from time to time. He nuzzles them and she thinks, *I know who they belong to.* He looks less of an ogre without the tights, and she tries talking, as if she is not afraid.

"You've made a bit of an impression, haven't you?"

"Is that what they're saying?"

"You're wanted . . . your picture in the papers . . . Where did you sleep last night?"

"In a hole."

"And why did you come to us?"

"That fecking chopper."

"Everyone is asking about the missing people."

"What missing people?"

"A woman and a child and a priest."

"I know nothing about a priest."

"So you do know about the woman and the child."

"She gave me a lift a week back . . . I got out at a shop . . . that's all I know."

"That's not what people are saying."

Suddenly he is shouting at her to go left, go left, and she is on a dust road, pouches of it splashing the windscreen, as if it had not been trodden in centuries.

"People must have lived here once," she says, pointing to gable walls of fallen cottages, mere attempts at normality.

"It's my area now."

"And that's why we're here?"

"I want to get to France."

"What the hell happened to you to turn you into such a raving lunatic?"

"They put acid into my brain. They doped me first with sleeping pills and poured melted plastic over my feet so as I couldn't move."

"You better have that head of yours seen to."

"I don't want to. I'm in with the top man now."

"Who's he when he's at home?"

"Man with the horns. He'd suck your titties any night . . . or that sister of yours, or your old dopey granny."

"You've seen too many horror movies, O'Kane."

"My arse is bleeding. I cut it going into your place."

"That's because you hadn't the manners to knock."

"You're funny. How are you feeling anyhow?" and he nudges her in the back.

"Freezing. Could I have my jacket?" she says, and as he passes it to her, her hand comes off the wheel, and in that instant the car swerves to one side and slides into loamy ground, the wheels slurping, then sinking down into a swamp.

"You done it on purpose, you bitch."

"If I done it on purpose . . . I would have done it on the main road."

"Reverse."

"I can't reverse. It's stuck," and they get out to push it, and he tries raising it onto a ridge of stones, all to no avail, and finally he gets newspaper out of the boot, rolls it furiously into twists, and as he opens the nozzle to dip them in the petrol, she lets out a cry: "Don't. My father loves his little car . . . his little Minny."

"He'll get another little Minny," he says, and as they walk away from it, she can see by the haltingness of the flames, the way they hesitate, that Minny will not catch fire. She will stay put and be a clue when her parents and the guards come on their trail.

Nothing, only emptiness, no cattle, a round, rusted, empty cattle feeder in the middle of nowhere, and they walking over boggy ground, the stones and the thorns cutting her bare feet. There are telegraph poles to one side of the bog, the wires sagging down, wires onto which birds fly in and perch for a few moments and her whispering to them, "Tell them, tell them where I am."

"My fucking feet," he said.

"My fucking feet," she said back. She tried to stop, but he pushed her on, and way way down below they came to a view of lakewater rippling and glinting.

"You can see the Shannon," he said.

"I don't need to see the Shannon . . . I live beside it . . . How long more do you intend to keep me?"

"For as long as I want."

"If you're thinking of killing me, you better know that I'm not ready to die."

"Are you afraid?"

"Everyone's afraid of death, sonny boy . . . even you . . . acting the big fella with Jeremiah Keogh's gun."

"Who told you about Jeremiah Keogh's gun?"

"His sister did. He's too chicken to go to the guards."

"What else are they saying about me?"

"They're saying you'd be as well off to give yourself up."

"Never . . . I'll never do time again."

"The priest's car was found burnt out on the pier . . . People saw it for miles . . . they knew it was your work . . ."

"They'll never get my dabs on it," he says in triumph. She stops and grips his arm to hold up one of her feet to show him how it is bleeding. He goes berserk, telling her to wash it, wash it or the fecking dogs will smell them out.

"I can't wash it . . . there's no water anywhere. We might as well be on the moon," she says.

"You're a cheeky bitch."

"You're not going to kill me, Michen, are you?" she says in an almost comradely way.

"If I have to I will . . . it'll be a fast end . . . you won't feel any pain."

"Jesus. Them that love me will feel pain . . . Anyhow, if you kill me you'll have no cover . . . I'm your cover."

"Bitch."

They walk and walk. Bronze bracken, tough tawny grasses, and furze bushes cutting her feet. Bouts of talk and bouts of silence. All of a sudden he stops, thinks, a storm going on inside his head, and decides that they will turn back, they will take a different route. She realises that he is starting to panic.

"Look . . . we're going around in circles."

"Shut up."

"You won't get away with it, you won't."

"Shut the fuck up."

He starts to shake his head, shakes it violently, cursing at some sudden apparition, and then he staggers, as if he is drunk or blind, and blunders towards her.

"I can't see you . . . I can't see you," he is shouting.

"What's wrong with you?"

"I've gone blind."

"I'm here."

"Lead the way," he says, gripping her arm, and she thinks as she leads him along in that wasteland, *What a deceptive picture, what a tableau, pilgrims, tired, footsore, making their way to the inn.*

"There's a rain barrel here . . . I want to drink," she says, stroppy.

"Where . . . where?"

"Put your hand out," and she guides him towards it and he plunges his head into it and drinks at the same time, like a caveman, then tells her to wash her fucking feet and keep them sniffer dogs away. She cups the dirty water in her hands and drinks it. It tastes of iron. Then she pours some over her feet. His sight restored, he watches her, grinning.

The sound of the helicopter, abrupt and thundery, comes from beyond, scoring the sky, a giant bird, the engine roaring, the rotor scissoring the air, and her eyes drinking it in, following it as it comes up from the rim of the horizon, coasts over Cloosh Wood, and veers across the range of bracken ground towards them. Unable to suppress her joy, she waves a white-sleeved arm and hollers, "Here, here."

"Get the fuck down."

"I won't get the fuck down" and he pushes her down with a violence and strikes her across the cheek and they lie in the wet hammocky ground, O'Kane slouched over her, believing his green jacket to be a camouflage, their hearts, their warring hearts like the hearts of lovers, beating violently. It dances above them, coming down, closer, closer, so that the crew are within calling distance and she is thinking, *They'll pick us up . . . they'll pick up our heat,* and it hovers and dips, undulates, and all of a sudden it roars away, happy with itself. In the wake of its passing the most awful silence, only the shivery vibrations of the telegraph wires.

"Thank fuck," he shouts.

She closes her eyes, not wanting him to see that she is in tears. Finally he eases his chest away from hers and she staggers up, disconsolate.

They go on down, limping, no longer arguing, the sun beating down, the odd house in the distance, ponies in a field sparring over sops of hay, life as it should be. He needs a car. Fast.

"You'll have the drive of your life," he tells her.

Coming to a two-storey house, he warns about not doing or saying anything stupid. She sees his finger on the trigger, sees the roof of a hay shed, him kicking open the double wooden doors and dogs barking from inside. The dogs are chained. In the courtyard next to a tub of flowers is a big new Jeep with a sheen to it, a readiness, a yen to go. He shouts for the keys to be handed out. Above the baying dogs comes the voice of a man whom they cannot see, ordering them to get off his property. His accent is foreign.

"Throw out the keys," O'Kane shouts up.

"I do not have the keys."

"Throw out your fucking keys," and now they swear obscenities at each other, the selfsame words sounding different in each tongue, and then the barrel of a gun juts through the upstairs window, and as shots are fired two orange cartridge shells land on the gravel near her and the dogs go berserk. O'Kane grasps her, his anger unabatable now, and holds her as a shield as they back away towards the gate, which is swinging open and shut.

"Tell him we will be back for him and his wife and his kids."

"We will be back for you and your wife and your kids," she says, her voice high-pitched. She is like a puppet, no, a robot; she is witnessing everything as if it is not happening, as if she is outside it — their going down the drive, him making her jump over barbed wire, his eyes now bulged and rolling.

The birds are busy, flocks of them darting in and out of the hedges, foraging, one with a very yellow beak carrying a worm back into a nest, to its young, birdsong so gay, so spry, soon to be silenced in the ensuing pandemonium, a fleet of patrol cars coming up the road, an older man emerging from a small cottage, refixing his cap as if it is just another morning and he going a few miles to fodder his cattle, and she thinks, *Oh, you poor man, you are for it in a matter of a minute and you don't even know.* They crawl under more wire, down a steep slope onto a cattle grid. Everything is eerily clear, the older man getting into his car and reversing, blue string with an assortment of white car-

rier bags to keep animals out, and underneath the grid a
pool of rainwater with cress growing in it—then a fleet of
cars coming up the road and guards jumping out, more
than thirty armed guards on the road, on the wall, calling
in loud, brisk, but still reasonable voices, "Let the girl go,
let the girl go," and O'Kane answering that if they come an
inch closer he will blow her fucking head off.

"I've seen your face on television . . . you're wanted,"
the older man says from his car, dazed, disbelieving.

She is pushed into the back of the man's car, O'Kane
hovering over her with the gun as the guards yell, "Throw
out your keys, Pat."

"I can't . . . you see, I can't," Pat answers, helpless.

They drive over the grid and away from the convoy of
cars and men, O'Kane, Kitty, and the driver all shouting,
mad tossing shapes beyond the window, and then a crunch
as the car veers towards a drain, comes to a halt, and Pat ex-
claiming, "We've been shot at . . . we've been shot at."

The back door is opened and a body thrusts itself over
them, a multiple scream as the gun explodes inside the car,
and she opens her eyes to see Pat grasping the raised barrel,
clinging to it, the cloth roof dropping down in shreds and a
smell of gunsmoke. "We have him . . . we have him." The
guards' shouts go up as though from one throat, passing
through their ranks, in glory and disbelief, and he is pulled
out of the car, his wild scoriated face, his wild unspent
voice, shouting, in a brief and fading burst, "I know nothing about the woman and the child."

He moves with a staggering and undefeated bravado,
this, for him, just an interim until he is loose again, a free
man, them hunting him down, this never-ending chase
of them and him, hunted and hunters, the victory he

had dreamed and re-enacted down the butchered years.

As he is put to the ground and his pockets searched, other guards rush on him exultant, anger and frustration wiped out now in this melee of jubilation, vindication, his cursing, kicking frame there on the ground, being reined in, his rampaging at an end. But where are the missing people? Where are the missing people? Where . . . are . . . the . . . missing . . . people? They ask from different heights, different vantage points, different degrees of desperation, each thinking he will be the one to worm it out of the bastard. Guard Garvey is already a hero, being punched and congratulated for having had the presence of mind to jump forward from behind that wall and immobilise the back wheel of the car and bring the chase to a close.

"Good work, Michael."

"Pure luck," Garvey says, his face scalding with pride.

"Where are the missing people?" She comes, the mercy woman, from some hidden dwelling, loose grey hair, in nightgown and wellingtons, cuts her way through the swath of men and kneels by him, placing her hand along his forehead, motherkind. "Where are they, son?"

"I can't tell you . . . with these fuckers around."

"That child is in nappies . . . his bottom will be sore . . . his poor mother at her wits' end. You can tell me . . . I'm your friend . . . I knew your people."

"They'll be left outside the shop tomorrow night."

"Are they safe?"

"They have food for two more days."

"Are they alive?"

"They're in a house . . . they have television."

"They're safe . . . they're safe," she says, her hands clasped in gratitude.

"Listen, my dear woman, I have to ask you to move out of here," a detective tells her.

"Don't take him . . . give me a few more minutes . . . He wants to tell me . . . he needs to tell me," she says, and as they move him forward, her voice goes on begging, like the long, sighing sound of the banshee, up there on a road where nothing had ever happened, just the seasons, branches choking each other in summer and reaching out wanly in the wet winters.

He is cuffed to two detectives and in a lather of curses is led away, his bunched arm muscles have the crazed and supple fury of a python, and even as they hold him, they fear that he will in some way elude them still, some phenomenal ingredient will transport him back to the empty woods and his murdering haunts.

He jerks fiercely on the cuffs and stands above Kitty, who is sitting on a wall with a blanket around her.

"The fox is finished," he says, his last utterance to the landscape he has violated.

Reckoning

SUPERINTENDENT MCBRIDE stirs the white stomach medicine in the beaker, keeps stirring it in order to delay drinking it, because the taste disgusts him. He is a big man with a bit of flab, his hair grey before its time but his eyebrows thick and sleek and black where he puts a lick of boot polish on them, something his favourite daughter, Sile, jeers at. He can scarcely believe what has hit him. Five days of searching, five days of pillory and criticism from press and public, and finally O'Kane captured in the early hours on a mountain roadway, with not a drop of blood shed. The heroism and euphoria of the capture are short-lived, because now all eyes are on him and his team to find the three missing people, before they die of exposure or starvation. Rumours abound. Tip-offs abound. They are near the lake, they are in the woods, they are in the mid-lands, they have been seen driving around together, the woman, the child, and the priest. He has thirty-six hours to find them, thirty-six hours to hold O'Kane, thirty-six hours with the eyes of the world beamed in on him, thirty-six hours of scalding pain in his gut and probably no sleep. He is lucky to have got O'Grady and Wilson, whiz kids at their job, the two most experienced interrogators in the land, famous for their strategy, their softly softly and then wham-bam. Never known to fail. A moment of respite as he imagines reading over the confession, when his attention is alerted to the commotion in the street outside. Beyond the grimed windowpane he sees a guard pushing back spectators as they try to surge forward over the metal barrier. He has given instructions that there be no ugly scenes, no booing, no weeping women with rosary beads beseeching O'Kane to confess. Journalists jump on windows and rooftops to catch a glimpse of the infamous figure, and in the corridor he hears doors banging and footsteps flying. The "Fox" has arrived. He does not go out to have a look. He waits until Flann, a young, conscientious guard, puts his head through the door and then indulges his curiosity: "What does he look like, Flann?"

"He looks like any other young lout in an anorak with five days of dirty growth on his chin."

The superintendent broods, winds his watch, listens to the lisp of the little tick, examines the sleek black hands, like sewing thread, as they meet over the digit eleven. In three days he and his team should be congratulating one another on having a confession and he will celebrate with yet another glass of his milky medicine.

Interrogation

THEY ARE on first names, Gerry and Frank and Michen. Easy does it, as Gerry says, he being the smooth-talking one. He is younger, informal, pulling his shirtsleeves up to show that they are all mates together.

"Bit of a rough ride over, had you?" he asks, and knowing there will be no answer, he says to understand that the boys get a bit hyper once there's press and cameras around. They sit at a varnished brown table, their three sets of elbows leaning on it, the castors wobbling this way and that. As Gerry explains in a soft, reasonable voice, all they want is to make things as painless as possible for everybody.

"How long will I be kept here?" O'Kane snarls.

"That's up to you," Frank snarls back.

"We'll help you if you help us," Gerry adds.

"I'm entitled to a solicitor," O'Kane says, then holds up his wrists, pink and ridged from the way they had handcuffed him on the drive over. He licks them.

"Of course you're entitled to a solicitor . . . no one's stopping you . . . but if you take my advice, we'll work it out here between the three of us. A solicitor will complicate matters at this juncture. Look, we have no papers, no pens, no notetaking . . . It's a nice easy friendly atmosphere . . . You and Frank and me," Gerry says.

"Where's Father John?" Frank asks.

"Precisely, we start with Father John . . . The whole diocese has gone hysterical . . . Masses offered for him every morning . . . very popular man," Gerry says.

"What the fuck are you talking about?"

"We're talking about three missing people, a woman and a child and a priest."

"They must be joyriding," O'Kane says, and sneers.

"Don't give us that shit," Frank says.

"Easy now, Frank . . . Michen here has had a tough life . . . packed off to a home at ten or eleven . . . your poor mother dying. Do you want to talk about your poor mother. It'll help. They say a grief like that, bottled up, is a bad thing for a child . . . What age were you?"

"She was smothered in her coffin and I know who did it."

"Where's the priest?" Frank asks, leaning in close to him.

"You have the wrong man," O'Kane tells him.

"But you know they're missing."

"You fuckers set me up . . . I've never heard of these people."

"A gun was taken off you at approximately nine-thirty-five this morning . . . it had been fired a few times. What were you shooting?"

"A hit from a bullet doesn't always mean that people die . . . it can be a shot in the air."

"Mich . . . what's the story. The sooner you get it off your chest, the sooner you will be out of here. The superintendent in this unit is as decent a man as you could find . . . a family man . . . if you cooperate so will he . . . he's no sadist," Gerry says.

"I was shooting vermin."

"What kind of vermin?" Frank at his most sarcastic.

"So you were in the woods . . . Maybe you came across people in the woods . . . or you might have heard them crying out for help." Gerry, still solicitous.

"I want cigarettes."

"You'll get your fucking cigarettes when you answer these questions. Where are the missing people?"

"You won't get my dabs on them and you can't keep me here much longer. I know the law . . . I'm here under Section 30."

"Section 30, my arse . . . Where are they? Either you tell us or we'll drag it out of you."

"Now now, Frank . . . we're all a bit het up. You see, Michen, there's a fierce responsibility on our heads. The whole country is asking, not just two men in uniform. These people have to be somewhere in this locality and you're the one that knows where . . . you were seen with the woman and the child . . . people saw you in the back of her car, crouched down."

"She gave me a lift a few miles up the road . . . Then I got out, because I don't go near towns."

"Where did she go?"

"Ask the assholes in the town. She was a mover and shaker . . . ye should have found her by now. Get me my fucking cigarettes."

"Look, if you don't level with us, the boys from Dublin will handle this and they'll put the squeeze on you . . . up in the upstairs room, if you get my drift."

"Knackers have them."

"What knackers?"

"I'm not telling you. If I tell, I'll be framed."

"Are they alive?"

"The woman and the child are alive. I saw them Wednesday . . . They had food, they were watching TV."

"So they're in a house."

"I'm not saying."

"Are they in this locality?"

"No . . . they're hundreds of miles away."

"And they're hostages?"

"I told you all I'm fucking going to tell you."

"Is the priest alive?"

"It was a robbery that went wrong. The bathroom window was open, and Joe and I waited inside . . . Joe conked him with an iron bar . . ."

"Who's Joe?"

"I can't tell you."

"Cunt. You'll go down one way or another . . . You saw that crowd waiting outside when you were brought in. There are men who will be more than happy to take you for a ride."

"I'll get your wife and your kids, scumbag."

"You'll be behind bars for thirty years, scumbag."

"Look, Frank, why don't you go and get a cup of coffee and Michen and myself will sort this out . . . Oh, and ask one of the lads to go get cigarettes."

"Bastard," O'Kane says.

"He's a tough man, Frank, but don't get on the wrong side of him. Anyhow, to get back to business . . . if Joe conked the priest, does it mean that he killed him?"

"I saw the blood pouring out of his head . . . He was not afraid to die."

"So he's dead?"

"He didn't die straightaway . . . They put him in a laneway in a wood and shone the lights of the car on him.

He tried to run away, but he couldn't . . . God's brother."

"Who shot God's brother?"

"The knackers . . . If she's not dropped outside a shop by midnight tomorrow, I'll grass them up."

"In the name of Jesus, grass them now."

"Off the wall . . . off the wall," Gerry says as he flings his jacket down in frustration.

"We know he's off the wall, but what have we got?" the superintendent asks him.

"He shot the priest. He turned the car lights on in a lane in the wood and made him kneel down . . ."

"We have him . . . he's admitted to it."

"He won't sign it . . . he won't fecking sign it."

"Go back in. Bring Kinsella with you, all twenty-two stone of him, hold the pen in the fecker's hand and tell him it's us or the Dublin crowd . . . the rat pack. No, on second thought, this is country business . . . we're running this. He's a country boy, he needs country muscle."

Absolution

THE ELDERLY PRIEST and O'Kane shake hands and stand in the little visiting parlour, each waiting for the other to take a seat. There is a tray with cups, saucers, and a plate of biscuits. He is an old priest, Father Christopher, kind, quiet-spoken, happiest when reading his missal, spring-cleaning his soul for eternity.

"How are you, Michen . . . how are you doing?"

"Bad . . . they're bastards . . . I met you in Killarney . . ."

"I don't think so."

"You were at the tote window . . . you didn't have your collar on."

"Well, I'm glad to see you now, to see you're bearing up."

"I have things on my mind . . . a lot of things."

"Yes, Superintendent McBride said you asked for a priest."

"I did . . . I do."

"Is it in a confessional sense, Michen, that you asked for a priest?"

"What else."

"Now, before we continue, I want you to understand something: It would be a very onerous position for me to be put in, a position I would prefer not to be in . . . if . . . if for instance you had something of import to tell me."

"Is God like you?"

"Oh no . . . God is God. He is above everything, everyone."

"Is he understanding?"

"He is. He is also all-knowing and all-seeing, omnipotent, omniscient."

"I don't like the Pope . . . he's a bastard, I wrote to tell him."

"Do you pray, Michen?"

"I said a prayer for them missing people. Did God see what I done?"

"He'd see what you did and whatever you did he'd understand it."

"Will I be forgiven?"

"I believe you will. Remember Jesus in His agony in the Garden of Gethsemane . . . how He asked forgiveness for His executioners: Father, forgive them, for they know not what they do."

"I'm not a psychopath . . . I'm not mad . . . it's them fuckers that's making me mad."

"Tell me, Michen, did you know Father John?"

"Not well."

"But you called on him."

"He was wearing a gold watch that had writing on the back of it . . . it was given to him as a present. I thought of fecking it off him, but then I didn't because I knew they'd frame me . . . He was a good man."

"As a lay person would you like me to act as a mediator between the guards and the detectives and yourself?"

"They're assholes . . . I want you to hear my confession."

"I would rather not."

But O'Kane is already kneeling, blessing himself, saying the prayer that he said as a child when he went into the confessional: "Bless me, Father, because I have sinned." The priest takes the purple stole that he carries in case of coming on any accident and puts it around his neck and kneels and closes his eyes, dreading what will be revealed.

"It was last Thursday. It was a gang doing a house and it went wrong . . . pissing rain . . . We found the top of the bathroom window open and the curtain pulled back. The priest drove the car into the garage and came around the side of the house . . . Joe hit him with an iron bar. We tied him up and put him in the back seat . . . I drove him to a car park. Joe followed in his car, because he wanted no shit . . . I had to drive the priest to my own area. We spent the night in a house . . . I had a sleep. The birds wakened me in the morning and I brought him out."

"Did he take long to die?"

"No, he went fast."

"Did he say anything?"

"He asked me to spare his life . . . The woman is dead, too."

"And the child, is the child dead or alive?"

"I don't know . . . with the knackers you can never assume . . ."

"Where are their bodies?"

"I won't tell you."

"You can tell God . . . it's God you're talking to through me."

"You're not to tell them out there . . . you can't break the confessional oath."

"They must be told."

"You can't . . . I confessed before God . . . I'm not confessing to them . . . I'm not, I'm not, I'm not."

"There's a child, maybe alive. Just think of God's rejoicing at this eleventh hour if you save a little lamb from the slaughter . . . just think."

"I don't remember shooting him . . . maybe he ran away."

"Why did you kill the priest?"

"I had to . . . he was going to baptise the devil's child. The woman was a devil, too, a she-devil, a sinner."

As the priest intones the words of the absolution they seem hollow, they seem a blasphemy to God, and having finished, he gets up shakily and goes out, torn between his duty to God and his duty to mankind.

The superintendent and the others know that the priest knows something but that he cannot tell them; so shaken was he when he came out that a guard was sent to the public house to fetch a large brandy and ginger ale. He is sipping it slowly, twirling the glass, looking out the window at people passing by, and all he seems to see are young mothers with children and all he can think of is a child screaming over a dead mother, trying to bring her back to life. He can see the guards looking at him and respecting his plight.

"So it's bad," the superintendent says.

"It's a shocker," he says quietly.

"I have only ten more hours . . . then I'll have to let him go."

"I'd tell you everything if I could."

"I know that, Father. I know that. Can you tell us if you think he would take a life?"

"I think he would, but then again it could be just fantasy . . . He comes out with strange remarks. For instance, he said he saw me down in Killarney at the tote window with my collar off . . . I've never been to a race meeting."

"That's baloney," Frank says. "That's to put you off the scent. Our little twister O'Kane knows his stuff . . . he's been juggling the authorities since he was eleven years. In one of the homes he was shown a piece of paper that said 'My future,' and asked to finish the sentence, he wrote 'is very bad.' Send him out to the street corners of any slum in any city and he'll see kids whose future is very bad and they haven't turned criminal."

"What is it that warps a child . . . what is it that changes a child from being a child?" the priest asks.

"I can't answer that, Father. But if somebody had taken that pup, his father or an uncle, and given him the hammering of a lifetime . . . we wouldn't be crawling on our knees begging him to tell us where missing people are. The state spoils them . . . all this pussyfooting, all this hand-wringing . . . his childhood, his loneliness, his mother . . . lots of kids with no mothers who don't steal cars and don't burn cars and don't take women at gunpoint . . . Little creep, little coward."

"Time, gentlemen, time," the superintendent says, holding up the watch he has had to remove from his wrist on account of a rash he has developed. His insides are scalding.

"There's something I feel I want to say," the priest says, rising, lifting his hands helplessly. "The day I was ordained, there were five of us, and afterwards we were all told to hold hands and so we did. We held hands, and then there was a white linen cloth wound around each of our hands, like a bandage, and we were told to take it and keep it and give it to someone very special when the need arose. My mother died last autumn and I put that cloth in her hands in the coffin. If I had it now I would put it into that boy's hands, but I don't have it, I don't have it . . . and I am telling you in the only language that is permitted to me."

"I see . . . I do see," the superintendent says grimly.

Then laughter started up, loud peals, a baying, and their heads turned to the door.

"It's your man . . . it's one of his stunts," Frank says, and they wait, expecting it to stop, except that it doesn't; it mounts, it magnifies, growing more macabre, more threatening with each bout, and they look from one to the other in dismay.

"He has been laughing now seventeen minutes," the superintendent says, holding up his watch.

"I make it eighteen, sir."

"Eighteen minutes of animal laughter."

"Bizarre."

The laughter went on unabated, and there was something terrible, something eerie in it, as if it would never end and they would never stop hearing it, and even when it did die down, it would be like a poltergeist along those corridors, O'Kane's curse on them.

A Plea

HE IS with his grandmother. Through the observation hole they see them kissing, embracing, crying, and then sitting close as the grandmother takes clean socks and underpants from a pillow slip and lays them tenderly on his lap as if they are gifts.

"How are you, son?"

"Not so bad," he says, and suddenly starts to laugh, and the laugh frightens her because it is as if his insides are being laughed out of him. She holds him to contain it, to calm him in some way, and eventually does.

"Why do you laugh, Michen . . . is it because you haven't slept?"

"I fucked up bad with that gun . . . it wasn't worth a fuck."

"You'll tell me, won't you . . . you'll tell me what you've done."

"I've done nothing."

"Don't lie to me. It's known that you took the woman and the child in a car."

"There's another man involved . . . why don't they find him?"

"Look, you can deny it to them, but not to me. It's written all over your face."

"They're cunts . . . if I go down I'll bring them down with me."

"But where are the people?"

"I don't want to talk about them people . . ."

"You don't have to talk about them. You just have to say, they're in Meelic . . . they're in Mohara, they're in Derrygoolin or in Derrycon, Clonoila, Clonrush, Coose, Allendara . . ."

"They would be places where they might be."

"Are they alive, son?"

"Oh yes."

"How do you know?"

"Because a gang have them and they've put a price on their heads."

"What gang?"

"A hardened gang . . . Dublin, England . . ."

"Tell me more. If you can't talk to me, you can't talk to anyone . . ."

"I've no one in the world."

"You have me, son, and your sister and your poor mother looking down from heaven on her little boy."

"My mind is gone, Gran."

"In what way . . . Like, can you see me . . . can you tell the colour of my eyes . . . Can you tell the day of the week?"

"Why didn't you come sooner?"

"I did come sooner . . . I came the moment I heard. I wanted to be near you . . . I asked them to put a bed in here beside you, but they wouldn't. I was awake all night with the bells ringing . . . did you hear them?"

"I did."

"They're from the abbey. The poor nuns get up two and

three times a night to pray . . . three hundred years of prayers and penance. They're praying for you now, love, and I'm asking you as your truest friend, Where are the three people?"

"I can't tell you what I don't know."

"You can tell me, you can. Get it off your chest. I know you're in pain . . . I see it in your eyes, in the way you're smoking, in the way you're fiddling, in the way you eat the cigarettes."

"They think they'll break me . . . they'll never break me."

"We're all broken, son. We're all of us broken by this and we won't mend . . . we won't ever mend."

"Fuck you . . . they've twisted you against me," and jumping up, he pulls open the door that is already ajar and flings her out, telling her to fuck off home, traitor that she is. She shakes her head at the two guards that have been standing outside. She doesn't have to tell them what they already overheard.

Old Times

THE TOWN was dark and dormant, the drawn blinds smack up against the tiny windowpanes above the shops and public houses. The limestone fortress of the convent solid as a mountain range. Dogs slept and snarled under the gates of the side yards and little streams came rushing down out of nowhere.

A long, cylindrical globe of cold blue light shone above the barracks door, and inside, a team of guards and detectives from across the country paced and mulled and argued, waiting for O'Kane to break. Thirty of the thirty-six hours had passed and nerves were beginning to feel rattled. They took turns to go in pairs, even twice going into the cell to waken him with just that one question: "Where are the missing people . . . just tell us where they are." At times he has roared back at them, other times threatened them, and still others laughed, those bouts that sent shivers through them and made them fear for their wives and children at home alone. Their hopes now are pinned on O'Mara, one of the guards that tried to help him in his young days.

"You must excuse my attire," Guard O'Mara says, shaking hands with several of them who welcome him like a prophet. His pyjamas dip down under his trousers and he is wearing no collar or tie. Hs is excited. He's been retired for a few years, his days spent looking at television, looking into the fire, eating too much, especially cream buns, and now he is wanted again, intermediary and hero. Superintendent McBride briefs him on the events so far: the priest's visit, the grandmother's visit, admissions, countered a minute later with denials, with "bullshit" threats.

"I can handle him, sure I know him since he was a child, a gorsoun."

"One of the lads will go in with you."

"Christ no."

"Christ yes . . . he could knock you out in a split second."

"Let me do it my way . . . Me and him go way back," and he drinks a mug of coffee before he goes in.

"You remember me?" he says to O'Kane, who is on the floor hunched, talking to himself. Getting no reply, Guard O'Mara sits, rocks his body back and forth, and commences on the reverie that he has told to himself in the twenty-five-mile drive along the dark roads, past houses with frightened people, their lights left on. He talks in a soft fatherly drawl. "You remember you took a bicycle from the doctor's shed, a lady's bicycle, you didn't do it for gain, you never did anything for gain, I'll say that for you; it was more like a game, a prank. Next thing you broke into the holiday home of a Dutch woman and you found tins of paint and poured them onto the floor and onto the chairs and the sofa. That's how I got your first fingerprint. It was on the bottom of a tin, and I lifted it off with a bit of cellotape and sent it up to Dublin to headquarters. You broke into houses and took cushions and pillows that you hid up in the woods. You were going to live there, that's what you said. Your father asked me to talk to you, to caution you, and I did, but you went on with your blackguarding. There was no holding you. I could have arrested you the time you broke windows, but I didn't, I let you off, I said there would be no summons if you agreed to stop running wild and to go back home, back to your father. I drove you down there and I watched you go up the path and you were a grand little lad with your curls, a bit afraid but a grand little lad. I drove on back home and it was pouring rain and a fierce gale. There were trees down. 'Twas one of them stormy nights. I can see it now, every second of it, the wipers getting stuck on the windscreen of the car. I declare to God, I'm at home in my own kitchen in front of the stove drying myself when my wife, Mary, goes to let the dog out and there you are under our ash tree like a drowned cat, not saying anything, not asking anything, just looking into our lit house. She comes back in and says, "That youngster is out there and he'll catch pneumonia," and I give her the nod and she brings you in. She sends you into the bathroom and hands you a bath towel. Later she dries your hair and stands you in front of the stove next to me, the two of us with towels around us like Roman senators, like Nero, my wife, Mary, not able to do enough for you, making you cocoa, heating scones, and imploring you to speak. You wouldn't speak. You wouldn't tell us why you came to us. Maybe you thought you could stay with us, my wife and me. Is that it, Michen, is that it, is that what you thought then?"

"They're bastards, they're pigs, they're jumping on me."

"They're not bastards . . . they're just doing their job . . . They're very anxious to find these people."

"Their time is up . . . I won't be long more here . . . they can't keep me."

"You know me, and if you trust me, I'll make a deal with

you. You and I will go back out into the woods and we'll find the three people and we'll restore them to their poor heartbroken families. It's days now and these people are gasping with hunger and thirst . . . Hostages, as I presume . . . The young priest trying to give them whatever comfort he can, the child yelling. You've proved you can scare us, now it's time to unscare us, Mich."

"They'll never be found . . . never . . . none of them."

"Why not, son?"

"I can't tell you. I'm not going down for what I didn't do."

"But if you didn't do it, you won't be going down at all. Your only crime will be the unlawful possession of firearms and abducting Kitty Boland. They're not heinous crimes . . . you'll be out on bail . . . local people will go bail for you."

"Bullshit."

"You've built up a lot of rage since you were a youngster, but just think — that woman, that child, and that priest never did you any wrong."

"I know that."

"I'm glad to hear you say so. How 'bout me arranging for you to get boots and clothes and the two of us go out?"

"I'll go if it's only us."

"Jesus, Mich, it can't be only us . . . there's forty men on this case."

"You fucker . . . it's only a stunt."

"It's not a stunt. I'll see to it that you're sitting in my car next to me and you're not cuffed."

"I'll come tomorrow, not tonight."

"Tomorrow could be too late."

"The priest is dead . . . he's buried three feet down . . . I took a leather jacket out of his car . . ."

"Oh God Almighty, where is he buried?"

"I can't tell you . . . they'll link me to the killing. Will the ballistics show that the bullet came from the same gun as I had?"

"Where is he buried?"

"Awful thing to see blood flowing from a man's neck . . . spouting."

"Are the woman and the child alive?"

"They should be."

"I'll put it to you hypothetically."

"What's that?"

"Say you're not you, you're an observer. If a person was going to dump a body in that wood, give me a clue where would be the best place . . ."

O'Kane thought about the question and for the first time seemed to show some interest, then asked for the door to be closed.

He whispers it: "You go up from the crossroads, towards Derrygoolin. You pass the first two barriers and you come to a third one and in a bit there's an old hut that had a dead goat in it . . . There's drains there . . . That would be a good place to dump a body."

Evil

THEY HAVE SET OUT early, to preempt the crowds, five men squeezed into a small unmarked police car, the air stifling because the windows have to be kept shut, the two detectives on either side of O'Kane recoiling from him.

"Feeling better . . . feeling a bit more relaxed?" Detective Morgan says, turning to O'Kane, but he does not answer. Solon, the driver, keeps looking in his mirror at the weirdo, slumped, his paws on his lap, like someone in a daze. Morgan has agreed not to cuff him. At unexpected moments he comes awake, and taking note of a shopfront or a tin sign flapping over a filling station, or a field with gorse bushes, he says, "I bought sardines there . . . I bought buns there . . . I had a good shit there," and then reverts to his torpor.

"You were a great hurley player . . . won the O'Donohoe shield for your school . . . scored the two goals . . . great stuff," Morgan says, and again O'Kane is listless.

Passing a glass shrine with a statue of the Virgin and a crown of artificial red roses, Detective Lahiffe, attempting to diffuse the tension, says, "Who puts them up, I wonder . . . is it the state?"

"Not the state . . . the locals. That spot is where there was a terrible accident . . . five people killed . . . tragic altogether," Brophy says, proud of his knowledge of the area and familiar with every house, every hay shed, every car or tractor.

"Is it the Blessed Virgin that's always in the glass case?" Lahiffe asks.

"Oh no . . . if you go towards Mayo you'll find they have St. Patrick," Solon says.

"Is that a fact, Joe?"

"Beautiful . . . especially at night . . . lights around him like a halo."

"Of all the vandalism that's around, these shrines are never harmed . . . Isn't that a marvellous thing?" Detective Morgan says.

"Marvellous."

"I want to go to my mother's grave," O'Kane says sharply.

"You can go later . . . we have our bit of business first," Morgan says, overfriendly.

"I want to go now . . . I have to talk to her up in heaven . . . she has a message for me . . . she whispered to me."

"Listen . . . we go to the wood first and then we go to the grave."

They drive on, in a taut silence, until they come to the crossroads with a sign that leads to Cloosh Wood and Morgan lets loose a stream of heated curses at the sight of so many cars, cameras, droves of people, and a helicopter landing in a nearby field.

"Ye bastards . . . ye fucking bastards . . . ye said no press, no cameras," O'Kane shouts.

"They won't see you. I'll go up and talk to the super on duty and have the area closed off . . . You lie low here with the men," Morgan tells him.

"Cunts . . . I'll bring ye down . . . I'll bring the whole

fucking lot of ye down with me," and he whirls and punches Lahiffe, knocking him sideways, then kicks on the door to make his escape. Brophy pulls him back by the coat, then by the torso, and while O'Kane is head-butting him with quick rolling thrusts, the shrill pips preceding the morning radio news, then a woman's voice, strangled, emotional, says, "Word has just come in that the body of a female has been found in a shallow grave in . . ." Then the reception is gone, because they have entered the wooded region, and Solon searches frantically, twiddling the knobs, the others craning, hearing only static and their own shocked exhalations. O'Kane begins to cry, quiet at first, then less quiet, sobbing, a seepage of tears, as if now he is only his tears; his flesh, his fury, his bellowing, all gone, only tears as he puts his hand out for one of them to hold it. No one does.

"We'd better go back, lads," Morgan says, and as Solon starts to turn the car, a guard on a motorbike comes rushing down, flashing them to wait.

"What is it, Pakie?" Morgan says, winding the window down.

"They're after finding the girl in a furrow between the trees, with twigs and brush over her," he says, his voice hasty and breathless.

"Oh Jesus Christ," Brophy says in a choked cry, recalling his brother telling him about delivering stones to her from a quarry and her getting upset because of the way the ground swallowed them up.

"Who found her—one of our lads?"

"No, a forester . . . he went up a few hundred yards and jumped the security wire . . . by himself."

"And the child?"

"No sign . . . they're intensifying the search," Pakie says.

"Take me to my mother's grave," O'Kane shouts.

"You sonofabitch . . . you thought you'd get away with it . . . you thought a couple of months and animals and insects would have eaten her . . . missing forever."

"Let me out . . . let me out . . . I want to go to my mother . . . she knows I'm innocent."

"Cuff him," Morgan says.

"We can't cuff him unless we get him on the ground. And if we open that door he's gone . . . he's back in them woods, period," Lahiffe tells him.

"Put your foot down, Joe," Morgan says to Solon, and as the car is turned, Cleary, a second guard, has arrived at the other window, his face streaming and red: "They just found the child, it was under the woman when they lifted her up."

"A fucking animal," Solon says.

"You're looking into the personification of evil."

"Get him out of the area fast. There's people up there baying for him . . . people that knew him . . . that fed him," Cleary says.

"I'd like to throw him to them . . . to the gladiators . . . it's what should be done," Pakie says.

"Now, lads . . . we keep the cool, we play this by the book . . . otherwise it could affect the trial," Morgan reminds them.

"You realise what he's done . . . a woman, a child," Lahiffe says.

"I do and I shrink from him . . . 'Touch not the murderer lest thou too be touched,'" Morgan says solemnly.

"Unreal . . . unreal," Brophy keeps saying.

"Fecking not unreal . . . real," Cleary says, gripping the

handles of his motorcycle, shouting to include the warm day, the soft countryside, young buds, hawthorn blossoms, and, a few hundred yards away, a scene so gruesome that he vomited.

"You saw her," Solon says helplessly.

"I saw her."

"What state are they in?" Morgan asks.

"They smell. They smell."

"Picture it . . . and picture him. He killed the girl, he reloaded the chamber and he shot the child . . . an animal . . ."

"No animal would do such a thing . . . an animal kills for survival . . . this is bloodlust . . ."

"I want my mother," O'Kane says, throwing himself across Lahiffe.

"You sonofabitch . . . your mother won't help you now or ever . . . you're zeroed."

"Take a back road, Joe . . . the word will be out," Morgan says, and thanks the two messengers with a grim nod.

It is a narrow road, rutted and grassy from disuse, the drive so frantic it is like a hallucination—dust spattering up, the fleeing countryside, the occasional cottage garden, horses, a television mast, O'Kane immersed in himself, in some bottomless cavity, like a grieving animal. Soon now they would enter bedlam, but they did not know it, and perhaps he did not know it either, because he was sitting with his head down, sobs reaching up out of his gut, when suddenly the car starts to veer from one side of the road to the other, Solon not yet realising what it is and then feeling that he is being choked as O'Kane has caught his tie and is jerking it violently. The car comes to a skidding halt and lurches up onto a bank where there are geese and goslings pecking. The cramped car, filled now with shouts, urgent, harried, afraid; the two detectives in the back locked in a clinch with him, like wrestlers in a pit, his strength prodigal, their fists not even denting him, as if they are hitting leather.

"Lie on him."

"Restrain him."

"Get him to the floor."

"Cuff him."

"We can't cuff him."

"Get him off me . . . he's biting my ear," Brophy roars.

"Jesus, as if one madman isn't enough," Morgan says, hoists himself over the front seat, grips O'Kane by the hair, pulling it with a long, practised traction until the teeth are loosed from the bloodied ear, and O'Kane's face getting whiter and whiter: "You're breaking my fucking neck."

"No one cares if we break every bone in your body," Morgan tells him as Lahiffe pulls his arms behind his back and handcuffs him, still butting, still vowing that he will bring them down.

The car rocks from side to side, with Solon struggling to get a grip on the wheels as they slurp on the mossy bank, and beyond, the geese in a wild consternation because their young have been slaughtered, bits of yellow lifeless furry rag slung there.

O'Kane sits between them, a lethal presence; the only weapons left to him are his fingers, his thumb tearing the opposite thumb, dragging the flesh away, and then each finger picking the flesh of its opposite finger, the shredded flesh, spurts of blood and the grating of the cuffs as if they too are about to spring open of their own accord.

As they near the town, the two detectives in the back look from one to the other, comparing their slashed jackets, their bruises, their cut lips.

"Longest eighteen miles I've ever driven."

"How's the ear?"

"Deadly . . . I can't tell my wife he bit me."

"Cover him up, lads. They'll be looking for his horns here," Morgan says, and throws a blanket over O'Kane to hide him from the throng.

They have gathered outside the station, milled, grave, appalled, but when he is bundled out, the voices break into an instantaneous wail of repugnance and revenge, the same words again and again: "Murderer . . . child murderer . . . butcher."

The likeness of the dead woman stares back at him from raised posters, stares from several points, her face with an unwonted calmness, the eyes soft as cloud, a long rope of hair under the upturned brim of a straw hat, gazing at them, at him, at the summer day. He is not seeing it, not hearing their heckles; he has gone back into himself, into a hulking frozenness.

A legion of guards converges around him, and he is pushed forward, a bunched and damned silhouette passing into the gloom of the hallway. Then in some monstrous and antic aftermath he turns, head butts the blanket off, and he begins to laugh, a mad, mocking laugh, and they draw back, a shaft of terror passing through them, witnesses to some medieval grotesquerie: his grinning face, his loathesome eyes with a dead yet murderous glare.

They are afraid of him now, the Kinderschreck, one of their own sons come out of their own soil, their own flesh and blood, gone amok.

Bart Glynn

IT WAS like I dreamed it. It was like I'll dream
it all my life. I seemed to have known where I was going,
my steps led me there in an orderly, unfussy motion. I
didn't salute any of the mob around the crossroads, they
were as invisible to me as I to them. I was a phantom in
search of a phantom and I would find it. To call it weird is
to belittle it. I even think I envisaged how the woman
would be. I'd seen her once playing pool in Boyce's bar
and sensed this glow around her, amberish, possibly because of the red-gold hair. She played like a pro and the
men riled her. I had known it before I wakened. To my
wife I said, "Leave the dinner till evening time," and she
didn't question me. She never does, which possibly ac
counts for our being together. I am described as a loner.
My favourite place is a mobile home thirty miles away by
the seaside. I walk and I walk and I need no one. I've never
been one to believe in signs or portents or dreaming. I am a
rationalist. After I passed the two barriers and little knots
of guards stationed here and there, it seemed to me that
everyone was running in different directions, somewhat
clueless. Strangers to the wood. It was a warm day and in
the breeze there was the smell of spring itself, a tender
smell. The wood was fairly dark and I had to crawl along
under the low branches and under the trees that had fallen

athwart. Strands of dead moss dipped from their branches. I sensed something in the instant before I saw it. Then that rapid contraction in the chest, that onrush of adrenaline. The exposed calf of one leg was the whitest white, the coat was black, and she had thick purplish socks. She was in a furrow face down, and the pine needles had fallen on her like decoration, fine, thin needles, rust colour. I knew she was dead, the smell alone told me that. She looked so remarkably lifelike that a person might be forgiven for thinking she could be brought back to life with a touch. There were flies on her hair, moving in and out of it and lodging on the crusts of dried blood. They were merciless. Nothing else moved. Not her. Not I. It was her repose that I found the most unbearable, the wisdom of it, as if in those last moments she saw what was coming and somehow she met death. The picture just kept going in and in, a gruesome canvas inside my head, forever.

"Up here . . . up here." I went out shouting it. I shouted like a madman, but Cornelius said that when he came towards me, my face and my beard had the pallor of a ghost.

Grief

"WHY didn't he overpower the bastard? Why didn't he take the gun off him? Why didn't he run off into the woods? Why did he die like a lamb to the slaughter?"

It is Jack, a second woodsman, asking the detective who has just been winched down. Asking it relentlessly, as he has asked it from the moment at dusk when, after the searches were called off until the morrow, he came on him alone, Father John, with his head placed over a limestone slab, his hands folded for prayer, his priest's collar unstained.

"Why, just tell me why he didn't fight back?"

"No use in whys . . . because the creatures are all gone," the detective replies, and then genuflects for a moment in lieu of a prayer, and then it is the cold grim task of identifying the body and noting every detail for his report.

The same woods, that filtered green, the constant leafy murmur, and yet not the same, no longer the harmless place it once was, marked now as a human can be marked by its violation, its wood memory, the habitation of their frightful pilgrimage, their hapless cries; three bodies soon to be wrapped in plastic and brought down to the waiting hearses.

Bluebells

THE SMALL COUNTRY CHAPEL has the
smell and leafiness of field and woodland. Garlands of fern
and ivy, bluebells in jugs, their bells a clouded violet blue,
close together as if they might just accidentally tinkle; car-
pets of flowers along the aisle and by the altar steps where
the two coffins are placed on either side, the larger brown
coffin for Eily and the smaller white one for Maddie. The
chapel is filled to overflowing; the sermons, eulogies, and
songs drift out along with the smell of bluebells and wood-
bine, out to the grounds and the adjoining fields where
hundreds of mourners stand, stunned and teary.

Cassandra spoke for her entire family when she said
that their spirits should now be allowed to go free and
looked at the coffins as if she was talking to the bodies be-
neath, bodies that had been cut and sawn and scalped and
weighed and swabbed and pieced together again, dressed
now in garments of eternal glory.

"Free them," she said, and cupped her hands, and as she
raised them, people looked up to the rafters believing they
were witnessing the transmigration of the two souls.

An estranged father stood apart. That was his child inside the small white coffin, his feelings locked inside his
own brusque and taciturn nature. Herself and the child
were one, indivisible, and O'Kane, the outcast, had seen

that and had wanted it and had had to destroy it in his hunger to belong. The ultimate loser. An estranged father who wanted to cry but did not cry then. There were tears to be shed, but they would be shed elsewhere, him imagining them forever in the woods, their true resting place. He thought, *What can I do to prove to myself that I am that bit bigger than I was before this struck. I can't bring them back. I can think of those last mad minutes until thinking is empty of thought, but I can't bring them back, ever.*

What he did then was to search out O'Kane's father and shake his hand, and the man looked at him, perplexed, uncomprehending, his sunken eyes like holes in his face, two fathers outside that boundary of mother and child, their hands briefly touching, touching on things that could never be said.

Blood

"TELL ME that you didn't rape her, Mich . . . just tell me that." It is Aileen, teary and unslept and waiting since dawn to be allowed in, travelling almost a hundred miles, since he has been moved to a prison halfway between home and the city. She has brought him the clean clothes, bar of soap, and bananas he asked for. The guard outside has explained to her that he has refused to give blood and asked her to tell him, as they have told him, that it can be taken forcibly. Her brother looks at her as if he might kill her.

"Tell me," she says, beseeching.

"They set you up . . . They want to blacken me with every crime in the book."

"Then tell me that you did not rape the woman, simple, simple, Mich."

"Fucking voices . . . won't shut the fuck up . . . Get me a radio . . . get me anything . . . get me a gun . . . get me out of here."

"Mich . . . Michen."

"She loved me . . . she was my girlfriend . . . she sucked my cock in the woods . . . we had a tent up there . . . mad for me."

"She was not your girlfriend. It's all in your mind, and there's only you and your mind for the rest of your fucked life . . . Jesus."

It is as they are arguing that a young prison officer with pale, almost albino colouring comes in; clean-shaven, a crew cut, his eyes the washed blue of cornflowers, dangling a syringe and making imaginary stabs in the air as he dances around O'Kane.

"We don't need your blood, scumbag . . . we have it. You cut your bollocks on the glass door when you broke into that house . . . we have your DNA on our files. They flushed you out of her, above in the mortuary . . . She's dead but she's clean, and you're unclean and you stink."

"Is that the woman on the shore?" he asks.

"No, it's not the woman on the shore, scumbag. It's the woman you brought to the woods. How come you forget the most important data? You don't forget to ask for bananas or a change of underpants, but how come you forget that? You're a monster, but you can't hide behind the devil's apron strings any longer . . . Do you want to know why? Because you are him, hooves and horns and all . . . It's been a farce, a roadshow down the country . . . everyone willing to help you . . . a bishop no less, priests, dignitaries, VIPs, wringing their hands . . . poor you . . . you never had a chance . . . the system failed you . . . we failed you . . . St. Michael's, St. Joseph's, St. Bridget's, St. Patrick's, St. Finian's, St. Teresa's, St. Anne's, Spike Island, Clonmel Rugby, Featherstone, Wolverhampton, all failed the little coward who so loved his mother that he had to take an innocent woman and fuck her and kill her and then kill her child to complete the tableau and kill the priest that was brought to give the last rites. It's all a blur inside that football of a head . . . It slipped your memory somehow. Well, I'll tell you something, the bishops and the priests and the VIPs will run like rats from you now, repulsed . . . Your visitors from now on are Us . . . state visitors . . . state plate . . . state blanket . . . state funeral . . . Welcome to hell, O'Kane. It's been waiting for you."

"He's a fucking liar, a fucking liar," he says when they are alone.

"I think you did rape her, Mich . . . I think you did."

"Do you want them to lock me up?"

"It's the only thing . . . after what you done."

"Your own brother."

"You're not the brother I knew . . . you're an alien," she says, fearless, despairing.

"Don't leave me," he says, running to her, grasping her.

"I have to . . . I can't stay here a minute more."

And he did not try to stop her, he just backed away in frozen immobility, seeing the shame that welled up in her eyes.

O'Kane

IT WAS AFTER I had sex with her I came downstairs to the kitchen. She had the kettle on. I heard the voice of the devil saying, *Kill her, kill her.* I said, We have to go to the woods. She tried to defy me. The gun was hid outside behind a tree. She didn't like it, she didn't want a gun around the child. I'm only after getting it, I intend to raid a post office, I said. I didn't think of killing her before that. I had no reason to. She used to come up to my tent in the wood every other day and bring me food, and we had loads of sex there. She sucked my cock. She wouldn't let me go to Tullamore. I made her drive to Cloosh Wood, and when we got there she said, Where's your tent. I said, I burnt it, I had no more use for it. I said then, I'm going to have to kill you. She said, Don't be raving. I brought her way in from the road at gunpoint. She was nervous, panicky. She was holding the child's hand. I told her if she tried running away I'd shoot them both. She let go of the child's hand and sent it to play. I brought her up into the horseshoe of trees and she said, You're frightening me, you're scaring me, give me that gun. She took it off me. She unloaded it. We were struggling. She hit the bolt and that automatically unloaded it. I tripped her. She fell on the ground and I loaded the gun. She tried to get back up. I shot her in the face. It was messy. I had a problem with the

child. What was I going to do with him? He was screaming. He had no mother. I couldn't bear to look at him. I
shot him in the side of the head or somewhere around
there. I forget. My mind was gone. I came out of the wood
and sat in her car. The keys were missing. I went back to
the wood to get the keys from her pocket. She'd gone
green. The colour frightened me. I covered her with pine
needles and left the wood. I slept in the car a long time,
maybe a day. I burned the car somewhere and went to my
grandmother's. I was sweating. I threw up. I was hearing
the devil's voice. He said, Burn your grandmother's iron
gate, burn her hay shed. I don't remember going out from
there, but I did; I was walking along the road with the
gun. I heard a voice say, Burn the lockkeeper's house. He
wasn't there. I took a blanket. It got dark, so I went on up
towards the lights in the village and saw the church. The
priest's house was beside the church. There was no light in
it and I waited. When he came I kidnapped him at gunpoint. He said, Oh my God. He asked me what I wanted.
I said I was in a mood to kill. He said, Relax and don't kill
me, I'll drive you anywhere you want. I brought him to a
house in the wood where I lived as a kid. I'd hid in a closet
there, pissed in it. My mother thought that very funny.
Someone had sunk a well there since we lived in it. The
priest said, What are you going to do to me? I said I was
waiting for orders. He said I was a sick man. He said
that he knew my grandmother, that he went to see her
sometimes, heard her confession. He had a wallet in his inside pocket. He went into the toilet and hid it in his
trouser pocket. I ate cake with sugar on top. I went to
sleep.

It was six in the morning and the birds were singing. I

234

said to him, Come on, time to get up. I took his wrist-watch. I gave it to some fucker in Limerick for hash. I laughed at the blood coming out of his head like a water pump. I got a great buzz, a great kick out of that. I liked the jump. I'm possessed.

Christmas

HE LAY in his own shit. He lay in his own dark, cursing and conspiring. He hated the screws. The screws hated him. He made their lives hell, refused to use the bucket that they passed in and shat on the floor to spite them. Threw his arms out as if they were oars or javelins and told the fuckers he'd be leaving very shortly, going through the roof. The "Jumping Jesus show" they called it. They were afraid of him. He roared and harangued, and they believed that even if his head came off from roaring, his lopped head would go on persecuting them. He called them Ambrose. They called him Fattie. "No hamburgers for Mr. Fattie." "No radio for Mr. Fattie." "No walkies for Mr. Fattie." He'd hold four fingers up in rotation, and they knew what it meant. He'd killed three people and there would be a fourth. Sometimes he sat as if he was in a trance, sucking his thumb, staring. His laughing was a kind of roaring also. He could keep it up for hours.

The staff shot the pheasant that kept him company because they were jealous of it. He got his revenge. He had birds coming in the window whistling tunes and he whistled back. Then one day six or seven red hens from home came and he talked to them and asked them if they were laying well. He had great times with them. He learned the chookchookchookchookchookchook that they did after they laid. One morning they didn't come and he cried. Pigs came, but they got stuck, they got wedged between the bars, their pink hairy rumps not able to get in and not able to get out. They taught him grunts, and the screws listened outside the cell and looked through the spyhole, made bets whether he was or was not a pig. Instead of Fattie they called him Piggy and he still called them all Ambrose.

He was brought for a walk each day, around a closed yard with a high wall and one tree with dead, papery leaves. There was a lavatory bowl in the corner with no chain and no handle and he shat in it, even though he was not supposed to. He saved his shit for there so that they would come with bucket and broom, cursing him and making him clean it up. One day there was a new nurse who gave him a funny look and he struck at him in a long lunge, got him to the ground, and then started hitting his skull on the edge of the bowl, his face mired in the shit. It was the padded cell after that. He'd hurl himself against the leather wall and be thrown back and rehurl himself, because nothing would convince him that it was not going to give in to him.

That's when Dr. Macready was called. Dr. Macready had the distinction of being the only one that was not afraid of these nutters, afraid of no one. He agreed with the governor to see him, but only on one condition, face-to-face. He did not want to be in one room and looking at O'Kane through glass in an adjoining room. "I want to get to the real person," he said, and the governor smiled the smile of the disenchanted. It took five visits to break the ice. He was late for his visit and sat down, took out his handkerchief, began to clean his spectacles, and said, "There was a drunk Scotsman on the bus and he kept saying, 'No sweat, John, no sweat, John,' and he walked up and down the aisle and looked into people's faces and said, 'Peasants,' and then he came and sat beside me and said, 'Peasant.'"

"Are you in America a lot?"

"No . . . why?"

"I don't want a trial here . . . they'll be laughing at me . . . They'll make fun of me and fun of my mother. Could you get me out of here. Could you get me out a back door? I'll harm no one . . . I won't get a gun."

"Not a chance in hell, Michen. The only way I can help you is to come in here and see you."

"Bullshit."

"Yes, and let you bullshit me."

"I throw food on the floor . . . I go to the toilet on the floor."

"I know, I've seen it."

"I'm a sick man . . . aren't I?"

"Yes, you're a sick man."

"And what will you do for me?"

"Not much, but something. We'll try . . . together."

Dr. Macready is with him in the hospital; he has been sitting for well over an hour listening to him as he dozed and rambled: "There's a little gun in your exhaust, I was a colicky baby, I smiled at three months . . . I twitched at six" — his sighs getting fainter and fainter, a film over the eyes, and sudden jerking as his brain seems to fuse out, then another little garbled sentence, then a smile.

The light from the corridor is mellow, in contrast with the harsher light in the hospital ward, O'Kane's face gaunt, his skin yellow, his head lifted back against the iron rungs, his wrist no longer chafing, slack inside the handcuff, the guard cuffed to him dozing with tedium. Two other guards stand at the end of the bed and one at the door, their squat revolvers slightly obscene-looking, their hips waddling as they walk around to kill time.

Dr. Macready has a gift for him because it is Christmas. O'Kane has been on a hunger strike for over twenty days, no longer warring, quiet, shivery, talking of being lifted up into the sky, and at other times seeing orange men dancing on his bed. He is saying that he wants his sins on his tombstone, wants the world to know he is sorry. He insists that it was when the box of Holy Communion wafers was found in Father John's car that his luck changed, and that it was a good thing, because it meant he got captured. He said she was a beautiful woman, his dream woman in his dream world, and that was why he fell in love with her. He asked the doctor to say goodbye to home for him, because home was the most important place in a boy's life, a boy carried the woods into the world. He said his father should have come and forgiven him, and he should have forgiven his father, because a son had to be a father, too. But always back to the woman, still alive in some part of him, still alive in Cloosh Wood, animals attacking her and him trying to save her and turning her over and picking her up. And picking her up.

"Aren't you going to open your present?" the doctor says.

"I can't," he says, and holds up the cuffed hand and smiles. Quiet, dreamy, like someone lulled by a potion that has come not from outside, not been administered, but from inside himself, his own metabolism altered, making him serene, remote, his demons gone. Dr. Macready unwraps the crepe paper and holds up the cigar box with the beige-coloured picture of a South American potentate.

"Who's the man and who's the woman?" O'Kane says, staring at it.

"There's only a man there . . . can you not see?"

"Is it chocolate?"

"No, it's cigars . . . I thought it was time for a cigar."

"I won't come off the fast . . . so don't try asking me," he says very gently.

"I won't let you die . . . What do you think happens when you die?"

"You go to the other place."

"What if you don't like it in the other place?"

"I'll ask the way back."

"Michen, listen to me."

"You listen to me . . . I'm not mad now and I've no temper, and isn't that a good way to die?"

As the door is pushed in, Matron calls in a falsetto voice, "A visitor, a VIP," and Dr. Macready gets up and says to wait for a moment until he clears it, then leans in over O'Kane. "I think I told you . . . I asked my friend Bishop Cormac to come by. He's a lovely man, a sympathetic man."

"Is he an Orangeman?"

The bishop stands by the bed and puts his hands alternately on O'Kane's shivering forehead.

"Can we take off the handcuffs, Matron . . . so as he can talk in private to Bishop Cormac?" Dr. Macready asks.

"No."

"No?"

"I can't take responsibility for that. If he attacks and kills, I will get the blame."

"He can't hurt a fly . . . he's a dying man."

"I'll have to phone the governor of the jail . . . he may

not even be there. It is Christmas, after all," and she points glaringly to a strip of tinsel looped above O'Kane's bed.

"Oh Jesus, where are the courageous people," Dr. Macready says, looking from her to the guards and back again.

"You've no idea, Doctor, how obstreperous, how dangerous this man can be."

"I have."

"Then you're lucky you're not in a morgue."

"I'll answer to the governor, and so will Bishop Cormac. This boy must be persuaded to take a sip of something . . . or he'll be in the morgue."

She nods reluctantly and the handcuff is undone, then the guards file out, somewhat sheepish at the presence of a bishop.

Dr. Macready and Miriam, a young auxiliary nurse, are in the pantry waiting. A plate of sandwiches covered with a cloth is on a tray, along with tea things.

"It's an awful thing to say, but I'm starving," the doctor says.

"Me too . . . it's the thought of people stuffing themselves at this very minute with turkey and roast potatoes and little sprouts . . . and then the plum pudding and the brandy butter and a dollop of whipped cream . . ."

"Don't," he says, and lifts the corner of the cloth to see what kind of sandwiches they have been brought.

From time to time, Miriam goes to the door, which is still closed, and comes back with her index finger to her lip.

The bishop takes them by surprise because of his crepe-sole shoes and comes in smiling, his cupped hands raised in a little triumph: "He'll take a sip . . . he'll take a sip of sugar and water."

"Fantastic. What did you do?" Dr. Macready asks.

"I didn't have to do much . . . He's a broken man, a broken boy, I should say. We talked of what happened. You see, it's always coming back to him . . . the place, the woman screaming, the child screaming . . . all jumbled . . . so we made a kind of pact. I said that I'd take his thoughts for one hour every day . . . I'd pray and meditate and he could have a rest from them . . . that's how I reached him."

"So we're to feed him?" Miriam says petulantly.

"Only sips, you understand . . . little by little . . . That will revive him."

"My father says he'd shoot the bastard, and we're about to save him. It doesn't make sense," she says.

"It does, Miriam . . . it makes sense of some kind . . . You wouldn't have volunteered to be a nurse if you didn't have sympathy," Dr. Macready says quietly.

"Okay . . . I'll give him the sips, but I won't tell anyone outside . . . and I won't tell it at home either, because his crime is the worst ever committed and it'll never be forgotten."

"Why is that, do you think?" the bishop asks.

"We'll never know the ordeal these people went through . . . and that's why we keep reliving it."

"And he'll never know either."

"He knows," she says tartly.

"You're wrong there, Miriam . . . He makes no distinction between life and death . . . between you and me . . . between inside and outside. It's all the same . . . it's all dreamtime.

"Dreamtime," the bishop says, and looks at the evening sky, a marvel of pale violet, God's creation, just as the young man in the bed about to take a sip of something is God's creation as well.

242

Court

A YEAR has gone by and O'Kane has been moved from prison cell to hospital bed, back to prison again, sometimes in isolation, sometimes not, by turns abusive or opaque, while down at home his spectre haunts the place, and those who are obliged to give statements to the guards live in fear of his return, of his coming back to take revenge on them.

Then it is the time for the hearing, and a crowd stand outside as they will day after day to look and to harangue him as he is brought, handcuffed, from the back of the van, sometimes cursing, other times shouting out that he is being persecuted in the prison, that he is being made senile.

On the opening day his counsel asked the judge to go back with him to those early years, O'Kane the child, withdrawn, timid, flung in with city delinquents, institutionalised for most of his life, assessed but never helped, because no one, no one in the entire world wanted to help him. He described the abyss O'Kane lived in, was still living in, the tortured mind, worms crawling in and out of his skull, voices dogging him, a sense not just of alienation but of living hell. He was at pains to remind the judge and the crowded gallery of the Blitzkrieg that surrounded this very emotional case and, turning to the jury, tells them that theirs is a sacred task. He said the young man did not deserve to stand there alone, because the country itself was on trial, it had failed him, the system had failed him, as from the age of ten he was shuttled from one institution to another, motherless, fatherless, never with them and never without them. There were stares and looks of indignation. O'Kane sat handcuffed, bloated, with a blank expression, sleeping the hours away as if he were already dead.

Counsel on the opposite side painted a different picture, that of a lying, untruthful, cunning, self-interested liar with a bloodlust, a man who took pleasure in killing, a man fully aware of what he had done, who now feigned madness to have his sentence mitigated. He said they would hear of voices that plagued the defendant, but to make no mistake, these were gimmicks, *Alice in Wonderland* ploys, tall stories of devils spiking his food or voodoo priests governing his actions or so-called maggots crawling out of his brain. And so endlessly his mental state was batted back and forth between quick jousting surgical minds, and mostly O'Kane seemed to register nothing, except for the times when he laughed uncontrollably and some in the crowd tittered with nerves.

Day after day a re-enactment of the scene, the woods, the track, the twigs, the small branches, the brush, the partially covered bodies, the blowflies, the eggs of blowflies, the left foot, the right foot, the flexed knees, the black anorak, the blue anorak, the mother splayed over the child, listeners at once riveted and appalled.

There were tears when exhibits were held up, the priest's elasticized gold watch, a wooden pendant that the woman had worn and the child's sweatshirt with a motorbike pattern on the front. A neighbour of Father John spoke of his last tête-à-tête in her house, the half measure of brandy she had given him and diluted with twice as much water, the slice of sponge cake filled with cream which he ate and the sacred box of communion wafers he was carrying for children's first Holy Communion three days hence. A cry of pathos was let out at hearing how he had removed his wallet from his jacket pocket and tucked it into the back pocket of his trousers, as if he feared being robbed by his captor.

When the time came for O'Kane to be cross-examined, he seemed to emerge from a long coma, burning to tell how he got great with Eily, their first kiss on a couch in her house, the hashish they smoked, the times in his tent in the wood, and of those last minutes when she defied him. He said how she grabbed the gun off him and he grabbed it back and pulled the trigger and shot her in the eye and blood started squirting out and the child ran shouting, "Mammy, Mammy." On being cross-examined, he denied that shooting the child was a vicious deed. He said no. He said that he did not want the child to grow up without its mother, the way he had done. He described and enacted how he had hidden the child under the mother and put the pine needles over them to keep off the rain.

Cassandra did not know that she was about to do it, did not even remember herself standing up and walking towards the witness stand to where he stood.

"The last picture my sister was painting was called *Grief.* It was a woman and a child . . . with a man at the edge of the canvas looking in."

O'Kane stared at her, baffled, vacuous, and then asked if the typist would read out to him what had been said. He heard it and shook his head repeatedly, as if to recapture something that had gone astray in him; then:

"I watched only one woman."

"Why did you watch her?"

"I was in love with her—that's the truth."

There were gasps and hisses of outrage.

"You don't believe me, do you?" he asked.

She paused, the pain, the horror, the sorrow, the anger, the loss, all compressed into this definitive moment.

"God help us all, you included," she said, her voice cold and unemotional, and she stood frail and unfrail, outside time and place, outside the shocked staring faces, not knowing if he had heard her.

Visiting Hour

HE IS HOLDING two soup spoons that are his friends. They have names. He is beating them hard. That steady hollow clang of metal upon metal, getting louder and louder and queerly hysterical in the austerity of the small dining room. Aileen is sitting opposite him. He has not said a word to her, he is in one of his blankety-blank moods, as she remarks. Others have got up as soon as they came in, shunned by all, even a black retriever which comes over to sniff them and goes off again. He has put on weight, and only his eyes bear resemblance to the youth that he was, just a year before.

"So how are you?"

"I'm in hell," he says.

"You're not in hell. You're in a mental hospital, and you prefer it to the jail . . . You prefer the food, the walks, the exercise."

"The chef is poisoning me . . . they're all out to get me, tormenting me."

"Do you want me to talk to the doctor?"

"You're thick . . . a thick head."

"Look, it's a three-hour journey . . . the trains are woeful . . . I had to get a babysitter for Ben . . . You don't even ask how he's doing. Well, he's first in his class, and his best subject is English . . . so there."

"I want a . . ."

"A what?"

"A medal."

"Oh, are you religious now, is that what they done to you?"

"St. Christopher. I want it in gold. It's for a journey."

"Where are you thinking of going?"

"Tullamore . . . I'll build a small bungalow . . . get the balance back."

"I never know whether you're mad or acting mad."

"Does your heart break?"

"Sometimes."

He is crying then, his teeth eating his tears; pitiful sounds coming from deep within, a child's despair imprisoned in the bloated being he has become. She leans over and takes the spoons from him, then very gently: "What is it, Mich? If you don't tell me, I can't know and I can't help you."

"No one will double up with me . . . they're all afraid of me."

"You attacked nurses . . . twice."

"Why did I kill them people?" he asks vacantly.

"That's between you and God."

"She's there," he says, and jumps back terrified.

"She's not there . . . there's only me here."

"God isn't talking to me. He says I'm an animal . . . Am I an animal?"

"I brought something to cheer you up . . . a poem you wrote to me . . . You wrote it in the first place that you went to. It was in a jug all these years . . . Ben found it:

> *Each night before I go to sleep*
> *I hope that you my heart will keep*

"Bullshit," he says, and snatches it and tears it up.

"It wasn't bullshit . . . it was before bad got into you . . ."

"I want to die."

"You can't die until you die . . . no one can."

"Would you help me if I asked?"

"You know I would . . . I love you no matter what. I'm your sister and nothing can change that."

"Get me back out into the woods . . . I'll bother no one . . . I'll live on berries."

"That's daft talk."

"Who hunts there now?"

"I don't know . . . I've never been in them woods and I never intend to and don't think that I don't blame myself for that night at Granny's . . . you unwrapping and wrapping that gun . . . Up in Mars you were and I did nothing."

"She was dead then and so was the child."

"You can't keep going over it."

"Will you do it for me . . . ask the knackers?"

"Look . . . there isn't a hope in hell . . . there's gates, there's locks, there's a sentry tower, there's dogs, there's guards . . ."

"You want me locked up for life, you're one of them . . . you gave evidence to the scumbags."

"I only told them that you sometimes flipped . . . They had me plagued, coming to the house."

It happened quicker than thought, the mug flying and the tea and the teabag running down the white wall, a sugar bowl smashed and two nurses coming in quietly and cautiously so that they can see him: "Come on now, Michen . . . cool it . . . let's go for a walk," and each one takes an arm and she gets up to follow.

"Keep back now, miss . . . keep a distance . . . this could be dangerous," and that was the loneliest moment of all, to see him gone into himself, dead to the world around him.

Heaven

THEY HAD put him down for the night. He had had his quota of pills, the blue, the yellow, the purple, and the white. The nurse wished him sweet dreams.

It came down like hail and he sat up excited, thinking the gang had come to rescue him. He'd prayed to them and now at last they'd come. But it wasn't them. It was a big television, so big that it filled the cell. He sat up and the picture came on; first there was a snowstorm and then there were trees and low bushes. It was the school and the Eamonn fellow shovelling shit and the woman carrying a tray with the little loaves of bread on it. People came from behind the trees and the prefab houses, people that he knew, and he wanted to shake hands with them, but his fingers had turned to dough, his fingers were all glued together. Nobody recognised him.

Then the picture changed to heaven. It was heaven. He knew it was heaven because of gold walls and lamps. Jesus was there, and his pet fox was there, too. There were angels flying around with trays of biscuits and oranges. There was music. It was playtime in heaven, and they were all there, the woman and the child and the priest and his mother. The child picked up a bucket and spade and began to play on a bit of sand by the edge of a lake. He wanted them to talk to him, but they wouldn't. The priest was in shorts and he had a tan. His mother was on a deck chair knitting, keeping an eye on the child. He tried to break into the screen, but it wasn't glass, it wouldn't break, it was gooey like putty. Then the woman came out of a doorway and looked straight ahead and then turned her back on him. Her hair was loose and it had grown, it was down to her ankles. There were animals and there were birds, thrushes and a load of blackbirds. His fox trotted across to where the child was playing and he called to it, "Ruben, Ruben," and it spat at him.

When it got to be dusk in heaven, the sky became navy blue, people started yawning and white garments floated out for his mother, the child, and the woman and pyjamas for the priest. Beds were wheeled in, wooden beds with acorns on the headboards. The child got into a little bed, and the woman leant over it and kissed it and then rubbed its tummy the way she used to down at home. He knew that she'd talk to him once his mother and the priest had gone down to sleep. He moved closer and closer so that she could hear.

"Will I go to heaven?" he asked. He asked three times. She turned and looked at him. He thought she was going to say something nice. Her eyes were a fruity green like the lights in a slot machine. She screamed suddenly and one eye slid back into her head and an angel that must have been a surgeon squeezed the two lids together and began stitching them with fawn thread. Tears began to run down her face, and then they were not tears, they were drops of blood, and she wiped them with her hair. She got into bed next to the child and the music finished and there was nobody in the room, only him, and he was wide awake now.

He began to bite bits of the mattress, tore minute strips

and began to plait them together, his eye on the peephole, and he was happy because he was moving on, away from there.

The court was told of it first thing the following morning. Dr. Macready stood before the judge and said he had unpleasant news to relate: the defendant had made a serious suicide attempt the night before, had tried to strangle himself with bedcovering in the hospital after Eily Ryan had appeared to him crying. He said he had examined the neck and that the marks of the strangulation could be seen very clearly, as they extended three-quarters of the way round his neck and were blistering. He said it was why the defendant was not wearing a collar and tie as he usually did and asked permission to have the defendant excused from the court because of finding the trial so stressful, hearing people talking about him, and about his mother and her attempted suicide. As he was saying all this, O'Kane began to laugh, and now he was in a full spate of laughter at the people looking at him, curious, appalled, while Dr. Macready tried to point out that it was not laughing laughter, that it did not mean that the young man was feeling good, far from it, that instead of being repulsed by it, they should look on it as the laughter of the damned.

"He is not fit to plead, your honour," he said, and the judge deliberated and called for an adjournment to give him time to consider the matter.

Crossing the floor, the judge stopped and said that he hoped in his heart that the case would not drag on as it had done; it had opened wounds that were too deep, too shocking, too hurtful; it had been a human haemorrhaging and the country was depleted from it.

· · ·

He appeared in court weeks later as his life sentence was read out, but he sat, dead to it, dead to the woman in the jury who sobbed openly at the verdicts, dead to the mother who for fifty-two days had sat with the stillness of an archetype, in her brown clothes, her brown hair tied back in a bun, and who simply said to those comforting her, "I can go home now and be alone."

Aileen

SURE IT WAS a Thursday on account of my being late going to bed after the bingo night. Ben was playing with his Lego when the doorbell rings and Queenie, the landlady, calls up, "The guards are down here in the hall for you." I knew she was raging at having the guards around again, thinking all that was over and done with and that we were nice respectable people now. I jump up and put a few clothes on and Ben follows me out onto the landing.

"Has that child toys to play with?" the guard calls out. He's sheepish-looking, a new recruit.

"Of course he has toys to play with," I say.

"You might want to give them to him," he says, and I take the hint and push Ben back into the bedroom and close the door.

He is wringing his hands to get it out: "I have bad news for you. We heard it over the nine o'clock news, but we thought it was a hoax . . . They found your brother, dead, in the early hours of the morning. You have to come down to the sergeant."

"Don't be raving . . . I saw him less than a week ago and he looked okay except that he had gone from a size sixteen to a size twenty-two . . ."

"It was a peaceful death."

"Did he get his hand on tablets, or did he cut his arms trying to get out a window?"

"He died in his sleep . . . They changed his medication and it seems he reacted to it . . . It was one chance in a million."

"So he's out of their way now," I said.

"It seems it was a very rare phenomenon," he droned on.

"They doped him up, that's what."

"His heart stopped . . . miss . . . they tried resuscitation."

As they crossed the green, the busybodies began peering out from between their curtains; the two terriers that sparred all day were at it and that Minnie on her new bicycle scooting up close to us so as to hear what he was saying. Him repeating the same rubbish about a peaceful death and the very rare phenomenon of my brother's heart.

When I got to the hospital they didn't want me to see him in the morgue. I insisted. A warder held my arm. "Let go of me . . . let go of me," I said. My brother's hands and everything else were tucked in, and all I could see was his bloated face. I leant in over him and talked to him: "Have you legs, have you arms, did they dope you up?" The warder was right behind me in case I did anything extreme.

When I came out I told the doctor that my brother's last wish was to be cremated. The doctor said cremation was okay by them. I waited and waited for the ashes, and when they didn't come, I rang up and was told that there was some confusion. I rang and I rang, and eventually I was told that our father wanted the ashes. I shouted down the phone, I said, "I'm the one that was close to him, him and his father were daggers drawn for years." They said they'd have to think about it. In the end I had to go up there again to get them. They were in a little box. They'd halved it. That was my brother's lot, halved in life and halved in death.

Grotto

THE SUN broke into the showers and lit them with a rainbowed radiance, and the showers carried on, festive, larky, bluing the road and spattering watery diamonds on the plastic bags around the silage and on the top bars of iron gateways. The sky was pink and lilac and powder blue; stone walls and patchwork fields, then more ragged undulating country, hazels, poplars, forts of oaks, hilly mounds. O'Kane country.

Dr. Macready had been thinking of him since he came west a week before for a court hearing. O'Kane, the lost prodigal son that he believed he could have saved if he had been given time. He thought of him often, the ravelled mind that hopped around as if it were on a hot spit, running from hate to love, to murder to repentance, fantasy and truth all one. Once, in a moment of searing clarity, asking for his brain to be taken out and washed and then buried thousands of feet in some bog where neither man nor machine could dislodge it.

"But you'd have nothing then," he had said to him.

"I'd rather nothing . . . I want to be out of my skull . . . I want to be empty," he had said, and repeated during those endless hours when they tried to pick out the pieces of his life, the milestones large and small that culminated in the abyss. In less furious moments he would talk of the places with their funny little names and the piers where local people who didn't hate him would fear to let him indoors, left tea and bread for him. Dr. Macready remembers him re-enacting walking backwards in his cell, remembering the winds he walked in, backwards, on account of their being so strong, so cutting. Now he was in that territory that he knew only from O'Kane's lips and reams of evidence.

It was Friday and he was heading home. He realised that he had taken a wrong turning but didn't bother to turn around, believing that eventually he would come onto the dual carriageway and the city.

As he was coming up to a crossroads, the name sprung out at him — Cloosh Wood. His absentmindedness had brought him there. Parking the car by the entrance barrier, he felt not fear but a city man's confoundedness at the stoicism of those living by and trothed to such a friendless place. The path was easy to follow, mementos all along the way like stations to a sepulchre. There were bits of mirror, ribbon, broken rosaries, seashells all whispering their whisper: "This way, this way, ladies and gentlemen."

When he got there, he found to his surprise that he was not alone. A woman kneeling in prayer, her body bent over, then at moments stooping to kiss the earth. He coughed so as not to frighten her and waved his hand in a reassuring gesture. It was obviously where the woman and child were slain, quite different from the rest of the forest, and the sight of it moved him. A garden had been planted, rosebushes, dwarf trees, wildflowers, and their little belongings — a gnome, a tortoiseshell comb, a vintage toy car, and a nailbrush with the likeness of a frog on its handle. Two tiny white crosses with their names painted on them seemed so childlike and belonged not to death but to moonlight and enchantment. On a lintel of stone a bog oak carving. Pine trees in a half circle, their branches soft and empathising in a semi-sway. From one branch there hung a set of chimes.

Eventually the woman turned and looked in his direction, and he whispered if by any chance she was a relative. She shook her head. She was wearing a headscarf which she had drawn over her face and a country coat, like a man's coat. Her eyes had that startled, highly strung look that he had often seen in patients.

"A sad place," he said.

"The women of Ireland want his blood," she said quite quickly, and repeated it with such force, such emphasis, that he thought, as she stood, that she was about to strike him.

"And what will they do with his blood . . . baptise it . . . bottle it . . . sprinkle it . . . put it in the tabernacle?" he asked, overcalm.

"Who are you—some do-gooder?"

"No . . . I treated O'Kane . . . I was one of the doctors during his trial . . . I was one of the few people at his funeral."

"His death was too good for him . . . he should have been hanged from these trees."

"You will not believe me, but I heard him once express great sorrow . . . great guilt . . . about everything that happened here."

"Sorrow," she shrieks, and she is above him now, her arms dangling, her piercing eyes, asking him to recall the woman's bruised limbs, her torn undergarments, her defilement before death, before meeting her God, and a hundred yards away a priest, his head on a stone slab, a butcher's block.

258

"I do recall . . . but I want you to know that he did re-pent one time . . . He had had no food or liquid for over twenty days . . . he was a changed man."

"Tripe." She shrieks it.

"Madam, is it not better that he showed repentance than that he never showed it at all? Better to atone for one minute than live in a vortex of despair?"

She turned away and muttered, her breath rapid and rasping. It was in that taut silence that a breeze started up and dislodged a piece of paper from the wedge of the joined crosses. It blew this way and that, as if deciding where it might land. Eventually it fell close to him, and he unfolded it and read it. Then he offered it to her to read, but she refused. He read aloud, he wanted her to hear it: "Darkness is drawn to light, but light does not know it; light must absorb the darkness and therefore meet its own extinguishment."

He looked to see if there was any softening in her fea-tures, in her stance, but there was none. The silence was killing. He could feel it magnifying and confirming itself in their separate beings, their irreconcilable natures. Suddenly she put her hand out and she was swaying and he thought that she was about to fall. "I picture her when I come up here as if she is still alive . . . as if she is within calling dis-tance," she said, her voice muted.

"I know . . . I do know that," he said, and reached to steady her but without touching, knowing that she was aching for some kind of consolation, like desert earth empty of rain. Then the chimes started up, brazen, arbi-trary, their strikes hitting and grazing one another, sudden jubilance in that hallowed place.

He led the way down, splotches of light and shadow

from a harvest moon that seemed to follow them. It would be winter soon, that ground far too soggy, the steep track sheer with ice and snow, and no mourners would venture up there for months to come.

After that it would be spring.

Scallywag

THERE WAS a boy and he was around four and he made a plan that he told no one, not even his friend Elmer. A big adventure. He was an only child and played by himself with sticks. He went that bit farther from home each day, and then one day he could only see just the slates and then the next day the copper beech tree brushing them, and then he came on a fort and there were purple flowers nearly as tall as himself and he picked them and played war with them, but they broke because they were not that strong.

The night he stole out there were thousands of stars and he crossed the fields and climbed over the town gate and walked and walked until he came to a big wood where there was all sorts of activity. It was buzzing. There were bats and game birds and badgers all doing the things they could do only at night: scaring each other and fighting and eating their suppers and rolling around in the leaves, basking and having fun. Hi ho, hi ho, it's off to play we go.

When it was time to sleep, he got into a big bed of pine needles and thought, *I'll be a potato, I'll be a spud and snooze down here.* He slept a beautiful sleep and there was no telling how long he slept and it didn't matter.

Meanwhile, there was major Sosesses at home: his mother, his father, the guards, the whole country out looking for him. They called in water divers because he loved going to the lake for picnics but he could only swim with armbands. They were demented.

He came out of the wood, his clothes all crumpled and pine needles in his thick mop of brown hair. He could see a house with the roof gone, nettles and cows in the front garden grazing between the broken statues. Fawn cows and spotted cows. They just went on grazing, they didn't pay any attention to him. Sometimes cows look cross and have glum faces, but these didn't. He walked in and out between them. They were far taller than he was, their coats were silky and they had big soft pink diddies. It was amazing the amount of grass they could take in their mouths, but of course they spilt a lot of it. Their tongues were rubbery. A farmer came and said, "Are you the boy that's missing?"

"I dunno."

"Yes, you are, you scallywag."

When his mother and father arrived with a guard and a man, there was a big reunion, kissing and crying and his mother wrapping a tartan rug around him in case he caught cold. "Where were you?" "Brazil." "Weren't you afraid?" "No." "Did you miss us?" "No." "Just say you missed us a teeny little bit." "A teeny bit."

They'd never know, they'd never get to the bottom of it, and they shouldn't.

Magic follows only the few.

AUTHOR'S NOTE

In April 1994, Imelda Riney, aged twenty-nine, and her son Liam, aged three, went missing from her isolated cottage in County Clare. Father Joe Walshe, a curate in County Galway, disappeared a few days later, and when their burnt-out cars were found, suspicion pointed to Brendan O'Donnell, a local youth, home from England, on remand from prison. O'Donnell was captured after six days, having abducted another young girl, Fiona Sampson. Later, the bodies of the three missing people were found in nearby Cregg Wood; all had been shot at close range. Brendan O'Donnell was charged with their murders and in 1996 tried in the Central Criminal Court in Dublin. He was jailed for life. In July 1997, he was found dead by nursing staff in the Central Mental Hospital in Dublin.